ADAM P IESCU

NIMA

A NOVEL

The Unnamed Press
Los Angeles, CA

AN UNNAMED PRESS BOOK

The Unnamed Press
P.O. Box 411272
Los Angeles, CA 90041

www.unnamedpress.com

Library of Congress Cataloging-in-Publication Data is available.

Cover Artwork by James Chia Han Lee
Designed & typeset by Jaya Nicely

ISBN: 978-1-944700-85-0
eISBN: 978-1-944700-96-6

Distributed by Publishers Group West
Manufactured in the United States of America

First Edition

1 3 5 7 9 10 8 6 4 2

NIMA

1

IT'S STILL DARK, BUT WE'RE ALREADY WALKING WITH FILLED baskets on our heads. Wicker baskets filled to the brim with yak dung cakes, some frozen, some still the faintest bit warm, we bend and scoop and pile our baskets high. It's easier to pick them when they're flattened like stones, but tonight is a cold night, and there's a frost covering the earth. Stuck in the frozen ground, we have to dig them out, clumps of dirt and grass coming along with them.

We work without seeing, over trails we've walked so many times, forever collecting these gifts. Gifts that give us fuel to burn our fires, to keep us warm, to cook our food, to keep us alive, we fill our baskets high, we fill them until the baskets' thump lines dig into our skin.

Second, the one born right after me, her basket's strap cuts into her forehead, and she tries to adjust the weight and bends too low, spilling everything. We all turn to look. In the dying moonlight we can just make out Second, down on both knees, scooping and heaving the dung back into the basket. My sisters and I all crouch and help her while Mother looks on, clutching her tokma, the T-shaped walking stick we all carry and use to prop up our loads during rest breaks. She shuffles toward us, basket steady, round eyes squinting.

"Every piece," Mother commands. "We need every piece."

She bends and gathers the spilled dung, flattening it with her palms, then placing the pressed clump back into Second's basket.

"The thinner it is, the more we can collect. The more we collect, the longer the celebration."

Second nods apologetically.

"More pain only means we've collected more for the stove, and that's good," Mother advises as I help Second readjust her basket, pulling a rag from around my neck and placing it under her thump line.

"This will feel better," I whisper.

Cakes of dung, grainy and thick and musty, burn longer than the timber that we've long ago cut away. At this altitude, we're just where the tree line ends. Life has been like this for thousands of years. No roads, almost nothing from the outside, all we own is what we can haul on our backs. We live by the season, man and beast as together as sap sliding down the bark of a tree. Forced together.

"Thank the yaks for leaving us these gifts," Mother goes on. "Auspicious gifts, gifts that will bring us great fortune. Tomorrow will be a special day."

I still can't believe that it's happening, and Second seems to read my thoughts. "We could have been matched with someone worse, Eldest. At least we know him. And he is from a good family. And handsome!"

"He is."

"But worth picking dung cakes before dawn?" Second laughs.

I still can't see her face, but I know that she's beaming with satisfaction. "In three days, we'll both be married," she whispers to me.

Married. Today we are gathering supplies and cleaning our home. Tomorrow we are visiting with the family of Norbu, the man I—the man Second and I—will marry. The day after, I'll become his wife, and so will Second. Two women for one man. It's not unusual for Sherpas to take more than one bride, yet it's usually one woman for two brothers. Even that doesn't happen so often now. That's the old way. It's Father, all because of him, dragging us backwards. Here I am, a bride-to-be, hauling yak dung. *Do brides down the mountain do this?*

"Are you nervous yet, about the wedding night? Do you know what we'll have to do?"

I nod to my excited sister, the one I'll soon share everything with. Of course I know, I've seen it done in the fields. And by my parents. Three bodies will be more warmth for the night, and I won't be jealous if my sister goes first...or maybe I will. Maybe I'm already possessive of a man who's not even mine yet, one I'm not even convinced I want.

"We've worked very hard to bring the six of you to this day, Eldest," Mother tells me. "We're happy for both of you—and for all six of you." All my sisters nod. Then Mother comes close and inspects each of our hauls. "How much have we gathered? Are your baskets full?"

Numbers. Everything a number.

How many yak dung cakes can we collect to keep the fire going?

How many pounds of barley can we grow, how many of millet? How many pounds can we keep to feed us and our animals? How many can we trade for rice? How much rice will feed us all? How long will the winter last? How long will the drought last?

So many numbers—even we ourselves are numbers.

Six sisters. Five of us here, the little sixth is at home, too small to work. Six sisters.

Six girls.

I am called Eldest, the Dremu, in ours, the beautiful language of the Sherpas. I'm also called Chig, which means the first. But my true given name is Nima, though I never hear it said. It's easier to call six daughters by numbers than by names.

My second sister is Nyi, the third is Soom, the fourth is Shi, and the fifth is Nga. The youngest, the suckling sixth, is Doog.

It's always "Eldest, Second, Third, Fourth, Fifth." Never "Nima, Nyi, Soom, Shi, Nga." "Six daughters," my father crows almost daily, from behind his bottle. "Six mouths to feed."

When I was small, I thought all Sherpas were like my father: a climber, helping the mikarus up the mountain, a weight-bearing porter to white-eyed foreigners, leading and opening their trails, laying ladders over crevices, tying ropes to pull them up, feeding them when they're hungry, helping them when they're sick. The people of the East don't get altitude sickness. Just mikarus. But not all Sherpas are alike. Not all Sherpas climb.

Trekking work is the only way to make real money on the mountain. Enough to not have to rely on the yaks—on the old ways—enough to not have to worry about what we can eat, what we can barter, what we can grow, where to find good pasture. And for many years we didn't need to worry because Father made good money as a climbing Sherpa. Now when we're around him, we speak softly, avoid eye contact. When we're alone we're always wondering: Are we such a curse to him and Mother? Ever since Father stopped working, he wants lay-koh in the house: zero mouths to feed.

There was no reason to be afraid of him before it all changed. Before he came home with his right leg broken in three places. Before that, he wasn't hobbling around like a cripple. He hadn't become a zi—a short-tempered drunk who beats me, my sisters, my mother. He beats all of us, all save Doog, the baby.

It was another life when he carried loads on his back like most Sherpa men do—like they wish to do. The pride, the respect, the honor, the money. All of it was good. Better than good. It was *enough*. I remember how he would come home at the end of a trek, the mark from the thump line branded deep on his forehead, his belly hungry, and his pockets full. He was happy when he was on two feet. Eager for Mother's cooking, he even played with his daughters sometimes. At night, always on the first night of his return, no matter how tired he was, he took his wife to bed, hoping to fill her with a son this time, not another little girl.

A Sherpa that only makes girls is a Sherpa who can't have climbing heirs. And there's a reason girls are only allowed to carry supplies but not lead treks: girls are bad luck on the mountain. We knew all this from my father's own mouth. He talked about everything, it was his right to speak without minding anyone else's feelings but his own—the master of his home. Once I tried to run after him as he started on a trek, I wanted to be like him—but he sent me home with a slap.

When my brother Ang was finally born Father was overjoyed. Ang means beloved, and he was. By all of us. He was like a living doll, that tiny man—someone to play with, someone different than us. We shared the same blood, but he wouldn't be like his sisters—no, no, we all were well aware of that. We live the Sharwa way, the Sherpa way, us, the people of the East.

My brother Ang was called by his true name, not by a number. I was Eldest already to my family, but Ang would always be the true first, thanks to the little manhood peeking out from between his legs.

So happy to have a living heir, Father invited all the male neighbors in our town into our front yard, to raise a cup of our home brew, drinking to the mountain spirits who finally blessed him with a son. His fourth child. A life that lasted four years. For four years, my father worked like never before, he was on the mountain every day of the season, all for the chance for the highest—and most lucrative honor—to be part of an expedition to Jomo-langma, the place mikarus call Everest. My father had a son now, and when he moved it was like his feet never touched the ground. Like he skipped across the air.

In Ang's fourth year, a team of British explorers hired our father and he got his chance. He wouldn't be the lead, an older Sherpa, a sirdar from our village, was chosen instead, but Father would still get to climb the roof of the world and look down on us all. The trip was scheduled for the coming year, permits were bought, and Father was happy. We thought he would rest in preparation, but then he was hired for one more trek, the last of that season—fourteen days round trip to Base Camp.

It was nearly spring, more than three years ago now, a joyous time. Light snow flurries at night but sun in the day. A good time for our family, a good time for the whole village. My sisters —there were only three of them then—we were all working in the field with Mother. Father was supposed to come home later that day, and we kept looking up at the trail. We could see it from where we were working, waiting to see him rush down the path. Sometimes he came home with presents, things the mikarus had given him—chocolates, gloves—and he would give them to us.

We had been crouching since dawn, harvesting carrots and potatoes. My back was aching. I straightened, looked up, saw no one. Every time I would rest, I would look up. Around midday I saw him, finally, loping down the trail, a brown dot on the mountain getting closer and closer.

He saw me and waved. I squinted as I waved back. He was holding something, I couldn't tell exactly what it was, maybe a gift for me and my sisters. My heart leaped—and then it hung in my chest, frozen. Behind him, farther up on the trail, I heard a sound like thunder on earth, a deep *tuuuuungg*, like the blow of a hammer against a bell. A sound all Sherpas know.

The piece of mountain Father stood on fell right off into white nothingness and Father disappeared with it. I watched the way a rat watches a cobra before the snake strikes. Fixed on that piece of mountain where my father was swallowed, slabs of snow, ice and rock kept growing, kept tumbling down toward us. I watched— we all watched it—and didn't breathe.

There's a Sherpa saying that there are as many types of ru' as there are people. Wet and filled with sluffs and slabs, or ru's that glide when the entire snowpack moves as one, or slush, like a flash flood of permafrost. This was a hard slab ru', the most deadly kind of avalanche.

So many things can cause a ru'. Layers of fresh snow weighing down the ice crust, or a bed of large-grained, wind-hardened snow made loose by heat from the sun's rays, ice calving in the heat of the day, or rain which can make a melt-freeze, or an ice surge. Wind, trekkers, climbers, so many things can be the cause, and in a flash I thought of them all.

One moment my father was there, coming down the trail, waving, calling our names, did he realize he was in its path—*or was he realizing who else was in its path, further below?*—then it took him and he was gone.

Strange, the ru' had seemed so far away, much too far to reach us, we all watched as the white surge kept coming closer, growing wider as it advanced. I knew how dangerous it was, we all did. Avalanches kill more than disease, famine, trail accidents, all put together. They kill every year. None of us could move—or stop watching that thick sheet crashing, a tumbling white pile swallowing birch trees and boulders, anything and everything in its path, tumbling closer and closer.

Then I realized what would happen next. The village, our village, was at the foot of the mountain on a valley plateau, right under the path of the ru'. Khumjung, made up of a dozen Sherpa homes. The climbers were on the mountain that day, most other villagers were in the fields for the potato harvest, but their families, the very young and very old, were there. In between us and the mountain. We watched from the field as the white blanket rolled right over Khumjung and settled with a deafening *whoomp*. And then there was silence and I couldn't see anything. The sun disappeared, blocked by a stormy white cloud. A single thought raced through my mind: Ang.

2

FOR A LONG TIME WE STOOD STILL, TRANSFIXED BY THE CLOUD. ITS most frightening part was its silence. The most deafening. One moment Khumjung had twelve homes: half a dozen built with wood, stone, clay and mud, homes huddled together under the foot of the mountain for protection from wind and weather. And the rest of the village, perched up on a hill, that's where those lucky Sherpas who could afford more had built their homes. A village full of people I had known my whole life.

All I could hear was my own breathing and weeping, then the screams that bounced off the peaks, echoing down the valley, screams from voices I was afraid I might recognize. The spell ended then, and we rushed forward with our field tools in our hands, crying out.

Ang.

We ran into the cloud of snow. He had been all alone, playing at home, having just recovered from a cold. My mother thought it best to let him rest that day. We ran like scared animals, crying and shouting and screaming, we ran towards home—or where we thought our home had been.

Ang.

There were blocks of ice where the village had been, stones piled as high as my shoulder, tree trunks split in two, shards of broken wood and glass, our whole village smashed—all except for the lucky rich who built their homes on that spared hill above us. I saw a horse, just its head and neck, sticking out of the snow, eyes empty. Dead yaks, goats—and dead people. People I knew, I recognized their boots, sticking out of the snow. Ngwang, the old man who liked to leave out millet for the deer to come and eat, and Namba, the widow who would sit on her porch all day, no matter how cold it was, sipping her tea deliberately—I recognized them and couldn't stop to help.

"The lucky ones die quickly in a ru'," my father used to say. "Without suffering."

The unlucky ones found themselves in pockets of air that would only last a few minutes. Trapped out of reach and out of sight, below the snow. Alone. Suffocating. Dying.

Ang.

Our home was gone, all that was left was the tip of the juniper that grew in our front yard. That morning that tree had been taller than our home. Now it was just a stunted shrub poking out of the snow. We dropped to hands and knees, my mother and my sisters and me, blindly punching through the surface with our hoes and rakes. We dug and dug and dug where our house was—where we remembered it was, just beneath the ridge where the rich Sherpas lived. There was no ridge anymore, just flat land filled with snow and ice.

We dug until our tools broke and then we dug with our fingers. We dug until our fingers bled and our nails cracked, the ice sticking to our bleeding hands. And still nothing. We couldn't break through the cold slabs. So much had fallen on our home. Too much to remove. All around us, where there had been homes and plots, everyone was fighting the mountain. Everywhere it was all the same: panic and death.

My arms were so tired, I couldn't lift them. And then the sound of a shovel—when Norbu Norgay stabbed its tip into the slab it made a cracking sound, and then he stepped on the shovel's head with his foot, scooped, and heaved. Not a word, just stab, scoop, heave. Stab, scoop, heave. Stab, scoop, heave.

We all worked, side by side, not saying a word, clawing at the ice until the sun hid behind the peaks. But even with our neighbor Norbu helping us, we could not lift the mountain. Too much time had passed, far too long, we all knew that, but we didn't stop. Not until my mother stopped digging and cried out loud. In her hands was a tiny shoe. Then she fell on her hands and knees, screaming and pounding furiously.

We dug harder, *he must be close, if the shoe was found, surely he was close*—then, Second pulled me near her and grabbed my hand.

"Mother left the shoes outside this morning," she whispered. "Remember? Ang had gone out in the morning, in the snow. And his shoes got wet." She shook her head. "Mother left the shoes out to dry."

That little shoe, made from yak hide, sewn by Mother just a month earlier—she clutched it and *she knew*—and she sat wailing up at the skies.

We all fell apart.

I don't remember everything that happened next, as if it was a bad dream I have yet to wake from. Norbu took off his jacket, wrapped me in it, took my hands in between his and rubbed them. I remember his hands were so big and strong. Norbu's father and mother came too, as did other villagers, helping my sisters and me, trying to take us away, to stop us from starting to dig again. Women tried to console my mother, but she pushed them away, still clutching that shoe, hysterical.

I freed myself from Norbu's arms and dropped next to Mother. She tried to push me away but I held her, my face pressed against her heaving chest, both of us streaming tears. All of my sisters gathered around us, holding each other and weeping.

When I looked up I saw a ghost. A living ghost. I wiped my eyes to make sure I wasn't imagining things. I hadn't even thought of him, so focused on my brother.

My father had dug his way out of the snow. He dragged himself to where we were and knelt down next to his wife, one hand holding hers, the other reaching for the shoe, and he screamed something without words and they both rocked back and forth, the snow under his right leg now a dark crimson. And then he fell over and passed out.

He should have died that day.

The avalanche had pinned him between two boulders, a shelter that kept him alive. But one of the boulders crushed his right leg. He still found the strength to dig his way out with his kikuri blade, and he was found by neighbors of ours looking for survivors. They gave him water, and he half crawled, half walked his way to the village. Of the men who were on the mountain with my father, five died that day. But the highest toll was in Khumjung. Twenty of our villagers were killed when the ru' struck.

Father should have died right next to Mother, he was bleeding so heavily from that broken leg. It was his grief alone that kept him going. We could see the white of the bone sticking out of the skin, the muscle hanging off the leg, peeled, a red mess. Again, Norbu, without speaking, without hesitating, lifted my father with the help of two other men, and they took off down the valley. My sisters huddled around my mother, still on her knees clutching Ang's shoe, but I turned and followed the men carrying my father.

There's no hospital on the mountain. And none of us had enough money to take Father or anyone else down to Lukla, to fly them to the capital—not that a helicopter would try to land up here right after an avalanche. Sometimes the sound of the blades can trigger another ru', shaking free what snow and ice didn't hit the first time.

Over my shoulder, where my village once was, only the hill with the rich Sherpas' homes was still recognizable, survivors crawling like ants, pulling and lifting other ants out of the white mess.

Don't look back.

The men carried Father to the only place where we could find help: the infirmary at the Sir Edmund Hillary High School. I had studied there for two years, making my hour-long walk in snow or in sunshine, from my home to the school, all to learn basic English, history, mathematics. The school serves the whole Khumbu region, teaching mountain children for a year or two before their families pull them out and send them hauling goods to make money. Goods they will never use, for tourists they'll never know, so their families can buy the rice, barley and grains that won't grow in our sterile soil. It's the only place for miles with a nurse and a supply of Western medicine. The school itself is nothing but a few rooms, each with a blackened stove that we would gather around while the headmaster taught us the geography of Nepal, the home of eight of the world's tallest peaks. We took turns passing the single lesson book, sharing pencils made black from fingers used to feeding yak fuel to the flames.

"Keep your body warm to keep your mind warm," the headmaster was fond of telling us.

When we entered the infirmary, Father's eyes were completely shut from the pain, his cracked lips mumbling something I couldn't understand. Norbu and father's two climbing friends stared in silence. But they weren't staring at the man lying on that narrow cot. They were staring at the figure standing beside my father, an apparition—a female nurse. By their terrified looks, it may as well have been a yeti looming above my father. The nurse smiled a mix of sympathy and scorn. I had never seen her before but I believed in her ability. Instantly, I loved this woman.

I had stopped going to school that year, even though my father was doing well on the mountain. My mother was starting to show with Fifth, and we still had a field to plow and animals to take care of, jobs that fell to me and Second, the two oldest. There was no time for school. So many things I learned from that sole lesson book, so many pictures of lives unlike my own, they felt so far away now. It was difficult to believe there was another world beyond the mountains. When I looked up from the schoolyard or from the village, from anywhere in the Khumbu, I saw the peaks. What else could exist beyond the Himalayas?

Once, the headmaster had held up a mobile phone and given us a lesson about an invisible force called *wifi*. I decided then that I would have a mobile. I had no one to call, but I knew the device could conjure some sort of power, and help me find my luck. I remember the headmaster letting me touch the mobile. It was so small, so light, I didn't want to give it back. He ended up yanking the thing out of my hands and giving it to another student to examine. The headmaster kept on talking until my head became dizzy, and when I told him so, he sent me to see the nurse, a man with a large mole on his cheek and a single long black hair growing out of it. I hated that mole hair touching my face when he got close, hated his cold hands when he felt my forehead, hated him ogling my neck, my chest.

But that man was gone now. In his place, a woman in a white coat, she couldn't have been that much older than me. A female nurse with a look of knowing, a confident expression of belonging. Thankfully, my father's eyes were still closed, I knew how he would have reacted.

The other men didn't say a word, they just followed the yeti's friendly orders and helped hold him down as she straightened the bone on a wooden splint, Father gritting his teeth and moaning so loudly she finally stuck a spoon in his mouth. "So he won't bite off his tongue."

I watched from the doorway as the nurse put two delicate hands on Father's leg—hands with thin fingers, nails painted the color of a blood pheasant—and when those small hands pushed down with all her weight and set the leg, I heard the *snap* and looked away.

Eyelids fluttering, words garbled with that spoon between his teeth, a web of saliva on the sides of his mouth, how could he recover from this? I felt like running out into the cold until it was all over. My fingers were wrapping around the doorknob, but Norbu pulled me back and held me close. I remember his smell so well. Like outside—like the mountains—and when he stroked the back of my neck I didn't recoil like I had with the mole man. I pressed my face into the crook of his arm and cried and cried. And though I was thinking of my father, my brother, the destruction, I couldn't help but marvel at this unknown woman. Confident, capable, even in a moment like this.

I wanted to know more about her. Clearly, she wasn't from Khumjung. She must have studied in the capital, but if she was working here, then she couldn't be a mother. I broke away from Norbu's grip. The nurse's slender fingers held a long sharp object that she filled out of a tube of clear liquid. She held it up, squirted some out, then pierced my father's arm. A prick of blood swirled inside the tube.

She saw me looking and pulled out that pointy thing from his arm. "It's called a hypodermic needle—it has medicine in it, to help with the pain. It won't hurt him, I promise, it's just sharp in order to go into the bloodstream quickly. It will work very fast, it will help, please trust me."

I watched my father become still. He looked like he had died, and I remember feeling nothing. Nothing at all. That scared me more than anything that day. By then, Father's friends had departed and abandoned him to the yeti, unable to watch and surely fearing bad omens. But Norbu had stayed. In this worst of all moments, a small laugh was caught in my throat, and I swallowed to push it back down, almost choking.

I took a step closer and touched my father's face. It was burning hot.

"Don't worry," the nurse said. "He's resting now. Just resting. He's still alive, still breathing. The fever will pass, the medicine will help."

I watched his chest rise and fall. But so slowly.

"It's from the pain and stress. The leg is broken very badly, and in more than one place. I gave him something to put him to sleep and I set the leg straight again, but it will take time to heal. It won't be easy."

I didn't know what she gave him or how it worked, but I was relieved that my father's eyes were still closed. Those wild, red eyes. And the way she spoke soothed me. So calm, so sure of herself.

There were two plastic chairs by the cot, and I sat in one and Norbu in the other. One of the cot's legs was held up by three medical books. I twisted my head to read the only visible title: *Leprosy & Infectious Diseases in Nepal.*

"Do you still go to school here?" Norbu blurted unexpectedly, looking straight at my father, as if afraid to make eye contact with me.

"I plan to return. And you?"

He shook his head. "No. Nothing left for me to learn here. What do I need books for?" he declared, stretching his arm and pointing at what propped up the cot.

"Can you read?" I asked. He shook his head again. "How about your name? Can you write it?"

"What for? Everything for me is on the mountain." It sounded so strange to hear his dedication to the mountain after it had just destroyed our village. "Every year, she takes revenge. She doesn't always give, sometimes she takes away."

"And my brother?" My voice rising. "Why did she take him? What did he do wrong?"

The nurse held up her hand towards me: *quiet, girl,* her face said, *your father needs to rest.*

Norbu whispered to me: "Your brother was an innocent, that's true. And the loss is deep. Sometimes she takes innocents along with the guilty."

So simple, so cold. Norbu sat with his arms folded, not knowing what else to say. The nurse held her hand on Father's wrist, mouthing something. It looked like she was counting.

"Where did you learn... ?" I asked her. I didn't know the right word for what she was doing.

She laid Father's hand down. "Good pulse, his heart is strong. I learned to be a nurse at the Model Hospital in Kathmandu."

The capital. Even its name, it sounded so like another country. So foreign. *Kathmandu*. I'd never been, of course. I'd never been off the mountain. "What's it like there?"

She held up a finger to her lips. "Please, be quiet for your father. I will tell you, but we must whisper, and let's speak over here."

I nodded, getting out of the chair and walking to the doorway after her. Norbu remained seated, but leaned towards us to listen in.

"Kathmandu is very flat," she explained softly. "So flat, there are no mountains at all." She paused. "And it's a very different place for women. Very different from here..." She trailed off, like she had revealed too much.

"How different?"

She took a breath. "In some ways, it's much easier for women there. And the trouble with the Maoists has passed, so there are no more killings. The streets are safe now. You can walk by yourself, shop at the market, there's running water and electrical power everywhere—you can drive a car—you know what a car is, yes? It's like a mechanical carriage, except there are no horses pulling it. Kathmandu is very different from here."

"But you can work? Women can work?"

"Women can work and do almost anything men can do."

A place where women can live and work as men do. I glanced at Norbu, arms still folded, but listening.

"What's it like to live on flat land?"

"The air is different. You feel more of it when you breathe. And the ground," she held her palms straight in the air, "it's just like this. There are places in our country that are forever green instead of black and gray and white. Places where it's not just rock and ice."

"And Kathmandu is one of those places?"

"It is. Kathmandu is in the valley, and that makes life easier."

"How is it easier?" Norbu asked from his plastic chair. The nurse signaled with her finger to her lips, and Norbu rose out of the chair and stepped towards us. "I've been to the city. You can't see the mountains, you can't roam free, there are always walls keeping the sky out."

"Well, yes. But you can buy food and water—so many kinds of food, meat as well—and there are cinemas. You sit in a darkened room with many other people and a movie appears on a large screen, like a television program, but the screen is much larger."

"Why would you want to sit in a dark room with strangers?" wondered Norbu.

She smiled. "That's city life. It is quite different, yes, but Kathmandu *can be* a very nice place—"

"I've been," Norbu chirped. "When my grandfather was honored by the Nepal Mountaineering Association. It was dirty. And it was flat, you're right about that. The buildings block out the peaks—they even block out the sun. And it's loud, so loud, so many autos and motorbikes, I couldn't even cross the road. When my grandfather's ceremony was over, I didn't want to go outside again. I stayed in that room after everyone else had left. When I did leave, I couldn't stop coughing. I coughed all the time until I was back on the mountain. My lungs were full of black soot. I never want to return there. If I lived in Kathmandu, I think I would die of sorrow." A long pause. Norbu looked up at the walls of the small room, remembering. "I hate not seeing the sky when I look up."

"And what about women who work," the nurse asked, "do you hate seeing that, too?"

Norbu smiled. "The other men left when they saw you, but I'm still here, aren't I?"

"Did they think I was a lepcha? Will they tell the other villagers not to bring their injured to a woman nurse?"

"Some will call you a snow demon, no doubt," he answered. "But they're fools, there's no such thing as a lepcha."

I strained to hear our neighbors coming down the mountain, carrying their own loved ones. I heard nothing but silence. The school was empty. It was Saturday, Nepal's rest day.

"Where do you sleep?" I asked her. And she smiled and pointed to the cot where my father lay.

"All alone?" I whispered.

"All alone," she answered.

Not a line on her face, she was too pretty to be a snow demon or a yeti. "You look very young," I said, voicing my thoughts. She smiled again and said nothing. "Wouldn't it have been easier for you to work in Kathmandu as a nurse?"

"Believe it or not, it may be easier here. There are so few nurses in the Khumbu that when people need my help, they get over the shock of taking orders from a woman. I'm needed here, and there's less competition than in the valley." She riffled through supplies, opened a box of medicines. Even when squinting, not a single line on her face. "And thank you for saying that, but I am not so young. I am twenty-four."

Ten years older than me. "And not married?" I exclaimed, unable to withhold my surprise and feeling the blood rush to my face.

"Not yet. If I was, I'd be stuck at home cooking, raising children, and washing my husband's socks."

Norbu burst out laughing.

"See?" she countered. "Be careful—"

"Nima."

"Be careful, Nima. Some paths you go down, you cannot return from. Marriage is not bad, but marriage is forever."

"Even in Kathmandu?"

"Even in Kathmandu."

"Were you born there?"

"No, I was born not far from here, in Namche Bazaar. I'm a Sherpa, too. My brother lives in Kathmandu."

Brother.

"He let me stay with him in the capital, he was very good to me. If not for him, I wouldn't have been able to study in the city, I wouldn't have had the money. A very good brother."

Ang. A pain shot through me. My brother would never grow up. He would never—I started crying. The nurse must have thought my tears were for my father. She looked away, busying herself with picking through bottles and tubes and things whose purpose I couldn't guess.

"I haven't seen you before, at the school," she said to distract me. "I know all the boys and girls here. But you said you were planning to come back, yes?"

I nodded, wiping my face. I stared at her white coat, her hair pulled back smartly.

"Good, I'd like to see you again," she said, leaning over my father. She placed a shiny round device on his chest and stuck its other end, a pair of metal prongs, into her ears. "I'm checking his pulse," she explained. "This is called a stethoscope. It doesn't hurt him, it's only to listen inside, to make sure everything's okay. Would you like to listen?"

I nodded again, and she placed the cold prongs in my ears. I heard a deep drumbeat and then she moved the device on Father's chest and I heard what sounded like wind blowing.

"That's his heart. And his breathing."

"Norbu." I took out the prongs from my ears, offered them to him, but he shook his head. I placed them back in my ears. How could this be—listening *inside* my father's body?

"It's not magic. It's medicine, science. You seem interested, smart. Have you ever thought of becoming a nurse, Nima?"

I felt Norbu watching me closely. Still giddy from what I'd heard, I didn't care. "I...would like to go down the mountain and study there. To see for myself what it's like. What I can become."

"There are many things you can do at university, many things to study. But you'll have to spend a lot more time in school first. Right here."

"I will. Is it difficult? The schooling, I mean. Were there other Sherpas with you in Kathmandu? Did you miss home?"

I snuck a glance at Norbu. Silent, but with a thin little curl to his lips.

"It takes a few years, and there are exams to pass. But if you study every day, you can do it. And there *were* Sherpas in the university, Nima. Even Sherpa women."

I smiled, my first and only smile that black day. Norbu looked confused. It's not his fault, I excused him. He had never heard women speak like this. He grew up with his mother and aunts speaking about matches for their children, and yaks, and grain, and barley. Not about going down the mountain and working in a city he hated. At that moment I made a silent promise which I repeated again and again, until it became a mantra. I will leave this place. I will be free.

3

THE NURSE HAD A LOT OF WORK THAT NIGHT. MOST OF THE VILLAGERS brought the broken bodies of their fathers and mothers, their brothers and sisters, they brought them and stayed despite the fact that the nurse was a woman, they all stayed—*where else could they go?*—and as we waited for my father to wake, we listened to the moans and screams. Inside and out, the small school was filled with broken and bleeding bodies—there was no more room—bodies lining the school's entrance, bodies in the corridor, overflowing from the three classrooms, all of them begging for the nurse. No more time to chat.

Norbu and I sat silently by my father's cot, our bodies close. I could feel the warmth coming off him, smell the sweat and that special scent of the wild, the earth, the mountains. He inched his hand towards mine and all at once took it in his, just as Nurse Lanja turned back to us, her white coat stained dark red, and just as quickly Norbu dropped my hand.

She looked tired. And if she had seen us holding hands a moment earlier, her face wouldn't say, a hard mask over it now. She stood over my father, pulled his eyelids open, pointed a small light into them. The light startled him enough for him to wake completely, and then he began throwing his arms up wildly, bellowing at the unknown woman, "Who are you? Who are you?"

"I'm your nurse, Lanja Sherpa," she said calmly, pushing him back onto the bed with those bird-like hands, painted fingers splayed on his chest like feathers. "You've had a severe accident, sir. You must rest. This is medicine I'm giving you—"

But he was too strong, too wild. Norbu and I had to hold him down while Nurse Lanja grabbed the needle and stuck it into him again. With all of my weight pressing down on him, I could feel his power. It was horrible to see my father like this, but I couldn't look away. I felt just like when the ru' struck. To calm myself, I found myself thinking: *Down the mountain, in the city. A very different place for a woman. Very different from here.*

Father finally stopped fighting, the medicine taking effect. But when the nurse held up a bottle of pills, he slapped her hand away. The pills rolled onto the floor and I rushed to collect them. "He'll only listen to a man," I whispered.

Nurse Lanja nodded, handed the pills to Norbu. "These are antibiotics, to ward off infection. He must take all of them. He needs a proper cast and should come back when I get more supplies." She pulled out a wooden crutch from a closet. "Birch bark. Very strong, but very light. Tell him to use the crutch until then," she insisted. "Otherwise, he'll never heal properly."

Norbu nodded and took the crutch.

"I have other patients to tend to," Nurse Lanja said. To my father: "Please be well, sir." He turned his face away from her. Then to me: "Take care, Nima. I hope I will see you again."

"Blessings and good luck."

"Tashi delek," she responded.

"Tashi delek," I said back.

We left the infirmary, my father taking the crutch from Norbu, but refusing our help as we stepped past the wounded and injured who crowded the school. I tried not to look—I didn't want to see people I knew. Nor did I want to imagine how Nurse Lanja would deal with this all by herself.

It was worse to watch my father, already walking so soon after I'd seen bone sticking out of his skin, even with Nurse Lanja's treatment and the leg in a splint. It was madness. Hobbling on that crutch, mumbling about evil medicine, lepchas, snow demons, he seemed mad. He was mad. We followed behind Father as he limped back home. But there was no home to go back to.

"My parents have opened our home to your family," Norbu said as we walked through the cold.

When Father stopped in mid-stride I thought he was going to collapse, and I caught up with him and tried to fit my shoulder under his other arm, to help him. He shoved me away so hard I fell face-first into a patch of ice. Norbu helped me up. My cheek was bleeding. Neither of us said a word. Father just kept hobbling, his whole body shaking, his teeth chattering. He didn't want a woman—any woman, not even his own daughter—to acknowledge his pain. There was still power in him, a pride he wouldn't give up even if it killed him. He didn't want a woman's help.

On that birch crutch, every step, every wince of pain filling his eyes with fire, my father hiked back to Khumjung, with Norbu and I behind him.

The village looked like the mountain had fallen on top of it. People were still running with torches, still digging, still wailing their pain. But we walked past all that, past the digging and crying, to Norbu's home—one of the lucky few on the ridge untouched by the ru'.

Norbu's family had taken their animals from the ground floor and retied them in the yard, and every single rug and floor mat they had were laid out for us to sleep. Father fell on one of those rugs, his leg dripping. Norbu's mother didn't say anything as Father bled on that rug, she kept her mouth shut and her eyes down as she offered her guest a steaming tea that he took with a swollen red hand. Mother sat by the fire, close enough that it looked like her clothes would go up in flames. Still clutching that shoe to her chest, she stared into the fire. Huddled around her, my sisters looked like they had not stopped crying since we took my father to the school.

Father crept to sit next to Mother. Our family was together again, but without my brother, buried under the ice a few hundred yards away. *If you die in great pain, your soul is trapped—a prisoner of it—only a great act of compassion can free you from it.* Mother said words like this sometimes. Sayings she had heard from the lamas and nuns. No one said anything now, the only sounds in that small room were of the flames crackling and the sobs from my sisters.

We never were able to dig Ang out. We tried, and kept trying when spring turned to summer. The rocks and ice that the ru' had rained onto the village had settled so firmly that they were part of the mountain now. We couldn't free my only brother's tiny body. The weight of the ice, rock, stone, it was too much to clear, even with Norbu and the rest of the village helping.

There was no puja ceremony, no sky funeral, nothing to offer to the sky, nothing to give—not the wooden yak toy Ang loved, nor his favorite red cap my mother had sewn him. There was nothing to bury beyond that shoe, nothing else of my brother remained. So my mother kept the last thing she had left.

We left Khumjung without observing the customary forty-nine days of bardo, the period of judgment in which a soul is suspended between worlds. We had to leave the village and Norbu's home. We moved to Khunde, farther from the school, farther up the mountain, even more removed from the world I wanted to join. And we started again, with nothing. All but three of our yaks had died in the ru'. Our possessions were the clothes that we wore, and all the savings we had was the money Father had been paid on his last trek, brought home buried in his boot, as usual.

His last trek.

Armed with hammers, Norbu and other neighbors helped us build our new home, gathering wood and stone, shuttling from Khumjung each morning and shuttling back at night. We stayed in their homes a few nights at a time. And in Norbu's home more often than all the others. My father would never have accepted such charity, but that was before he'd lost so much, and there was less and less of him every day. He should have been resting, regaining his strength. But he couldn't sit still. His leg never mended right. Neither did his mind.

He used the pills that Nurse Lanja gave him. I saw him take them. The pain must have been horrible—what else would have made him take the "bad medicine"—but it didn't matter. He was always on that leg. Trying to lift stones, hammering side by side with Norbu and the other men. His pride the only part of him still strong—he kept fighting and working, and every day he got weaker.

At nights, after a meal of tsampa, balls of roast barley flour, and dal bhat—full of rice, vegetable curry, lentils, the meal all mountain people eat daily—we would sleep in the communal living room, sharing the fire with goats and chickens while our hosts slept upstairs. Every night, a little more of my father melted away as he stared into that fire, the flames swallowing him as he swallowed his nightly bottle of chang, the home brew that had become his cure-all elixir.

"Was the healer's magic not strong enough?" my sisters asked me.

She wasn't a healer, I had told them. She was a nurse. A modern woman. But to my sisters, healing is magic. It was to me, too, until I saw Nurse Lanja at work. And they couldn't understand the things she had told me about her life.

"You said that she was smart," they would say. "Why isn't Father healing? When will he get better?"

Perhaps he was no longer strong enough, no longer young enough, to mend? But we never said that in words, for what we speak may come true. Even words have spirits inside them, and lives. Other questions bubbled from my sisters' lips: "Why is Norbu helping us, Eldest? You think he has one of us in mind? Why else would he help?"

"Because he's a good man," I said. "That's why."

But Second laughed in my face: "He wants to marry one of us, Eldest, and who could it be but you?"

My sisters were right about at least one thing. Norbu didn't have to be there, and we never asked for his help, yet here he was every day, hauling heavy stones for someone else's new home instead of earning money on the trail. I began thinking of Norbu differently. He'd rushed over with his shovel to help us try to find Ang, and then he had helped father hobble to the school and back, not just from his good heart alone. He was a good man, yes. And good men need wives.

One day, towards the end of our new home's construction, my sisters were herding our three yaks in the hills, my mother was tending to my father, and we were alone for a few moments, Norbu and I. I had been helping mix the mud and clay to set the stones. We didn't speak much, we never did. We shared cold water from a halved plastic bottle, the mikaru trash we found everywhere and saved to reuse.

"Why are you helping us?" I asked him suddenly.

Cheeks reddening, eyes darting at me, then away, the face behind the mask showed through for a moment. Then Norbu took a long drink, and when he put the bottle down, the mask was back on. "Why am I helping? We're all helping, Nima. Everyone is helping, it's our way. Would you not help if my family was in need?"

He was right, but that wasn't what I wanted to hear. Though I wasn't sure whether I liked him in that way, I wanted to know how much he liked me. But I couldn't ask him that.

Crushed by the loss—my brother, my father, everything—I sobbed softly. "Why did this happen to us?" Like a little girl again, craving the comfort of kind words.

Norbu scratched his forehead. When he answered, it was with his mind, not his heart.

"Once, explorers came to the Khumbu. Heroes with white eyes and white faces. And when they came, we would help them. We were heroes, too. We would guide the mikarus, protect them, share in the glory together. Now heroes don't come anymore. Anyone with money can come. And they don't care what they leave behind.

Too many of us don't care either. Too many just want the mikaru money. One season on the mountain is worth how many in the fields?"

"Many," I agreed, disappointed by his answer.

"Many," he repeated. "We've forgotten the mountain's power. That's why Khumbi Yulha and Jomo Miyo Lang Sangma took revenge that day."

Khumbi Yulha, the deity of Khumbu, and Jomo Miyo Lang Sangma, the goddess of Jomolangma, the world's tallest mountain.

He was right of course. Even though people didn't like to talk about it, things weren't as they used to be. And I didn't really desire Norbu—*I don't think I did*—but I was so confused, so in need, all I wanted was for Norbu to clear things up for me. I needed someone close to my own age, someone outside of the family. But Norbu drained the last of the water, then got up and back to work. Always working.

"Work is good for the spirit and body," my Father used to say. "It lifts the spirit, it hardens the body."

Whatever seeds could have been planted right then between Norbu and I never took root. We built the new home in a fortnight. My family was so relieved to have somewhere of our own to sleep after weeks under the roofs of others. I thought Norbu looked sad when we left his family's home that last night, but he didn't say anything to me.

Our new home wasn't much when it was finished. One story, very small, and everything donated by our neighbors: beds, blankets, a blackened stove. They even made us a gift of a goat and two pigs, just enough to start a new life. And we still had three yaks, roaming in the hills.

Most Sherpa homes are two stories, the first for the animals, the second for the family. Ours was too small even for a modest altar. My father always said this home would be temporary. "Next season, I will be back on the trail and we'll build a real home. Maybe back in Khumjung."

I wanted to believe what he said. But it became harder and harder for him to move. Now, almost four years later, we still live in the same house. Father can still barely walk. And we still live on the same floor as our animals. The musky smell of the beasts clinging to my clothes no matter how thoroughly I wash them, my hands white and wrinkled from washing, and yet, forever I feel dirty. At our old home, the altar was a place where I could find peace—not in prayer but in having a moment alone with myself. Here in Khunde, we don't even have a place to give a simple offering!

It was a year after we left Khumjung that Father took me out of school officially. I had too many chores to have time to sit in class, but I had gone back to visit Nurse Lanja, a few minutes at a time, and we spoke of the outside world. I wanted to ask her to paint my fingernails like hers, but I was frightened of what Father would say. To even visit, I had to make elaborate plans and work twice as fast. My father may have been mad and lame in one leg, but he always had a sharp eye. And he noticed. I would finish my chores quickly, too quickly for my father's liking. "Where are you going?" he would ask, hobbling after me. And when I told him once foolishly that I was still so thankful to Nurse Lanja, the one who had saved him that day, the swift *smack* of his hand across my face told me how he remembered my secret friend.

Father forbade me to set foot in the school again, and Mother told me that whatever dreams I had, I must help the family first, and that meant either work or marriage. What point was there to dream of books and of places I would never go? *A woman should be like water, able to flow around anything.* My mother had often said that phrase when I was young. My mother, the stay-at-home abbot, always speaking the words from the dharma and never practicing them.

I had just turned fifteen. I alone out of my sisters could read, and only like a child. I wished that I had had more time to study, but there was none. I had to work because my father could not. I had to help feed my sisters. Father was no use for that. That's when he started to live with a bottle in his hand. He raved drunkenly every day, blaming our misfortune on the lepchas or the wicked gods on Mount Kailash. A man punished with six daughters— why would he give the gods his reverence?

Punished for having six girls. Girl after girl. Punished for breaking his leg. Never to work again. So he punished us all, too, for sharing his fate. He cursed the monasteries, the monks, the gods, he condemned them all.

Did that make the gods angry? Did it stir their wrath against us?

My mother slowly turned away from the faith also. She still chanted, still repeated the words of the lamas and monks, and it was hard for her not having an altar. Sometimes she traveled to her older sister's home, to make an offering for Ang, to help free his soul from our failure to mourn him properly.

I would pray for my brother in my own way. I would go back to Khumjung in the spring, on the anniversary of his death. A day of deep sadness which I marked with a white khata scarf that I left by the tip of the old juniper tree, the rest of it still buried underneath ice and rock, too much to ever dig out.

My brother's soul was trapped forever, and I felt responsible as the Eldest. When I went by myself to the old home, I kept my hood over my face so the villagers wouldn't recognize me. I didn't want to talk to them, I didn't want them to see my pain. My family may have already been cracked before we left Khumjung, but the ru' sent us flying in the wind. And we're still flying.

The one thing we kept from those days, found by one of the villagers, was a framed photo of my father, its glass shattered, but the picture inside it intact. It had been blown out of our home somehow and landed on the other side of the village. In that photo my father is a young man with a wide smile and ice chips in his scraggly beard. A proud climbing Sherpa, strong enough to take on Jomolangma, arm in arm with a Westerner.

My father was so happy back then. The photo hangs crooked in our new home, in the same broken frame, taped together. Father never looks at that picture. He believes more and more that the gods are against him. He's made me believe that, too. Many nights, squeezing my eyes tight, I try to pray. I should know better. The gods don't listen to me, I'm my father's daughter.

4

I LOOK UP, AND EVEN IN THE DARK, I KNOW EXACTLY WHERE EACH peak is.

Ama Dablam, Khunde, Lhotse, Taboche, the realm of Khumbi Yulha and Jomolangma, the holy mother rising above them all, her sides salt-gray, a white cap for a crown. The home of the supreme goddess Jomo Miyo Lang Sangma. The roof of all the world. Mountains that birthed the world and all of its people. Mountains that protect us, mountains that isolate us, mountains we worship.

The sun inches above those crests, transforming the valley, showering bits of light onto the six of us. But the sun can take away what it gives. When its rays thaw the ice, avalanches come. We're still picking dung as the sun climbs. And my sisters are all still talking about the wedding.

Second hums a tune, holding one hand over her face in a sort of tantric dance, alternating hands alluringly, one hand freckled, the other without a single mark. A beautiful mixture.

"Are you going to dance for Norbu on your wedding night?" Third chuckles as she picks dung from the grass. Second dances as she scoops cakes and tosses them in the basket. "Where did you learn that?"

"Don't you remember? We saw it in that Bollywood film, in the cyber cafe!"

"Shh, Mother will hear. You know what she thinks of that place."

"*Tanu Weds Manu*," Second confirms the name of the film. "It's the last one we saw."

"Shh!"

"I don't care," Second says, still dancing. "In two days I'll be married. And then—my husband will be the one to tell me what I can and cannot do."

Norbu and I and Second, all together in one home, in one bed. Wed.

"Are all your baskets full?" Mother calls, breaking the spell.

She'll need every piece we picked up, and she doesn't stop reminding us. The next few days will be crowded with relatives, friends, neighbors, strangers even, all eager to wish us good fortune and to congratulate my parents. And the ones with unmarried sons will be looking over the remaining sisters for a possible future coupling. It's what always happens.

All of my sisters are blessed with long, slender necks, firm legs, womanly curves. Each one believing they're ready to be a wife. Beauty is a curse in a place where you cannot choose your own fate. Maybe it's better to be born ugly. My sister Fifth will surely have the toughest time. She wears the mark of a tooth on her left cheek. It's not from a lepcha that slipped into our home at night, eager to snack on a young girl's flesh. Only fools say that, and they do. It's from a village yard dog she was trying to pet. I saw it happen. I beat the dog with a closed fist until he let go of my sister. Tears ran down her face, mixing with the blood from her cheek, her whole body shuddering as she screamed, and that finally sent the mongrel scurrying. That shriek was the last sound Fifth ever made.

She hasn't spoken since. She grunts, nods, but nothing else. She rarely laughs or cries but Mother and my sisters know exactly how she feels. Fifth has made up her own language. Aside from using her hands, she scrunches her nose a certain way when she's happy and another when she's upset. Sometimes I feel that she's the most expressive of us all, displaying thoughts with all of her body. All I have to do is look at her eyes, and I know what she's thinking.

Fifth wriggles her nose now, as if confirming my thoughts. I feel a rushing surge of warmth. She's my favorite, the sister I speak to without words. The others never stop gabbing. They're gabbing now about our deal with Norbu's family. It's a generous deal for our side. For each bride, the other family pays in yaks. Two brides means twice as many yaks, and more yaks mean a longer life for my family even though they lose their two best workers.

Second likes Norbu. She told me so. It's obvious even without her saying it. He's tall, his shoulders are as wide as a doorway, his gaze light and happy, his manner soft but strong. He's a man who can provide for a family. And with her young body so ready to give him babies, I understand why Norbu would like Second. But he couldn't like both of us equally. He has to have a favorite. The more I look at Second, the more I'm convinced that she's the one. She would be my favorite, too. I can find all sorts of reasons to like Second better than me. Yes, Norbu took my hand once, but maybe he only did it because my father was barely clinging to life on Nurse Lanja's cot. Besides, I was foolish to tell him about my dreams. Life in the valley, in Kathmandu, what man would want a girl who talks like that? He's being kind to take me, too.

The way he looked at me that night, it wasn't with lust or affection. It was pity, I tell myself. And when Norbu approached my father, the old man saw his chance. Two brides, more yaks. Success.

In the older times, before the mikarus reached Nepal, we were even more tied to the land and the yaks. We didn't have to collect their dung back then, we could chop down timber to satisfy our fires. Before I was born, the government made my home—the whole Khumbu region—a national park. That meant we could no longer touch the forest. Army patrols were busy with the Maoists, but if they caught you poaching it could mean prison if you couldn't afford a bribe. Few did. Change is slow here, and us

Sherpas are a stubborn breed. Most of our lives stay the same as they always have.

We still pick berries, herbs, roots, and yartsa gunbu—a cater-pillar fungus prized for its effect on male potency and frustrated husbands' moods—a gift that's saved marriages, no doubt, but destroyed whole communities. Erosion, jealousy, greed. Many children are pulled out of school to comb the hills. There's no law against taking this mushroom, but there is against other lucrative things. We can't take the timber, nor any of the rare creatures that fetch money over the mountains. Villagers still believe that every-thing here is holy, ours to protect. *At least most villagers.* Some still hunt for red panda, wolf, snow leopard. The government says they'll pay for reporting poachers but the government has no money. At least not for us. The bravest Sherpas aren't the ones climbing the mountains with Westerners, the bravest of us are the ones climbing the mountains to enter China. The Chinese grind up any and every bone to put into their wine.

Boar, tahr, fox, when the Chinese grind them, they're all tiger. And when they get a real one, from far in the south in the rice fields of the terai—they charge twice as much. Sometimes I imagine being a man and hunting those creatures, making that journey, a trip filled with so much worry, but so much adventure. If my father was well and able, he would—I don't know why I bother thinking about what Father *would* do when I know he can't. Wishful thinking is just that, something for children.

My father's misfortune doomed our lives so completely, my parents saw their daughters as their last chance. The only thing they had in abundance *were* daughters. For months and months, my father's and mother's worries were carved in the wrinkles on their foreheads and in the circles around their eyes. Worried that Norbu's family wouldn't give them enough for one prize, me, they upped the offer, adding my sister. They'd been negotiating since I first bled. Right after Ang died. My parents wanted to sell us both or nothing at all. Leaning hard on that birch branch, Father kept hobbling back and forth to the Norgay home. When he was too exhausted, he rode on the back of a neighbor's pony, Mother holding the reins, leading him along the trail.

Plans were at last finalized—for both daughters.

As far as my parents were concerned, getting rid of two mouths was a big step towards the survival of the rest of the family. The drought had stretched over a whole year, and people are harder to feed than pack animals. But with the two best workers soon gone, caring for the new yaks, working the fields, my sisters would have to grow up fast. They'd have no choice. If this were a Bollywood film, there would be some kind of miraculous answer, a charmed solution to make everything simpler. Nothing in real life is as simple.

I knew my place. I was tradable goods for my family. Something to be used. No one ever asked what I wanted.

My mother is talking to me now, but my ears are listening to the chirps of birds flying through the dawn. Doves paired with mates they choose and stay with for life. Mates *they* choose. I want to be like them: light, flying away from the old nest, never to return.

"Are you listening, Eldest?"

"Yes, Mother."

"Aren't you happy about your marriage?" Third asks me.

"Of course I am," I chime back.

All my sisters want a husband. All of them want their own families, their own lives. Desperate for a new yoke to replace the old one. I'm ready to marry with my sister, too, Fifth seems to say with the flash of her bright eyes. That could be the surest way to gain a husband. *No man wants a mute for a wife. Or maybe they do. To a man, that would probably be the best gift, the ideal in fact, as long as she could cook, clean, and make babies, why bother with tiresome chit-chat?*

Fifth wiggles her nose, the tooth scar twitching on her cheek. If she's worried about her future, she doesn't show it. My heart aches for her, and loathing for myself, the selfish Eldest who cannot be happy or leave the past behind.

"My future has so much hope now," I mouth to my mother, knowing that's what she wants to hear. No love marriage for us, not even an engagement stage. Some couples are engaged for years, even having children before the ceremony. Many couples now choose their own partners. Not us.

"Your future," Mother says firmly, "originates with your past."

I've heard this one before. My eyes shift sideways. They want me to replace Ang, as though I was the cause of the ru' that took him. Or if I made a boy with Norbu, that would replace Ang. I cannot help a thin smile: what's the point of bringing another life into this world when we have so little to give aside from life itself? So little to share aside from hardship? When my belly swells, so will my responsibilities. It feels like these parents of mine are truly mad, envisioning solutions nestled inside the problems themselves.

"With you married, it's going to be easier for your sisters. It will be a good sign, showing others that our family has value. This union is a good beginning, an auspicious beginning for all of us. If the gods are willing, the land and sky will come together and bring us rain."

"And the drought will end, Mother?" asks Fourth.

Mother laughs like the gurgle of an unexpected spring, pushing through a clog. "There has been a curse on the earth. And it will take time. But it will change."

My sisters—the three whose futures are yet to be arranged—share glances, the mysteries of their fortunes playing in their mind's eye. "How long must *we* wait?" asks Third, the next in line by birth.

Mother laughs again, differently, like a splash among stones. "Not so long. And when we marry the *last* of you, your father and I will be ready for our sky funeral."

My mother, like all Sherpa women: *die young, exhausted by work and childbearing.*

I shake my head, trying to drop the feeling like a dead leaf. When all their children are married, most Sherpa women are ready to lay down on the mountain and feed the vultures. Alms to the sky. *I don't want your sky funeral to be any time soon, Mother. But how could I not dream of escaping?*

The sun pokes beams of light through the clouds. The birds are louder now, their song of joy replaced by warning shrieks. A golden eagle swoops down, talons ripping at fragile feathers. The doves dodge and weave, never leaving each other. If they did, one—maybe both doves— would be saved. But neither abandons the other, and the eagle gets its chance.

I hate this hunter, this bird whose beak will one day feed on my parents. When it's my turn, as the Eldest, I won't have the heart to raise my kikuri to my parents' still warm bodies. Is this the key to freeing the soul to the heavens—the bodies of our dead chopped to pieces to make it easier for the birds to lift them beyond?

Mother's close-set brown eyes focus on me as if she's reading my thoughts. Then, as if to sum up my existence, my place, my role to serve, "Come," she commands, and I march forward next to her, my four sisters trailing behind me as the village comes into view with its hilly farms and rocky soil where even potatoes and root vegetables are hard to grow. The mud brick homes with thatched roofs made of bundled reeds and sticks, the pockets of air between the layers providing cheap insulation. Last night's dew trickles down angled roofs, collecting into plastic bottles, set around each home in supplication to a stingy water god. *Please bring rain.*

The ground is a mix of icy scree and yellowish grass, parched dry and frozen from the high altitude. A high altitude ice desert. An underfed river snakes through the village. Yaks graze in twos and threes on both sides, sucking up what's left of the short grass, some further up the hills, on midriffs once pine-green. Smoke billows from stone hearths, a rooster crows, then clucks in fear as if chased by a hungry tomcat. The sounds of early morning.

All around the towering mountains, with their thick snowy capes, keeping the outside out, and us in.

All my life *here*.

I look up suddenly into the purple-blue sunrise after a single high-pitched cry. A war cry. The eagle, its great wings flapping, whizzes directly overhead, its talons clutching both doves.

My sisters have already hurried on towards the village. My mother turns and yells and I run to catch up.

5

BACK HOME, MY FATHER IS IN BED WITH A BOTTLE OF CHANG. THE drink of the yeti, he calls it.

The drink yetis kill for.

I believed that as a child. That there were real yetis, crazed by the effects of the chang. I know now that it's just the home brew that keeps my father's mind as cloudy as the drink itself. A mix of barley and water, you can't even see through it when it's in a glass. Strong stuff, strong enough to not freeze through winter. Strong enough to turn a grown man into a demon child.

I know all too well what happens when the chang takes him. I know all about chang, I've made it for my father, on my hands and knees, mixing hot water into a cask of thick, fermented grain. I've made it too many times to count, barrels of it, one on every holiday for my father to make blessings with, to drink with the other villagers. Now I make one each month, a barrel he shares with no one else.

I've tasted it, too. Just once. I coughed so hard I thought my insides would burst. My sisters laughed. Luckily, my father didn't catch me sneaking the drink.

If you drink chang, you'll get a headache, so goes the song, *if you don't, you'll get heartache.* Men yell this as a toast when they celebrate and when they suffer.

When my father's eyes are low and his fists hot, he repeats that saying over and over, like a mantra for black deeds. Best not to be around at those times, but where can I escape to? Only one option. Along with my sister, of course. "Two down," he says, in between gulps.

My gaze moves from Father as he is today to the yellowed photo of the proud climbing Sherpa he was not long ago. Almost four years ago.

I remember a mother yak we once had, back when we were in Khumjung and Father wasn't a cripple. The cow had broken a leg a few days after giving birth. Usually calves are vulnerable after birth—from frost, from starvation, unable to wean, from predators attracted by the smell of afterbirth and blood—but this calf was healthy. It was the mother who suffered from poor health. Or poor luck. One morning I found her still on all fours, and at first, I had just thought her lazy. But when I saw her leg, I was instantly reminded of my father. My sisters and I applied a moist poultice of herbs, and I remember the cow moaning, that little calf not leaving her side.

We tried to set the leg in a splint, but the cow went mad, kicking and bucking. And moaning. That sound, that wail. We had no choice. The other cows wouldn't let the newborn suckle, they didn't have enough milk to spare. Poor luck, the job fell to me as Father was gone on a trek.

My hands shook, the frost still clinging to the grass, crunching under my feet, my steps uneasy. And I remember the look she gave me. She knew. Strange, how even animals know what's coming to them. Her eyes were blood colored, like deep lava-filled lakes with a stone thrown in. All morning she was grunting and mooing, but she fell silent when I got close. Do it, her eyes said. Caressing the soft tuft of her nape, my hands steadied. And she was calm. I remember how hot the blood felt when it spurted out. A puddle at my feet, growing and freezing in between flecks of hardened grass. Even beasts deserve sky funerals, and I made one right there, offering the cow and her calf to the world beyond after taking them from this one.

My father's fate is crueler. He dies a little more each day. His life is a morning to night cycle: he sits and drinks, drinks and sits. When he does move, his fury is unleashed by the drink. Unleashed on all of us. Once I'm married, my sisters will have my example to contend with. I, as part of the Norgay family, will be rich, with six dozen yaks, and most of them producing milk.

Norbu is one of only three children, all boys, and the other two are already married, so my sisters will have to look elsewhere. Luck chooses harshly.

The impermanence of life, Buddha says. Always look forward, always be filled with compassion. But my mind is filled with doubt. And fear. Black thoughts on black days, I push our goat out of the way, and she bleats in protest. I sit on my worn wooden bench, rocking back and forth.

My fingers clutch the bench like it could come alive under me. I claw at its chipped blue paint, not feeling as it collects under my fingernails. Finally, I leave. When my mother goes to bed with my father just a few feet away and he begins—that leg hasn't diminished his desire—I leave when our home's four walls seem to cave in, when the stink from the open mouths of the animals is too much, when my sisters won't stop arguing, I leave. And I go to where my feet can't take me, down the mountain, to the valley below and Kathmandu. In a classroom with girls my own age. Ready to graduate from university in the capital—learning without having to do chores—*one day, I'll come back to show everyone, just like Nurse Lanja did.* Or at a festival, dancing with a boy, his hands on my body—and I smile, feeling no shame for wanting that touch, for enjoying it. For that thought alone, my father would hit me with a closed fist, and once would not be enough.

The crackle of the flames brings me back. Mother piles dung to prepare the midday meal. My silent sister glances at me as if asking: "Are you all right?"

The thick smoke from the stove fills the room and I imagine Father's chang-blurred vision. It won't be long before he'll wake and find fault with me again. There's nowhere safe in our small home. The hungry goat rubs against me, chews on my sleeve. I shove her harder now, she staggers back—and steps on the pig. She squeals. Then all the animals shriek, and the beast on two legs—well, almost two—awakens and roars

"Soon, very soon," Mother mumbles, glaring at my sisters, who jump into action. Crouching, leaning, bending, necks craning, limbs stretched. Second lights incense to purify the room and bless the food, Third lights the butter lamps, Fourth and Fifth take the steaming pot of rice off the stove. "Why aren't you helping, Eldest?" Mother snaps. "You aren't married yet."

I leap and get the rice bowls and cups.

"Your father first, Eldest!"

I pile the rice high into Father's bowl, then pour lentils and curry on top. I give it to him, but he almost throws it back at me. "Where's the roti?"

I turn, it's still frying, I burn my fingers as I grab it. "Here it is."

He takes it from me, crunches down on the thin doughy bread, sending crumbs onto the floor, the pig scurrying over right away. Father hits the pig on its snout, but it keeps eating the crumbs. "Eldest, hand me the birch."

I grab the crutch and give it to him and he beats the pig away. Father clumps food in the fingers of his right hand and eats. Mother unwraps her sash, opens her bakhu robe and suckles our hungry Sixth sister.

Birth, life, death, sky.

I daydream about a space of my own, truly my own, a place where I will be able to read, to learn more about life beyond the mountain—to *be*, in a way that I've never had the chance at home. And since Norbu's family home is full, we'll build a new one for ourselves. My instincts tell me Norbu is gentler than Father, but his expectations for women are probably the same. He is a man, after all.

A woman's role is simple, to tend house and make children.

It will help to have my sister there, and I reassure myself that Norbu is different than Father. We have at least one very important thing in common—he goes to the cyber cafe in our new village of Khunde, more than an hour's walk from here, and watches Bollywood films on the computer. Second and I have seen him there many times. Norbu would never admit that he goes there hoping to see us, but the cyber cafe is the only place for the unmarried to be together without causing gossip. When you cannot be alone with a man, there are no other ways for flirtation. And when a man cannot speak to you alone, when the business of love becomes just that, a transaction conducted by parents instead of the future man and wife, we have no choice but to resort to whatever inane ways we can find to see each other. How many young men go and sit there behind a machine, pretending to be enthralled by the artistry of Indian choreography and complicated love affairs, when they are really just waiting for their own real-life affairs to start?

When we saw Norbu at the cafe last time, he nodded, then quickly turned back to the screen. But his eyes kept glancing at us, then just as quickly looking away. Impossible to tell what he was thinking. Impossible to know what to do next. I couldn't talk to Mother about this sort of thing. She and Father forbade us to visit the cyber cafe. "Don't you have any useful work to do?" Mother questioned. We would finish our chores as fast as we could, rushing to watch those films when the generator worked, sometimes all of my sisters huddling around a single small screen.

"Do any women really live like that?" Third would ask, pointing to a brown-skinned goddess reclining on a throne while two men fed her peeled grapes.

"Some women have two men as servants?" Fourth wondered.

"Maybe some women have *two* husbands?" Third asked. "I saw it in another film. Didn't you see that one with me, Eldest? *The Two Husbands From Bangalore*, remember?"

I could never handle two husbands. Even if I wore henna tattoos on my hands, a ring in my nose, and I liked to chant and dance at any given moment to the sounds of sitars and drum beats, one is enough.

Once, on a rare occasion that I was alone, I discovered Norbu at the cafe. He sat up in his seat and looked at me so intently, I felt like a deer trapped by a wolf. When we're married, he won't leave me alone until he's put a baby in my belly. I'm certain of this no matter how kind he is. He'll make me and my sister pregnant at the same time. And if neither of us can give him a child right away, he could take another bride. Norbu's family has enough yaks to buy many brides.

Two days from now, I'll be a bride. Soon enough, I'll learn if I can make him happy. But the way my mother sounds on the nights my father isn't passed out, when he has his way with her—the sounds she makes. Sometimes she cries. More times than I can remember I've kept my eyes shut, pretending to be sleeping but wide awake, my hands balled into fists, a cold sweat all over me— is that what it is to be a good wife—to have a man on top of you every night?

If Norbu would let me study, maybe that would—

"Eldest!" My father pushes the goat out of the way, hops towards me on his good leg. His eyes are rolling. "Have you gone deaf, Eldest? What are you thinking about?"

"Maybe Norbu will let me go back to school," I say before I can stop myself. The blow is so swift, it knocks me down.

My sisters, crouching an arm's length away, barely look up. My mother holds the little one close, and by the way the baby cries, I know how hard she's pressing her breast into Sixth's face. It's a scene that's played in our home so many times, no one shows surprise—better to be done with it quickly. Mother breathes deep, stirs the pot. He hits me again. I'm so used to it, I don't even flinch. I go deep inside. Far away, to a place where I don't feel anything. Where I can't be touched. Father is puffing, sucking air through jagged teeth. He'll go on like this until his end. Not the first or last man to make chang his life until it's gone. He hops on his one good leg, one, two, three steps until he collapses back down to his bed and his bottle. The noble Sherpa.

The goat is back in my face, licking the salty tears from my swollen face. I don't even push her away. My sisters keep their heads down, best to stay low. Then Fifth, sweet Fifth, she puts her rice bowl down and comes and nuzzles her head against mine.

"Third, fill a cup with snow for your sister," Mother directs. "She's getting married the day after tomorrow. We can't have her face bruised. Eldest has to look her best."

6

I HAVE TROUBLE SLEEPING TONIGHT, AND IT'S NOT BECAUSE I'M SORE and bruised. Nor is it because I share my bed with my sisters. I'm used to that. I'm used to the stink of the animals and my parents' nightly sport. All normal.

What keeps me awake are my thoughts. I try remembering the last time my father was *my father*. The last time he was sweet to me. The nearest I can recall is when he bought a mobile phone, a Sony Ericsson J1332—I was so impressed, I memorized the model. Father bought it used, for seven hundred and fifty rupees. He never had a mobile when he worked on the mountain, but he told me he planned to make it a gift to me on my wedding day. This kindness was so unexpected, it was hard to believe. "For me?" I confirmed, astonished.

He nodded. He hadn't given me or my sisters a present since he'd broken his leg. The small, shiny thing felt so smooth.

"How does it work, Father?" I asked.

The lines on his forehead creased and rippled, and he started punching numbers on the mobile, impatient and wild, the way he did everything. The device uttered a string of sharp *beeps*, then fell silent.

"I'll show you on your wedding day," he growled, throwing the mobile into a chest at the foot of his bed. The chest where he kept his climbing flashlight, his special sunglasses, and other trekking supplies he no longer used. He hits the top of the chest with his walking stick—that's it—and limped off. I pinched my eyes shut and exhaled.

A week later, telling myself this *would* be my wedding present —*it was my right*—I opened the chest while he was asleep. Everyone was working in the field, all except for our patriarch, deep in the land, the empty bottle at the foot of the bed. I watched Father's chest rise and fall, a whooshing snore escaping his lips. And as I looked down at him, I thought of all the times he had stood like that over me.

Tracing his body, from the hard lines of his face down to those terrible hands. How easy it would be to end him, I thought, and then, as if cheering me on, the goats and pig began wailing. He didn't stir, though his chest kept rising and falling, rising and falling. Shame washed over me. Then fear and guilt. I shoved the mobile into my coat and rushed out, Father still snoring.

I ran to the fields to oversee what few yaks we had left. I felt as if I was being watched—*I'm a thief. No, I'm not*—making me work double-quick, filling the jugs with milk, piling the dung to collect, all the while, the little mobile in my pocket waited to be touched. I felt it throbbing like the heart of a newborn calf.

The elders—the real elders—they say yaks birthed our world. In the old days, we would use their hair to make tents and clothes. Now most prefer buying down jackets over sewing coats by hand. The Norgays have dozens of yaks, enough to make life easy. Or easier, as long as I'm not the one chasing them up and down the steppe. I imagine having to tend them all by myself, but no, that's not the way for a new bride. We don't have enough yaks, so we never have enough cheese and butter to sell, never enough to buy rice or flour, so I often drink water to fill the emptiness.

Too tired to worry any longer I sat under a tree, a silver birch, and finally pulled it out. My shiny little friend.

The weather had been pleasant enough that week, long days with the sun high enough to melt the morning frost. With the wide sky warming me, I felt safe, safe to sit without fear of the cold creeping up my backside. Or of anyone watching. Sitting under the silver birch, I read the letters and numbers on the back of the mobile, trying to sound out English words. *Made in China.*

I flipped it over, and my finger touched something that made a startling *beep*—startling enough that I dropped the thing. I let out a laugh, my first in so long, and the laugh turned to a slight cry, and I laughed and cried at the same time, free to let my heart sing under that birch. My head down, my shiny little friend filling my whole world, I felt the sun's touch moving across my face. My neck ached a bit, but I didn't move, I couldn't get enough of this toy. When the headmaster showed us his mobile years ago, I didn't know what I would do with it or who I would call, but I decided I would have my own one day. Now I did, even if for only a few moments. Recalling Bollywood films in which people tapped them with their fingers, I did the same: the screen growing bigger, then everything smaller. I couldn't imagine Norbu beating me for this. He had his own mobile, which I'd seen him use at the cyber cafe.

I raised the phone and pointed. Yaks chewing their cud blissfully at pasture. Salty gray and white peaks. I pressed down with my thumb. *Snap.* Looking at the screen, the mountains were now trapped in the machine. I turned the mobile around, then, looking at my reflection in it, I tapped down again. *Snap.* I barely recognized what I saw, prettier than I remembered, despite being covered in dust. I wiped with my hand, splashed water from my bottle, smeared and washed as best I could, then snapped again. Better. I kept looking at the photo: no child anymore.

One of the yaks grunted, but I didn't even look up.

Another time in the cyber cafe, a boy showed me his phone. His name was Tinga, the owner's son. Half my age and already connected beyond the mountains, to another planet, Tinga looked and spoke to me as if I was a child—and of matters like this, I was—addressing me with the confidence of an annoyed adult. When he crouched close, his finger brushed against mine, and our eyes met, mine scared, his suddenly filled with excitement. The hairs on my neck pricked and I felt my whole face redden. I left right away, knowing well what would have happened if I would have let Tinga show me more, how quickly my virtue as a woman would have been considered lost just from being alone with a man—even a boy like Tinga. Gossip is trafficked more than anything else in these mountains.

The yaks grunted again. A light snow flurry began falling, but I was too busy to care, nestled against the silver birch, its drooping shoots swaying in the mid-afternoon wind. Then I heard a twig snapping under the weight of something heavy, and I knew it wasn't the yaks. It felt like the rumbling of the peaks before an ice fall, and for a moment I thought it was a ru'. Then they grunted a third time. Yaks have many types of grunts—pleasure, pain, fear, as many as we do—this one was sharp and high, a warning call. Fear.

When I looked up from the mobile, I barely noticed it move, barely believed what I was seeing. It blended so well into the land, but there was no mistaking it. All muscle and spotted fur, silent in the falling snow, the fresh khaa perfectly masked the sound of its steps. But there it was, fifty yards away, a serken: the pet of the gods. A snow leopard.

The bardo of life, the bardo of death.

I froze. Its body wasn't crouched, it wasn't stalking. It moved carefully, almost frightened. Then I saw why. A tiny bundle of white fur and spots trotting at her heels. It was a mother with cub.

"Namaste, serken," I whispered, loud enough to let her know where I was, but not too loud, I didn't want to startle her. There couldn't have been a more dangerous place on the mountain—in the world—to be so close to a mother with cub. But the way she nudged the little one along, coaxing it through the field, it made me strangely calm. Without fear.

She looked at me and the snow stopped falling. Above us, the sun pushed through the clouds again, a good omen. The yaks didn't take any chances, though. Huddled together, they stood their ground and faced her, all three of them, even the oldest, the one who's been with us since before I was born, her legs shook in fear, but she held firm, head high. The mother leopard didn't even give them a passing glance. The way she moved, I didn't worry for the yaks, certain she wasn't here to hunt.

Perhaps she was moving dens or returning to a kill. No male in sight, of course. As it is in any other world, the mother takes care of the young while the father sires them, then does who knows what, likely never to return.

I felt a warmth radiating inside of me. Compassion. Perhaps she felt it, too?

Remembering the mobile, I held it up, waiting for her to get close enough to fill the small screen. She didn't even notice me— not until the *beep* returned, and the sound stopped her in mid-stride.

Still crouching under the birch, I realized how defenseless my position was. How exposed. And I started to worry. That mobile I was so hypnotized by, it's disrupted all of my senses. And now the mother leopard was staring right at me, three leaps away. Her eyes were so green. A pine tree in spring. No, carved jade, freshly polished.

Muscles tensed and rippled underneath her thick fur. She shifted her head, tongue tasting my scent, big green eyes shining even bigger as she focused on me. My heart banged like a monastery drum during the morning meal, hard and loud enough that I was sure she heard. But I didn't reach for my kikuri. I stayed still and kept staring back. She looked at me without fear or anger, and I felt my heart slow. Hers reminded me of a look my mother had given me when I was younger—and it calmed me—from one mother to one who will soon be one.

The cub, a few paces back, growled squeakily, tired. The mother flicked her tail, waited for the youngster to catch up, holding my gaze the whole time. Eyes so green, and something else

I noticed: a fleck of black in one of them. Then she prodded the little one with a padded paw, and they kept on.

Tashi delek. Good fortune.

Just as she passed by me, two steps away now, I picked up the mobile again. But the screen was black. And when I looked back up, the pair was gone.

Serken. Truly a ghost.

That night, I told my father what happened. (Well, I was careful to leave out the part about the mobile, and I was quick to replace it right when I got home.) First, Father didn't believe me. No animal is rarer, none holds more power. Father was furious that I didn't protect the yaks. Throwing rocks or sticks would have antagonized the animal, I said. I was so filled with joy from the encounter, I didn't imagine Father would grow angry. His hands didn't quiver, his breath didn't go short, like the beginning of one of his rages. I thought I saw it in his eyes, a tug at the sides of his lips, the beginnings of a smile that never materialized, a moment that still transported me back. I felt like a little girl in that moment. Even him not saying anything, I was sure there was some greater meaning. There must have been. Or perhaps it was all a little girl's wish and my father was simply too drunk and tired to raise his fist. What a foolish girl.

Now I can't sleep, so very far away from that wishful girl. My father's actions have spoken clearly this time. My swollen face throbbing, I want nothing else than to see that image of the wild, an animal no one has seen in these mountains since before I was born. Those deep jade eyes, the fleck of black in one of them, that massive tail almost like another limb. And the little cub, only months old...

I wonder if I *would* have been able to snap the leopard, and tried to explain to Father that inside the mobile device rests the gods' pet, what would he say?

"Blasphemy," he would cry. *Blasphemy!*

I know better now, I wouldn't share that image, I'd keep it for myself.

I close my eyes, thinking of her, a life filled with hardship and solitude, that we have in common. It doesn't matter what species you are, a low birth means suffering. I can hear Father now, snoring, deep in dream.

I imagine her: at rest in her den, lying on her side, cub suckling, or on a hunt, after tahr or musk deer. Is she thinking of our meeting? No. She's thinking of survival. Warmth, food, safety. Animal thoughts.

An animal lives in the moment, in the now, a high form of consciousness, even if they cannot speak. Being ever present is a major tenet of Buddhism. Forced to act, forced by circumstance, there are no luxuries in nature. And that's why the snow leopard, the tiger, the monkey, all can attain Nirvana.

7

DRESSED IN OUR BEST, THICK COATS OVER YAK WOOL SWEATERS, itchy, but warm, under red sashes and white khata scarves blowing in the wind, my whole family marches past neighbors who bow and press their hands together and whisper congratulations of "namaste."

At the center of our procession, the two brides, cheeks painted crimson, our heads covered by pill box hats trimmed with fox fur tickling my ears with each step, our necks weighed down by long-shaped pieces of bone set into metal grooves, protective necklaces worn to keep evil spirits from rising to the head. Over that, strung coral beads, studded with heavy stones supporting jantar box amulets, more weapons to ward off the evil that lives all around us.

"For protection against mountain spirits," my mother says. "Always eager to snatch the body of a wayward bride. Don't even think of taking those stones off until you've said your vows and your marriage has been sewed. Understand?"

I nod, my jaw still sore but covered with makeup, the redness from my bruises makes my cheeks even brighter. I'm not so sure I believe in these stories—or the power of what I'm wearing—but it is tradition. And in my next life, my life with Norbu and my bride sister, I welcome all manner of help to keep me safe.

"I can't believe this is happening," Nyi, my second sister giggles, and I force a smile in reply as my mother yells: "Quiet!"

We have been transformed—for once we look pretty—fully women. Worth being wanted. All around, every step, every tradition and ritual, is made to protect us. My sisters carry lightly burning juniper branches, the smoke flowing over us in the wind, part of our ceremonial cleansing.

My mother—with Sixth strapped to her back—carries our dowry, a silver box encrusted with two large pearls, she strums a blue-green turquoise necklace, fingers rubbing the beads, lips whispering good fortune prayers. And my father, in a long black cloak, felt fedora angled up on the crown of his head, riding on the back of a black pony he borrowed from a neighbor, even he looks transformed—almost happy. Two steps closer to lay-koh.

Tomorrow will be the ceremony, a feast, many glasses raising with the chant *"che, che, che,"* arms linked in dance, the exchange of gifts, khatas, vows. We'll eat meat, surely we will, the first time I'll taste it since...I don't remember when. Then, our bellies full, my sister and I— we will be transferred to Norbu's house. What follows after that, the work, the responsibilities, I know I can manage, but the idea of giving myself to a man is terrifying. I remember watching Norbu work, heaving stones with hands so big it's hard to imagine that they could be gentle.

Tomorrow, tomorrow, tomorrow.

The deal is already set, if either side backs out now much shame would come, and neither family would be able to save face. And yet, today is for both families to give the other one last look, to make absolutely sure. And if there are any other details to settle— *there couldn't be another sister added, could there?*—then they will be made today.

And so here we are, on display for all of Khunde to see our "virtuous beauty," as my Mother calls it. We walk slowly, slow enough for all to lay eyes on my sister and I—us—the living prize. We walk for three hours on a path that should take half that time, that's how much we stop, sharing tea with neighbors who come out of their homes, pressing their hands together and bowing,

Father never getting off his pony, trailing behind his flock like a shepherd. Everyone wishes us "tashi delek." Good fortune. A fortune that's tested when we finally come back to Khumjung, the first time we all return as a family, the first time in almost four years we're all so close to our brother Ang—our old home still forever buried, none of us look that way—*don't look back*. We stare forward, in the present, back at Norbu's parents' home, we're greeted by an old woman, her face holding as many lines as the mountain has stones. Beside her, her husband, a stick of a man with a wide fedora that swallows his small head, its brim almost touching his bony shoulders. They bend with bowed legs, smiling with missing teeth, beckoning us in, and we bend back and follow, both sides holding our smiles as we enter.

My father steps down from the pony, his coat long enough to conceal his limp and cane, high leather boots trudging over ice and rock. He stops and looks at me for a moment, and I'm that little girl again, if only for a moment. And then he keeps moving, shuffling to the door. It's time.

Inside, animals on the bottom floor, family above, we climb a small set of stairs, past the shrine room, a kitchen, *an indoor bathroom.* Merely a hole cut into the floor, but a luxury beyond our means. Even the wood and mud that make up the walls, the floor, everything looks shiny, newer than I remember it. Being here, I feel as if I'm from another caste altogether.

I'm not, of course. Even Sherpas do not marry below their station, but compared to our home, this is opulence. And instead of exciting me, as it does Second—her eyes shining—I feel fear as we sit on pillows scattered all over the floor, looking too ornate to use. I find a place in between my father and mother, Second through Fifth around us, little Sixth bouncing in my mother's lap.

The woman of the house serves us each a cup of steaming black tea, and when I look at her and her husband, I'm less sure that they're so different from us. Not much on their bones, the drought, the years of struggle, it's hit them just as hard as it has us, life's unfair fairness balancing the scales. Blessed and cursed all the same, like all people.

All the faces in the Norgay household are old—there are no children here, all married off, but it's still too small for the family to take on two brides. A grandmother and two aunts sit in the corner of the room, watching, stroking mugju prayer beads, sipping their tea. Above them, a picture of the fourteenth Dalai Lama and his unceasing smile, with the ancient kingdom of Kham in the background, where all Sherpas originally come from. His image gives me courage. Norbu is nowhere to be seen. Could he be gathering his own courage right now?

My mother and Norbu's mother exchange katas. My mother hands over the silver box, Norbu's mother opens it, revealing shiny jewels I didn't even know we owned. My father unfurls a brightly colored prayer carpet from his long coat—*how did he manage to hide it in there and how did I not notice?* I can hear my mother's stern voice: "Do not dwell on the past, do not dream of the future, concentrate on the present."

Words of the Buddha, whispered to my sister and me. Words usually filled with compassion sound like a harsh warning now as I hear them repeating in my mind. I would be calm, I should be calm, but my mind is a jumble. Where is the bridegroom? I turn to Second, she looks a bit worried, too.

My mother feels our tension. *"Steady,"* she whispers.

Norbu's parents flash that happy smile full of holes. We smile back. And then he enters.

Norbu Norgay, my—*our*—future husband. No holes in his smile, he has all of his teeth, and they're all still white. A round face, cheeks with a dab of red, flushed, he is nervous, too. His hair, as black as a volcanic stone, is slicked back. He—he's handsome, and this realization makes me smile my first real smile of the day.

Norbu holds a bottle, fills glasses. I can't stop looking him over, even though I'm not supposed to, not before we're kyo-ka kye-man. Glasses raised, the men buzzing *"che, che, che,"* then *"chang toong-na go-na, ma-toong-na nying na."*

The bottle is quickly emptied, the warmth from the tea and the chang surging. Norbu sits across from me, close enough that I can inhale that pungent mountain smell of manhood that reminds me of the day when he pulled me in close as Father's leg was being set. A day that feels so long ago. His darting, smiling eyes have a childlike aura to them. The very opposite of my father's eyes. But there's so much I don't know about Norbu, so many questions that make me unsure whether I could love this man.

Mother doesn't say a word. Neither does Father nor my five sisters, and not a peep from Norbu's family, just the sound of steaming black tea being poured again, Norbu's mother filling all of our mugs. She doesn't even let us put in our own sugar, she does everything. The process takes at least ten minutes, but it's still hot when I put it to my lips.

Good tea.

I put the mug down, I don't want to conceal my face—but I also don't want him to notice my bruises. Mother painted me over using crushed leaves of meshming pati. He's examining me, and I examine him in return. Under a yak fur coat, he wears a long-sleeved robe that falls slightly below the knee. Even with a shirt on, he looks muscled, like a workhorse. Well-fed. Ready.

Maybe I was wrong about him.

Our eyes catch. I want to look away, and I do. He doesn't. I finish the tea, place it down in front of me on the table. And then it happens, before I even realize what I'm hearing. He pronounces my name softly in a way my parents do, looking at me straight on before turning to my father. "Only Nima. Same amount of yaks, only Nima."

Only Nima.

The smiles disappear around me, replaced with wrinkled brows, narrowing eyes. Whatever is happening is happening to Father's surprise—to all of my family's surprise. Second looks as if an arrow has been shot right through her, she can't catch her breath. Mother's eyes go huge. Father adjusts the felt hat on his head with a strangled look on his face I've never seen before. Norbu's father parts his thin lips: "My son wishes to honor our agreement—but he only wants *one wife*. And I cannot argue with another man's wish, even if it is my son."

The veins in Father's neck bulge. We can hear him gritting and grinding his teeth. But he doesn't open his mouth, doesn't say a word.

"What have you done, Eldest?" he suddenly erupts.

I feel dizzy, cut up and set ablaze. Norbu's father intercedes. "We will honor the agreement, we will still deliver the six yaks as promised—but my son will only take one wife. Know that this was not my choice, I advised against it, but I must respect my son's wishes—"

"Why? Why do you spit in my eye?" Father asks Norbu, staring directly at him. Norbu drops his head. "Why do you break your promise? Who will want to marry my younger daughter now?"

Tears build in Second's eyes.

"People will talk, people will say something is wrong with her. What of our suffering? What of the pain you're causing us?"

With his thumb, Norbu brushes a drop of sweat from his temple. He clears his voice, and when he speaks, he keeps his gaze to the floor. "Most esteemed sahep, I apologize for your pain. I apologize for the dishonor I am causing you and your family. As my father said, we will honor our side of the agreement. I have always respected you, sahep. And I respect your family. If I may say, I feel I have grown quite close to your family in the last few years. I was there in your time of need, and I will be again. And I will take care of your daughter. Forever. But I have to think of my own life. My future."

The room is so quiet.

My father stands abruptly, and everyone braces.

"Please, sahep, listen, sit, please," Norbu urges.

Father collapses back onto his pillow.

Norbu swallows, speaking quickly. "It's normal for Sherpa men to take two wives. Even sisters. My uncle wed two sisters. When I made my decision to wed your daughters, my family wrote my uncle a letter. And he wrote back, asking me to visit him. I hadn't seen him in years, but he said it was important that we speak by face, not hand and paper. Last month, I made the trip to Gorak Shep. In the five years since I had last seen him, my uncle looked like he had aged five decades. He's younger than my father, but he looked so old, so tired. And why? His wives. Both had stopped speaking with each other—for the past three years—and barely to him, and yet they still share the same bed. Only one could make children. And only one son was made, and he came stillborn. That's when the trouble started, the jealousy. They wouldn't even speak to me when I visited. My uncle wanted me to see this for myself, he wanted me to see one possible future. It was a mistake to marry two women, even worse to marry two sisters. Both of your daughters are beautiful, and I say all of this with respect, sahep, but I don't want to make the same mistake as my uncle. I apologize for the pain I'm causing, but I cannot change my decision, sahep. Nima. Only Nima."

My mother grips Second's hand, her tears having ruined her makeup. The room is spinning. I can see Father's lips moving, but I can't hear anything. I feel the heat rising off his body. Norbu speaks again, then his father, but I still can't hear. I shift my gaze across the room, focusing on Norbu's grandmother and aunts—*help me*. I watch their bony fingers, rubbing one hundred and eight beaded bracelets, beads dedicated to mantras and sentient beings, dark beads, made from a tulsi plant or the seeds of a bodhi tree. Their faces are living chortens. Cheeks like over-tanned leather, long and saggy as though they'd once been fuller and became deflated, leaving deep trenches.

I look up at the picture of His Holiness, that cherubic face, forever laughing, as if at me. The eldest of Norbu's blood, fingering the pearls of life, they smile cautiously, and though I don't want to live with these mother hens, I smile back. *Esteemed aunts, I have not tried to ruin this deal. And even though Norbu's uncle's wives did not get along, I would always get along with Second. I wish you could say this to Father, please believe me, I had no idea of Norbu's wishes.*

My father sees my lips curl in deference to my future in-laws. No matter how this will end, one thing is certain in his mind: I'm at fault. The tension feels like the silence before the ru' strikes.

Norbu's mother begins to refill everyone's mugs, but her hands are so shaky that boiling tea overflows onto the wood floor. Steam wafts into the air as Second weeps openly now. This was the start of a new life for her, the start of everything. Now it's over. She won't even look at me.

It's not my fault, I plead, searching for any friendly face.

Third and Fourth look away. *Fifth, my favorite, Nga, my silent sister, what of you?* Not even a sympathetic nod. They all think I'm part of this plan.

I turn to Norbu, he knows the pain he's causing. He puts his mug down, bows slightly.

Norbu, make this right.

Will he speak now? Apologize? No, he says nothing. Instead he exits the room. *How could you leave me now? How could he do this to me?* I can feel Father's anger radiating off him and I close my eyes, sure that he'll start beating me right here. But when I open them again, Mother has her hand on Father's arm. She looks at him in a way that says: these people could still become our in-laws, *manage yourself.* Norbu's mother refills the remaining cups, hands firmer this time. No one is drinking.

Norbu returns—thank you—pushing in a black box on wheels. He adjusts it in front of us, positions two long metal ropes, connects a snake-like cord to an old generator.

Ze-nith, I read in glossy silver lettering.

"This can be run on a generator or solar power," he says, on one knee, cranking the generator by hand. "I haven't received the solar panels yet, but I will soon. They're being sent by plane, to

Lukla. Very expensive, but I'll bring them to you, sahep, in a few days. Ah, there it is now, the power is flowing. I'll show you." Norbu pulls an object out of his pocket and offers it to my father. Long and black, it looks like a wand wrapped in plastic. "Please," he says. "It's for the television, to watch programs on. Please, sahep. Take it."

Fathers eyes it skeptically, though the intentions are clear: this is a fresh addition to the deal to smooth over the new relatives. Not worth as much as another yak, or the food it will cost to feed my spurned sister, but for a man like my father, who has never owned such a machine, it's not a complete loss, right?

Father's not sure what to do. Norbu's eyebrows dance, as if Father accepting this gift frees him from guilt. Father holds the long black wand cautiously, like a serpent that might snap at his fingers.

"Allow me," Norbu says. He comes closer—I smell him again, and now I despise that smell—pushing down with his big brown thumb, and like that, the sing-songy drone of the device awakens and the Ze-nith's glow fills the room.

On-screen, a man with a black mustache and a dhaka topi hat hovers over a woman with a dark red bindi on her forehead. Her arms are folded, and there's a dramatic rhythm of Hindi drums. Second and I have watched this program before, in the cyber cafe—it's called Tito Satya, named after the star of the show. I think this is the first time my youngest sisters have seen a television set, but I'm not sure if that's why they are staring at it with wide eyes, or they're just too stunned from what's happened. Perhaps it's both.

When I turn to look at my father, he seems to be glaring right through the screen, eyes empty, but with a fire burning just behind them. A side glance at Norbu again. Hand on his jaw, sucked in by the sorcery, he looks proud.

The music changes, the drums end, making way for the hum of a sitar and a fat man with a rosette patterned shirt. He's spewing insults in Nepali, he and Tito push each other, Tito's wife sobs, her face buried in henna-tattooed hands.

Norbu's parents look on stoically, sipping their tea. Behind us, the aunts and grandmother keep strumming their beads. My mother bounces Sixth on her lap, she's getting restless. My other sisters look on ignorantly, half-confused, half-entertained. Second lets out a muffled yelp we all ignore. Then, broken by the glow of the box, *slap*, the fat man strikes the woman, and a piercing high-pitched laugh: Norbu's. No one else is laughing, just Norbu.

The veins in my father's neck look like they're about to explode.

When we step through the door back home, my father hits me with his cane. Hard. I hit the ground. "What did you do?" he yells, throwing dishes at me, pots, pans, anything he can find. "What kind of pact?"

"I made no pact, Father! I did not know—"

I look up as he raises a gnarled fist and his cane comes down. Will he smash me with the television, so heavy it took three sisters to wheel it back home?

"Have you made him promises with your body?"

Whack!

"Already given it to him?"

Whack!

"Broken your honor?"

Whack! Whack! Whack!

The goat bleats, the swine squeals, chickens flutter. My mother stays out of the way. Second, watching with such disgust, I'm waiting for her to start kicking me, too. Fifth, my favorite, is crying. Third and Fourth shake their heads at their dishonorable sister.

I knew this beating was coming. I could feel it, sitting there while we watched the television, and on the walk home when Father didn't say a single word, back on the pony, the vein in his neck pulsing like it had a life all its own.

"Why would you dishonor us?" Again.

"Why dishonor your sister?" And again.

He keeps going, again and again and again, but I feel it as if from afar, as if it were someone else's body. I curl into a ball and go deep inside.

Om mani peme hung, om mani peme hung, om mani peme hung.

I repeat the mantra over and over, rolling on the floor. Its meaning sounds so strange now: the true sound of truth, words made to invoke compassion and peace. What is the jewel in the lotus flower?

Father stands over me, exhausted, but I can tell he's not done yet. Maybe this is the best way to get rid of another mouth. One step closer to lay-koh...

Whack! Whack! Whack! Whack!

I don't know how much time passes. It's all a warm glow, new bruises forming over old ones, the familiar taste of blood in my mouth. Father is out of breath. Tired from beating me longer than usual, those veins in his neck still pulsating with each hungry gulp.

How hard would it be for me to rise and slice that neck open with my kikuri?

When I saw Norbu last, by chance, for ten minutes at the cyber cafe, we traded hellos, then bowed our heads to each other. No secret deal. No words. Now I'm suffering as if I'd planned it all, like a mindung, a soothsayer.

We are all bees in this world, buzzing alone. Father is back on his feet, and with strength I didn't think he still had, he lifts a heavy bag of grain up and over me. I imagine, suddenly, that this is my end, on the dirt floor of our home, a day before my wedding, killed by a bag of barley. I suppress a laugh, it's all so absurd.

Om mani peme hung, om mani peme hung, om mani peme hung.

I think back to the picture of His Holiness at Norbu's home: we do not have any effigies here, no pictures of the great lama, so none can witness this shame. I'm not even raising my arms to try to deflect the blow. Animals stop fighting when they know it's over.

Father's eyes are red, bubbling. He hangs over me, panting, a pose he's struck so many times, only this time he's going to crush me, maybe even take out his kikuri—but he drops the bag. It falls with a *thud*, dust clouding the room. Father staggers, whole body trembling as he grabs the bottle, tilts it, filling that hole inside him.

Om mani peme hung, om mani peme hung, om mani peme hung.

With the beast occupied, Third, Fourth, and silent Fifth all rush over. I feel wet rags on my swollen face, soft hands helping me up. And then Second comes close, touches my face with her fingertips, her nails lightly raking my cheek. Mother, having watched silently, at last turns to Father. "It's not her fault! Do you think she wanted this?"

He lies on his side, wipes his mouth with a still shaking hand, points his finger threateningly at her. Mother walks forward with such purpose, we're all startled, Father most of all, but she heads towards me, picks me up. My legs wobble as I stand, thinking of those old women at Norbu's home, stroking their beads, circling the prayer wheel. When you die, will faith alone help you ascend to a human body instead of an insect or a goat or something worse? When I die, what happens to my consciousness? Maybe nothing, maybe this is all there is. And if it is, what a fool I am to listen to others.

My mother is speaking to me now. "Do you want to be reborn as a lesser being?"

No, Mother.

"Do you wish to forever swim in the ocean of sadness?"

No, Mother.

If only life were as simple as a mantra. If we did just think and live in the moment, what would it all be like?

"Eldest! Eldest!"

I want to respond, but I can't. I look up, my mother and sisters all around me, getting smaller and smaller, like I'm falling through the earth, to Naraka. Then I can't see anything. The room goes black.

8

I GET UP, QUIETLY, AS IF IN A DREAM. MY HEAD IS POUNDING, AND IT'S
still dark, but I'm wide awake now. Careful not to stir my sisters,
or the light-sleeping goat and pig—I could reach out and touch
Second, despite all that's happened today—her future traded for a
television, she sleeps in peace. So does quiet little Fifth and Third
and Fourth, all so young, all so in need of more than this.

I take off my amulets, my strung coral beads and tengura
necklaces, placing them on the bed. Walking on my toes, I dress
in my warmest yak scarf and sweater, creeping through the dark
room, moonlight from the window guiding my steps. My bruised
fingers dig into the bag of barley that almost killed me, and I stuff
my pockets with that dried grain, then snatch cubes of hard dried
cheese, millet. I fill an empty plastic bottle with water—the water
makes a splash. I look up, expecting six pairs of eyes to open. Nothing. Everyone, even that goat, still sleeping.

Sweat collects on my temples and under my arms. I feel dizzy as
I bend and grab my kikuri, gloves, knit cap, down coat—it will be
cold tonight—and shove it all into a cloth knapsack I sling across
my back. Then I slip my feet into Father's boots, still almost brand
new and too big for me, but I lace them firmly. Good.

In two steps, I'm at the door, toes swimming inside the big
boots, but I stop before letting in the cold night. One more thing.
I turn and creep back towards father's bed. Standing over him,

watching the up-down, up-down of his chest, another deep and drunken slumber. I put one hand on that chest, feel how weak he truly is, how easy it would be. My other hand touches the kikuri, fingers dancing on the blade's hilt.

No, not like this. My hand moves down to the foot of the bed as I crouch, searching, outstretched fingers scanning. My pointing finger hits it and I hear the sharp *ting* of metal.

I raise my head—nothing, no one noticed—then duck back down. Inside the box are the mobile phone and my father's prized flashlight. I grab both. Then something else. Money.

Probably the last bundle of bills Father made, he kept it buried in his boot since the day we lost Ang. I may burn in Naraka for this, but it doesn't matter.

Mother always said a being is only born into that hell as a direct result of their accumulated actions. Their karma. Mine is ripe, I know it. I take a breath and then take three hundred rupees. I stick the bills into my pocket, place the box back under the bed, rise, and my heart stops.

Greeting me are two eyes, staring back in the moonlight. Mother. But her lips remain sealed. She doesn't even raise her head off the pillow. She doesn't call out, doesn't yell or try to grab me. We exchange a look of knowing, and in seconds we exchange a lifetime of unspokens. Then she closes her eyes. *Go.*

Out the door, into the night.

The wind sings, every note a high one. It sounds like my mother's voice, like her cries.

But I haven't heard her cry in almost four years, not since my brother died, and I don't look back. I keep going.

Bundled up, the wind still rips through my clothes, stinging my bruised flesh.

Kang gyok—like a body possessed—I race down the path. *Mother woke up Father and told him. He's coming after me. No. She didn't. He's not coming. My pain, all of my suffering, she saw it in my eyes. Years of holding back, years to make up for, my buffer.*

I have until the morning. Every few feet, turning at every rustle, every hoot and howl, every flutter of feathers, I don't know where I'm going, I just know I'm going down. Down the mountain, using the same trail I've walked so many times. But never like this. My feet hurt already, toes bunching together with each step. I shorten my stride, but the blisters are already forming. With the wind screaming and everything dark, the lepchas and yetis that I laughed at as a girl come alive. Anything can be real when you walk sightless, alone at night in the Himalaya. The moon helps, but after how long, an hour?—I have no way to keep time—Father's prized flashlight goes out, and I'm nearly blind again. Useless, I drop it to the ground and I hear it bounce off a rock and fall into oblivion.

When I pass a ridge that blocks the moon, it becomes so dark, I stop from fright. I'm cold. My face, my ribs, my whole body hurts. And around every corner, steep cliffs and sheer drops, I'm such a fool to be out here. I thought the weather would numb the pain. Instead, it feels like the wind is dancing on my wounds. I want to curl up, go deep within, my eyes are icy and burning, I wipe them and keep going.

The trail narrows, and I shorten my stride even more, a chore to raise my heavy boots, careful steps over loose rocks, then, so slippery, it must be black ice, I can't see—almost dragging my feet now, careful, careful, it's perfectly dark, and I don't want to slide on the ice. Slide right off the mountain.

The trail changes, the rocks becoming more jagged under me. I know this trail even if I can't see it, but still I bump my head on something hard and sharp. I'm not injured, and I reach out to touch a sheer rock face overhanging the trail. I'm lucky, my discomfort saved me—if I was traveling any faster that would have been my end.

With my right hand hugging the rock face, I feel the ground under me change again, from hard stone to slick ice. I pick one foot up, and then I feel my other leg lift into the air as I push off. For an endless moment, I'm flying. Then I feel my body turn and I hit the ground.

I'm on my back, more scared than hurt. No. That's not true. I take off a glove, touch my head with trembling fingers, feeling warm, sticky blood. A choir of wolves sings a sad chant. They must smell my tears. I wrap my shaking arms around my knees, pull them in close, and rock forward and back, curled up so nothing can harm me.

I don't know how long I've been sitting, rocking back and forth, when I touch the lump on the top of my head, the cut has hardened and scabbed. And I'm missing one of my gloves—my hand has gone numb—and again, I'm lucky, I find the glove, it's on my lap. But my hand is so swollen, I can't even get it on.

Get up.

I blow into my palm, massage and flex my fingers to get the blood moving, then open my jacket and stick my hand in between my arm and my side.

Get up. Now.

I no longer hear the wolves. Just the wind, a sharp cold hum that stings my ears. I pull my cap low over my ears. I can't go back even if I wanted to. It's too late, too dark, and I'm too tired to climb uphill—I couldn't take another beating.

Get up.

If death is what I face either way, I choose death below. In the valley.

Now.

I take my hand back out, manage to finally get the glove on. I try to rise, but my legs are too weak. I just want to lie back, my whole body is so tired.

You're going to freeze to death if you don't get moving.

It's said that before you die from cold, your mind and body transform—a warmth flows through the body before the end. Peace.

Get up.

Is Ang still cold, forever buried in that underground tomb?

I SAID GET UP.

I rub my thighs, calves, ankles, wiggle my toes in the too-big boots. Keep going. I plant my gloved hands on the ice-cold ground and raise myself up. The force of my movement sends loose stones over the side of the trail, just centimeters away, down, down, down, sinking into nothingness. I can't hear the stones hit, hundreds, thousands of feet below. But everything hits bottom eventually.

The wind returns, stinging my face with shards of ice. My steps are even shorter now, more uncertain. I trip on something in the path, but I don't fall this time. I pick up a birch branch and use it just as the blind would. And that's what I am, walking blind, pace slow and measured—but I can't stop, I'd freeze in place—and so I walk on.

Swallowed in the darkness, not a single light shines behind me. Good. Lights would mean that they're up, and if they were up this late, it could only be because they knew I was gone. But no one knows and no one is following me. I'm alone on this dark mountain, seeing without my eyes. What I can't see in front of me, I see in my mind's eye peaks that make rivers foam, the Dudh Kosi, the milky cascade that drains Jomolangma herself. I can hear its waters far below, the river snaking down like me, winding through the valleys, twisting and turning past some villages and around others. The waters run parallel to the trail now, and I follow past a still sleeping Khumjung, our old home, then on to a groggy Namche Bazaar—built into the lap of the mountains, home to nearly a thousand Sherpas, a hub I've visited many times to barter for supplies and wares. Then the river hides behind another valley, and I turn and trot past the waking village of Monju, just a speck on the side of the road.

Thousands of feet lower than when I started, below the tree line now, dust and rocks replace snow and ice. I pass wooden houses and empty fields that in a few hours will be filled with bent villagers. Birch branch in hand, I limp along like my father, toes pinched together and blisters swelling. Then the sun joins me, and when it comes, I'm so happy to feel its warmth.

Blood pheasants squawk in the early morning, horses graze, tails swatting the flies that build as the day gets on. Nobody raises their head as I pass. Brown dots cover the hills—only when they move do they come alive, their empty black eyes looking up, horns aimed. Many yaks, and no people. None at all. Everyone is still sleeping.

I cross a suspension bridge trying not to look, the river hundreds of feet under me. Hands clutching the chain-link railings, I bob up and down over the rickety wood and metal, stepping carefully, one foot in front of the other. And then I'm on the other side of the bridge, on solid ground, and my heart is still racing and I'm embarrassed—*a Sherpa afraid of heights!*—as I turn and head down another ridge, a switchback, up a slight incline, and finally another bridge. This time I look down as I cross.

On the other side, heart still speeding, the river disappears around a bend, again running just beyond the snow white stupa that marks the edge of the last village on the mountain. Every town here has these markers. And I'm thankful to see it.

I pass through the stupa. Hollow inside, it's big enough to walk through, and there's a wooden prayer wheel that comes up to my shoulder, its Sanskrit carvings chipped off in places. The wheel is attached to bells, of course, very loud ones. It's good fortune to spin the wheel, but I don't touch it, afraid to wake the villagers as much as the gods. On the other side of the stupa is a stone archway, a kani—the arches seen at the entrance of every village in the Khumbu.

I cross from gravel to stone street and walk past stalls and stores, still boarded up, past tea houses, lodges yet to open. Strange restaurants with English lettering and odd names.

Everywhere the word "Everest," everywhere pictures of the mountain on signs, painted on doors and walls, a town that is an altar to the great mountain. This is Lukla. And this early in the morning, the streets are empty save for a few mongrels who snarl at me hungrily.

I'm tired, hungry, too, but I march through the entire town in less than ten minutes, it's that small. But so different from my own. Here, everyone is a merchant, every home a place to sell something. These Sherpas are rich. Tourism has blessed them.

Only a few hundred live in Lukla, and most are businessmen —and business*women*. Many women run tea houses that serve as lodging places and meal houses. All steady jobs with a never-ending flow of foreigners. Much better than working in the dirt, tending livestock, lugging a case of Coca-Cola on your head, up, down, all day, every day, for only a few rupees and a short life. *This* is a good life for a Sherpa. Here. Just sit and wait for the money to come. Wait for the deep- pocketed mikarus. Run a lodge, feed the fire, drink tea, eat meat, get fat.

But to run a lodge, you must own a lodge. And to own anything means money—or marrying into it if you're lucky, a thought that reminds me my fate won't be that. I don't know what will happen, but with every step forward things grow more uncertain. If only I could get work and enough money. I could even go down to the capital, to make a new life in Kathmandu. I could study. I could do anything a man could do. And I'd be free.

But I have no skill to offer, no trade to earn. I am a fool's fool. There's only so much a woman without a skill *can* do. If I had walked up the hill, I could have made it to a shedra, a place of teaching. I'm fantasizing, of course, I could never really become a nun. Shave my head, renounce what little possessions I have, never take a husband, never have children, sleep in a meditation box, dedicate my life to learning the Buddha's teachings, maybe one day become the first female abbot? No. No. That way has never been for me. I've tried many times to prostrate myself, to pray to the deities in secret, and still I felt my father's hand, no matter how many times I invoked the name of the protector. Khumbi Yulha never protected me. And years of offerings to Jomo Miyo Lang

Sangma—when we had our altar in Khumjung—it never helped my family.

If only those gods were fair, not even generous, fair would have been enough. But none listened. Instead they acted cruelly if they acted at all. I'm no nun, I can't enter the world of compassion with a closed heart. I would still be running.

I pass poster after poster of the mountain, a strange reminder of my trap. And then I see the mountain paired with an English word I recognize: "Trekking." And "Summit." Yes. Women have done it. I can't think clearly, I can't remember their names, but I do remember.

Could I? Am I even strong enough?

A mongrel barks. I turn and a shiver runs through my tired body, waking me from fantasy. The dog lowers his ears and snarls. I snarl back.

Walking, keep walking, always walking.

I walk until I can't walk anymore, stopping at the top of a small hill of dirt at the edge of town. Looking down, I kick a rock and it lands not on dirt or grass, but on something gray and smooth. Man-made. White lines are painted on it, broad and long, as if sending a message to the sky. There's a single building with a wood frame, corrugated tin roof, the words TENZING-HILLARY AIRPORT in faded red paint, with the double triangle of the Nepali flag at the top of a flagpole.

I take out the mobile phone from my knapsack, the clock on the screen telling me it's seven in the morning. Khunde is just waking, just discovering what's happened. So many images rush forward at once: my father, my mother, my sisters, even Norbu. All of them realizing I am gone. What was I thinking, running away? Fool. I'm no nun, and I'm no painted woman or whore either—my only other real option.

I slump down, exhausted, take my boots off and then my socks, rub my battered feet. With what little water I have left, I wash them, wiggling my toes in the yellow grass. A tiny aphid mounts the top of a blade of grass, just next to my hand. Its small body looks like a white dot, a dot that cuts down the grass with a mouth like a living kikuri. I watch the insect eat more and more and more, belly not getting any bigger—*where does it all go?*—and then the tiny thing is plucked away by a green monster.

The mantis looks like a giant compared to the aphid. It has bean-shaped eyes, pure green, each with a red bindi in its center, each looking in opposite directions, one at the victim it slices with sharp mandibles, the other at me.

The bardo of life, the bardo of death.

I think of squashing the mantis, but I hold back. I still respect the balance, no matter what the truth is. Anything—even this little killer—could be the future reincarnation of a holy monk or a new-born infant. Anything. But could a creature like this really be reborn as the Buddha?

The flame of a dying candle serves to light the flame of another. Reincarnation is based on the merits—or demerits—of one's life. So surely this creature could not be anyone of true consequence. A jilted lover, returned to samsara. A runaway bride.

The mantis stares at me with both odd green dots now, each knife-like arm holding a dead aphid—it plucked another from this world and sent it into the next while I sat debating—those jade pinwheels stare back at me blankly while its long white jaws chew one of its victims' heads. I pick up my boot and slam it down, squashing the bug. Rebirth is immediate—if there is such a thing. And if it is, where is this killer now?

I've never done anything like that, taken my rage out on another living thing, and I feel a pang of guilt. I lie back in the grass, stomach aching. So much pain, I've pushed that part of me so deep, kept it buried like a rock in an icy crevasse. I eat a cube of dry, hard cheese, then another, and I think of the leopard mother.

Do snow leopards dream?

Staring up at the sky, scattered clouds peel off as the sun pushes its way through. *A white day.* She's hunting right now. Or sleeping, with her cub pressed against her, in her lair. If it was winter I would have frozen last night. I won't be able to last another night in the cold. Not like this.

Something cuts through the sky overhead. A bird of metal and plastic, wings like sticks churning the thin air. It heads closer and closer towards the narrow strip—coming right at me. The airplane flies by me, between patches of dry bushes and shrubs on both sides of the narrow strip, until the wheels hit the runway screeching. I've never seen one so close, but I know about this place's history, all mountain people know about it. Many mikarus have died here before they even reach the mountain. Lukla's runway is known to be the shortest anywhere, choked between peaks and ravaged by bad weather and air thin enough to make engines die.

In my language, Everest is Jomolangma. In Nepali, it's Sagarmāthā. Both mean "mother of the world." Everest was a British mapmaker who never even visited our country. I learned about him in my school, a place named after another mikaru, Hillary, the first and most famous white man to summit her.

I'm sure the people below—all the tourists coming from the valley—they don't know. And they don't care. They come, take pictures, then leave. They'll come as long as there is a mountain. Jomolangma, our gift and our curse.

We know that when an avalanche strikes, or a storm, an ice fall, lightning, at moments like these, she makes her displeasure known. Foreigners call it an accident. We know better, and still we tug her tail, all of us, because the mikarus bring money—and we need it.

The airplane makes a halting turn to avoid a stone wall. The strip looks about a quarter of the length of our pasture back home, and like a vision—a classroom's worth of children suddenly flock around the machine as it comes to a stop, gleaming in the morning light. I throw on my socks, lace my boots, and scurry down the hill to hide behind an oil drum, crouching low.

The door opens and little brown arms stretch to it, grabbing sacks of rice, salt, luggage, unloading the plane in seconds. They are blessed with a few rupees each, doled out by a fat man with a red nose and a wobble. Probably drunk from the night before, just like Father. In between yelling orders, he blows that red nose in a rag, checks it, then blows again. He yells to strong-looking Sherpa porters, men who grab the bags, toss them up and onto their backs, disappearing inside the rickety building.

Off the plane step white faces. I come a little closer to get a better look, scampering to a patch of bushes. They wear clothes that look too clean, the white of their shirts too white, stepping awkwardly in never-worn boots. Even their skin seems too clean, their faces look like they've never felt the sun. And among them, a woman. Her skin the color of freshly fallen snow. Lips pink, hair like light chestnut. She walks down the strip, shoulders back, head up. Two men follow her. Two husbands?

The Nepali boys fight over which one gets to carry her bag.

Could she be so different from me? I see her lips moving, pointing, smiling, but I can't understand what she's saying. I'm sure it's English. The men with her nod to this living goddess. And then she touches lips with one of the men. She puts her whole face into his, pressing against it just like in the climax of a Bollywood epic.

Sherpas touch the crowns of our heads to show affection, we don't touch lips. And we don't do it for all eyes to watch. I've never seen anything like this in real life, just in the cyber cafe. And yet none of the locals here seem to care, neither does this woman or the other mikarus. Normal behavior for them, but it still feels so strange to witness an act that should be private made public. I wasn't sure before, but now I am. Yes. Yes, she is different than me.

9

I TAKE MY PLACE AMONG THE BOYS, WHO ARE ALL STANDING IN
a line, ready to work. The oldest looks half my age. I'm a head
taller than all of them and the only girl. Even with my hair tucked
under my wool cap, I'm still obvious.

"Move," one of them yells. Every space is precious here. His
face is thin, angry—but he's still just a boy. Maybe eight years
old—the same age Ang would be now.

Behind them, the strong-looking Sherpa men squirt something
from a plastic bottle into a circular canister. Then one lights a
match and throws it in, flames erupting. The men hold their hands
up to the fire. It smells foul. I imagine Kathmandu, which is where
all these planes come from, smelled like this to Norbu, only many
times worse. That's probably where Nurse Lanja is now, back
down there, in the flat land.

The next man-made bird is in sight now. It lands in front of
us, moves down the strip, stops, and then its hatch opens. I put
one foot forward and am elbowed in the stomach by the boy who
reminded me of Ang, knocking the wind out of me. Another boy
trips me.

I get up, coughing, rush through a thick cloud of smoke. The
boys descend like vultures, some of them working in pairs to lift
the heavier bags. I manage to grab hold a sack of rice, but it weighs
too much, and the bag is quickly snatched from my shaking hands.

I look up, it's that same angry boy. He sticks out his tongue and drags the prize away. Palms outstretched, the red-nosed man throws him a few coins and then shoos him off as he warms his hands over the fire.

There is nothing left to take off the plane, and I limp back towards that dusty old building where the bags are stacked, hoping to warm up by the fire. But a hand goes up, blocking my path.

"Women aren't porters," Red Nose yells, strands of dark brown tobacco hanging from the corners of his mouth.

"Why not?" I say, my exhaustion erupting in anger. "If I'm strong enough, why can't I work here?"

"Women make babies," he laughs. "Women clean house. Women complain. This is not women's work."

The men around him laugh as he wipes his nose in that rag, then spits brown juice. He takes a step closer and grabs my arm. He reminds me of my father, and like my father, I'm sure he's looking for an excuse to cock back a fist and crush me. I steel my eyes over and let my face go slack, hoping to convey my fearlessness. My mask. But he looks right through it.

"What kind of woman comes alone to work? Huh? Women alone on the mountain is a bad omen and bad omens bring bad fortune. Go back to where you belong. Get out of here or we'll drop you into the gully. No one will find you, no one will care." He points that finger like he's holding a knife, and I pull back.

The fat man roars deep, and the men join him, and then the boys, all of them laughing.

One of the boys throws a rock that whizzes by my face. "Where are you going, Sherpa girl?"

I turn and trudge back up the hill, the laughs following. I'm afraid they will follow, but I don't run and I don't look back. Sitting in the yellow grass, I open my knapsack and eat the remains of my food, drink the rest of my water. The sun moves higher into the sky and two more metal birds come and go during that time, each bringing money to the porter boys.

I take my boots off, tear a kerchief in two, wrap part of it around my blistered toes, stuff the remaining shreds inside my boots. When I put them back on, they fit me. I try to steady myself by listening to my breathing—my mother's way. I remember watching her crying, when I was very little. She had just given birth, but too early. I didn't even know she was with child. She didn't show, no roundness to her belly, no fat. She had it in the house, of course, alone save for me. At first, I wasn't even sure what was happening. Mother said her back was hurting. Then her abdomen. Then she was on the floor, writhing for what felt like hours. But it could have been far less time, minutes even, I was so young, I didn't know. And I certainly didn't know what to do. I watched silently and waited for Father to come home to fix everything. But he never came. So I did what Mother commanded, anything to make the pain stop. I thought she was just sick. But she didn't double over and throw up like I expected. She loosened her bakhu robe and wan-ju shirt, squatted, and grit her teeth.

"Nima," she moaned. "Boil a pot of water."

Terrified, I huddled in the corner of the room, knees to my chest, my head tucked between them and my eyes half open.

"Get me a bowl!" she screamed. "Water now!"

We stayed up all night together. By morning, it was over. And somehow, without any help, she gave birth in that cold room on that cold floor. We were lucky the chickens were still in the yard and the yaks grazing in the hills, instead of clustered together in the house. My father in those times would bring the animals in for the night when he came in. But he didn't that evening, he was on the mountain.

Mother gave birth to a boy, years before Ang or my sisters. But it was all wrong. He was too small. And red all over, with thin skin, like all his blood had settled just beneath the surface. He didn't have any hair, and his eyes were shut, just two tiny slits that never opened—and his mouth—there was a wound somewhere inside him and there was so much blood, oozing out, how could such a small thing have so much blood? He didn't move. No life to him at all. I'm ashamed to say it, but the baby looked—it didn't look like a baby. It looked like something the elders would describe to scare children. Tales of demons and fallen deities. Gek and gdon.

He was so small, so unnatural, he fit in my mother's palm. And Mother held him there, cradling him for I don't know how long. She held a rag to his mouth, cleaning the blood, all the while chanting, calling the soul, repelling whatever spirits may have taken her child. If she was scared, she didn't show it. He never breathed. Was he ever alive, even inside her womb?

We ended up putting him in a tea tin. Mother, or maybe Father, I don't think he'd returned yet. I don't remember who did it. It couldn't have been Father—*was it me?*—I just remember that someone put him in there. Mother cried and chanted for a night and a day, clutching him and cleaning that wound—I don't know how we got her to let go. I don't know how she dealt with the pain. And then she stopped. She stopped crying and she inhaled and exhaled slowly, deliberately, suddenly controlled. She stopped chanting, and the tears dried on her face as she got up, took that little tin, opened the front door, and stepped outside. It was cold, nearly autumn, but she went out without a coat and stacked the wood and made the pyre by herself. And then she went back in to take the bowl with the placenta and the cord and placed it on the pyre next to the tin. *How was she capable of standing?* It felt wrong for me to interfere. This was at our old home in Khumjung, back when we had two stories and a window looking out onto our yard. And that's where I stood, looking down from that window.

When she lit the pyre, the flames shot up, flames as tall as the juniper in our yard, and I remember looking for my absent father. Was he seeking absolution or ultimate truth? Did he believe his firstborn son a demon, fated to burn away in the front yard, sent to the sky? Was that the first step for Father? The first step to becoming what he is now?

When Mother came back inside, she was calm. And that scared me more than anything I'd seen that day. She closed the door behind her, then walked right past me, not once looking at me. Her eyes were big, circles ringing them. She looked off into the distance, but there was nothing there, nothing to look at. I stood in the middle of the room, watching. She went to the kitchen, filled a pot of water, placed it onto the stove and lit a match. That rag was still on her chair where she'd left it.

"I'm making tea," she said finally. But she just stood there in front of the stove for a long while as if she had forgotten what she was doing. Then the calm passed, and she began searching for something—*where is it?*

She was looking for the tin where we kept the tea. And then she stopped and broke down, bending over, her face so close to the stove's open flame that I thought she'd be set ablaze.

My mother and father never spoke of what happened—they never even gave the boy a name. Ang was their firstborn son, not this thing. My sisters never knew. They still don't.

I run my fingers through the dry grass. I feel my heart slowing down.

"Every decision should be made in the span of seven breaths," Mother would say.

I breathe seven times. Slowly. In, out. In, out. In, out. In, out. In, out. In, out. In, out. It's a long walk back up the mountain.

Another aphid crawls just beyond my outstretched fingers, from blade of grass to blade of grass, and then me. It touches my palm, tests with one thin leg—safe—creeps up onto my thumb, all six legs moving in unison. The aphid doesn't worry about money or marriage or memories. All it cares about is survival, always in the moment, always now.

10

WALKING. PAST YOUNG CHILDREN PLAYING IN THE STREET, COVERED
in dirt, skinny, but with bright smiles on their faces. These are the
lucky ones who don't have to carry bags too heavy for their little
arms. The lucky ones whose parents can afford to send them to
school down in the Kathmandu valley.

The blessed children of Lukla dance in front of shops just
opening, shops run by their merchant parents who sweep dust
from their front steps, laying out jackets, sleeping bags, water
bottles, trail essentials for shopping mikarus. Others sit in old
wooden rocking chairs, tea in hand, waiting for the mikaru money
to arrive. Things would have been different if I had been born here,
with my family running a business selling to tourists: five hundred
rupees for a bottled water, eight hundred for a tin of crisps. I would
have been smiling just like these children. Me and my sisters might
have even been called by our names, not numbers. And maybe I
would have still been in school. Maybe I would already be in the
capital.

I feel the merchants' eyes following me—they must think I'm
a witch. If only I had the power of Milarepa, the first thing I would
do is give my tired feet a rest and fly out of here. And then...what
else would I do with my power?

I follow Lukla's single narrow street, past shops and restaurants
with names in English I try to pronounce. *Ss-tar-buckss Cof-feee*.
With a picture of a steaming mug up against a snow-capped

mountain. *Yak Don-naal-ddsss*. With a picture of a yak against the same snow-capped mountain.

Whoever can afford to eat yak meat must be very rich. Very rich to slaughter an animal that provides so much life. Each gives milk and cheese and hide for twenty years—how wasteful to make just one meal from it. And yet...what does that meal taste like? How special is it, to be able to eat something so few can, something that costs so much?

I put my hand into my pocket, finger the rupees I haven't spent, feel a rumble in the pit of my stomach.

I'm at the edge of the village, past all the shops, all the playing children. I can hear the river again, still out of sight, around the bend. Feet as heavy as two lazy yaks, I walk through the domed stupa, and this time I stop at the huge wooden prayer wheel. I grip the metal handle. It's surprisingly heavy. I have nothing to lose asking the gods one more time.

The wheel starts to turn. Unseen bells chime. I step through and under the stone archway of the kani. A painted English sign reads ENJOY YOUR TREK.

Standing under the sign, the bells still chiming, a little girl stares up at me. She is barefoot, cheeks pink and full, not more than four or five years old. She reminds me of my little sister, of Fifth.

Where did she come from?

She holds one hand up shyly, but her eyes are full, penetrating, older than the rest of her. She takes my hand and leads me down a short path, back through the stupa towards Lukla, but not into the town. We go down by the river to an old wooden home with a young woman sitting on an old chair, resting a mug on top of a swollen belly. We trade "namastes," and she holds up her mug. "Would you like some?"

Inside, the familiar smell of yak dung fills my nose. It's tight, dark and smoky, just like at home. The woman's name is Mashi. A toddler boy crawls over and climbs on Mashi like a forest monkey. "How is the tea?" she asks, freeing her breast for the boy.

"Very good, thank you." It's more bitter than what I'm used to—stale leaves probably.

When she tells me her age, I can't believe it. Mashi looks at me closely, her cheeks sunken and heavy, face ringed with deep circles. She is barely older than me.

"You say you're from up the mountain? The drought is killing us. Did you come to Lukla to sell at the market?"

I nod.

"Did you bring potatoes and cabbage? No? That's too bad. Too bad. This year's crop has been so expensive, we haven't been able to afford good vegetables for months. Or millet."

Rich or poor, no one in the Solukhumbu has escaped the drought.

"My husband would never let me travel by myself—why are you alone? You're of marriageable age. Excuse me for saying, but it's very strange."

Every time Mashi brings the cup to her lips, she pauses as if thinking of a new question and goes on chatting instead of drinking. It's like she's forgotten how to hold a conversation, no patience to wait for a reply. *When was the last time she had a visitor?* I take another sip, debating how honest I should be, trying to stay calm and count my breaths. *Let her do the talking.*

"I had a sister who used to travel a lot. By herself. Of course, she was unmarried."

Unmarried.

"People would always talk. And they were right, of course, they always are. Why else would she travel alone?"

"I'm not like that," I whisper defensively. "I'm a merchant. My whole family are merchants. But my father is sick, his leg was injured, so I'm the one who travels."

She smiles, finally takes a sip. Then she looks me over again. "Where is your tokma?" That T-shaped walking stick. *How could I have forgotten it?*

"I broke it yesterday," I muster.

93

"Broke it? From sitting on it?" She laughs. "You look far too skinny for that. Me, maybe, but you..."

"It was already cracked, it was years old, older than me. No use to keep."

"Mmm." Mashi nods, sips the tea. "My family must be the only one left in Lukla that aren't merchants." Pause, a sore spot. Mashi opens her mouth to continue, stops, presses her hand down onto her belly. "Ooh. The little one. I know he's a boy, that's why he's kicking, he's eager. He wants to see the world." And then she frowns.

"Very auspicious to have two sons," I respond.

Her eyes narrow, as if she reads my thoughts. "Do you know how difficult it is to walk down to the river to fetch water every day? With this?"

Mashi raises her shirt, belly protruding, white stretch marks around her middle, and...blue and yellow bruises on her side. Am I staring at the future self I ran away from? Alone, tired, filling my children's mouths while my husband is away. And when he comes back, he's not gentle. He fills me up with more and then leaves again.

Mashi holds her cup to her lips. "I hate Lukla. All the mikarus, coming, going. I'm from Machermo, but I haven't left here since I had Sia."

The little girl's face shines when she hears her name, and she tugs at her mother's skirt.

"She's six," Mashi says. "I never thought six years could go by so fast. Even with all the hardship, she makes me forget."

I thought the girl was younger. Her legs and arms are like twigs.

"Did your village support the Maoists?" Mashi asks suddenly.

"My father always said to spit on a Maoist if we ever met one."

Is it wise to be so honest? I blurted the first thing that came to mind—the truth. Mashi just sips her tea, slow to respond.

"My village was on the Maoist side," she begins. "But no one knows that because the Gorkahs killed them all. They came during the night, we didn't hear a thing, but in the morning, half the village was gone. The Gorkahs knew where to look. Someone told them. One day, you go to bed with everything seeming normal, then you wake up and so many people—people I thought were good people —*gone*. It was a bad time, I thought it would never end. And now I'm here. With drought instead of war. Has the monsoon ever been this late before?"

I shake my head. "I don't remember it ever being like this."

She nods. "Some days I can barely rise from bed in the morning. It's so cold, I feel the cold in my bones. How can it be so cold, and yet we have so little rain and snow? I can barely walk around the house like this, barely do my work. My husband"—I think of the blue and yellow bruises—"he works in the trekking. Always gone. And when he returns, always..." She mimics the act of tilting the chang, a motion I know well. "One good thing about him being gone: I don't have to sleep in a chhaupadi." Mashi shakes her head. Another centuries-old tradition so many are forced to suffer with. Impure, they call it, when we bleed. Not fit to be in the house with others. Not fit to take water from the public well, not fit to serve food. Not fit to even touch livestock. *Dirty.*

Mashi throws another cake into the fire. "A woman not far, a Hindu of course, she died from fire during a cold night," she says. "Burns and suffocation, just from sleeping in a chhaupadi. Count your blessings you were born a Buddhist."

The smoke wafting, Mashi gets up and the clinging toddler lets out a yelp. Mashi puts down her tea, picks up the boy. Hands full, she can't even wipe her tears.

Sia presses the crown of her head onto her mother's leg. And then I lay my hand on Mashi's back—something so foreign in our culture, to touch another person, it's something a Sherpa would never do—but I wipe her face as if she were my sister. And I haven't even told her my name.

Mashi touches her stomach, lets out a whimper. "Ooh. Again, always kicking, a little Gorkah in my belly."

I take the baby from Mashi's arms, cradle him close. The boy grabs my thumb with a tiny hand and stops crying. "You're the first woman to hold Jamling besides me. He won't let anyone else touch him."

A dash of light through the dark cloud.

"Jamling, like his father. Jamling Babu."

We share a smile, the first truly unguarded one since she offered me the tea. Not a frown, but a smile. A moment of peace, of compassion. Why do smiles mean so much? Why do they make us feel light, whole, trusting? It's just a movement of the lips and cheeks, nothing more.

Why does the impermanence of our faces have such power? And why do I care, why do I allow a smile to have such power over me? I'm still smiling when I look into the little boy's eyes. And then my smile is gone, just like that.

The impermanence of life.

The baby boy's eyes are completely white. Glossed over. Little Jamling is blind.

Mashi offers me a place by the fire to sleep. It's late, and I accept. And I tell her the truth, or at least part of it. I don't tell her I ran away. Or why. But I do tell her that I want a new life—she's seen through my half-truths anyway.

I'm hungry, and Mashi serves me dal bhat. Then she scoops clumps of rice and curry into Jamling's mouth, always watching but never seeing. She asks me what I'm planning to do, for work, for money. I tell her about my failed attempt this morning and she laughs, light, with a birdlike sound: "A woman can't be a porter, even if she is a Sherpa."

The meal over, little Jamling falls asleep on the floor. Sia rests at Mashi's knee. I reach out, touch Sia's face, just like with Fifth, my favorite Fifth, and Sia laughs, burying her head in her mother's dress.

"Why not? Why can't a woman be a porter?"

Mashi curls her lips as if I've asked why water is wet or why fire burns. It just is. "You can't be a porter because of this." She touches my long hair. "Or this," pointing to my breasts. "You're a girl. Men won't listen to you. They see all girls the same: something to take. And on the mountain, away from your village, that's what they will do to you. It's what they always do."

There's a hint that she knows from experience, and Mashi's words stay with me as I stare into the fire. Life is always set in a pattern, for man and all creatures. *You're a girl. Men won't listen to you.*

She's right. If I'm a girl, that's all I'll be, something to take.

I fall asleep on the floor, under wool blankets. The blankets are thick, but it gets so cold during the night I wake up and put on my coat. Teeth chatting, a dream takes me back to my village. It's a special day. My Second sister is marrying Norbu. Nyi will be happy, her path mapped. I feel like I'm floating, looking down from above Is this our near future? Second wanted Norbu as a husband. And maybe, given time, Norbu will become happy with her. And my parents will finally be happy.

I float above my father, his face soft for once, so unlike how I remember him last. Then I'm over my sister as she says her vows in front of a line of lamas. Each bless her. Nyi is beautiful: knee-length robe woven of yak wool, a white khata wrapped around her long neck, a bright blue turquoise necklace dangling, cheeks red from excitement. She looks so happy.

Everyone does.

My sister looks up—and she sees me, still floating above everything. She touches my face with an outstretched hand, a hand adorned in jewels, red coral glass beads, golden rings. Our foreheads touch.

"Thank you, sister."

I'm floating away now, up and through the roof, out of Khunde, into the mountains, floating, floating, floating, through wind and snow. I blink and I'm in a cave, above the mother leopard and cub. She licks her little one so gently. Maternal love. Wait. Something's wrong. She keeps prodding, and the cub doesn't move.

I stop floating, my feet drift down to the soft floor of the cave.

The mother leopard doesn't look up at me, she's too focused, and I look closer and see why: his little eyes shut tight, his little chest still. The cub is dead and she cannot accept it, she keeps prodding him.

I can feel her pain, and it's as strong as the happiness that I saw glowing around my sister. I reach out to soothe her, but when she looks up, finally seeing me—there's nothing in her green orbs. Nothing to comfort, nothing to soothe, nothing I can do to stem her pain. Just two empty shells that stare back, so big and sad, and I fall into them. I fall in and out of the cave, inside those green holes, and when I open my own eyes, I'm back in Mashi's home, the fire burning low and my heart pounding. In the dark, the mind has no leash.

I can hear Mashi's labored breathing all the way on the other side of the room. Her enormous belly heaving with each breath, little Jamling by her side, Sia only a few feet away, all bundled close for warmth.

Do not scorn the weak cub, for she may become a vengeful tiger.

Why would the gods give me this signal? What are their plans for me?

Fool—there is no point to thinking this way. What manner of gods mock us by giving us lives like these? I doubt there are gods. Belief is something we've created, a wish to make sense of all the pain. The tears running down my face are welcome—long suppressed thoughts bubbling up. But deep inside I know there must be more, there must be meaning, or why live?

Animals choose life and the pain and suffering that comes with it, and they do it with none of the trappings, none of the wealth or ego that we carry. Still they choose life.

Back and forth, I believe, I don't believe, I do, I don't.

Confused and tired, in between dream and waking, the span of seven breaths, I make my choice.

11

I LEAVE BEFORE MASHI AND HER CHILDREN WAKE UP. BUT NOT BEFORE
I fold half of what's left of my rupees under a rice bowl. *Thank
you, Mashi.* Marching back into Lukla, down the main street, every
step symbolic of my affirmation for change. The shopkeepers and
merchants, the children who play in the dirt, none of them frighten
me, none of their stares, none of their words, their fists, their jabs,
punches, kicks—none of it can touch me.

Yesterday was a black day. Today, my life force is high. But I'm
already famished.

I stop in front of the strange restaurant I passed yesterday.
The animal that's been part of every important moment of my
life poses on the sign: *Yak Don-naal-ddss.* Inside, there are pictures
of yaks everywhere. Animals I've lived with my whole life. Holy
creatures.

Lamas say that if we don't eat meat, we earn the merit of one
hundred fasting rituals. But I know the power of this animal will
help me grow—and I need the strength. Save for what they sell,
the restaurant looks like any other Sherpa tea house: small, with a
low, wooden ceiling, a stove in the center for warmth. There are a
few mikarus sitting at a table, and at the counter stands a girl close
to me in age, wearing a red hat with a picture of a yak on it. She
waits for customers—that could be me if I was born here.

"You're the first of the day," she says. "Well"—she nods at the
table of mikarus—"you're the first Nepali." She hands me a paper,

laminated in plastic. "Menu," she says, her teeth very white for a Sherpa girl. Maybe she's lived in the capital. Maybe her life is larger than just this place.

I try to read the menu, but it's full of English words I don't understand. The girl smiles once more, flashing those bright pearls, as if saying: *It's all a game, a game I've learned, a game between the people of the East and the outsiders, the ones who come with money.*

"What is a yak *burger*?" I ask finally.

"Yak burger: patty of ground meat, fried, served with bread and vegetables. A very large meal for one."

What is a patty? Without finding out, I dig my hand into my pocket, lay the rupees on the counter. Different notes, each denomination in a different size. A rhino, a tiger, a blood pheasant. The girl counts, nods, takes the bills.

"Okay, just sit, we will make it. It will come."

I sit, wait. Finally, it arrives, and she's right, it is enough food for two full-grown men.

My last rupees for a thick piece of yak meat in between two pieces of thick bread. I'm so hungry, I don't feel remorse or fear or sadness for eating this creature. The first bite, warm and tough— and wonderful. I've never eaten like this, gasping from hunger, juices trickling from the corners of my mouth.

My last rupees, I think as I chew and swallow. No more after this—but wait, I still have the mobile. I could sell it—how much would it be worth? Not the seven hundred and fifty my father paid, but perhaps half. I shake my head ruefully, imagining what my sisters would say if they could see me here.

There are three mikarus in the restaurant. They sit at a table right next to me, speaking in English. The two men have long hair and beards. The woman wears a knit cap over blond hair. Real mikarus, the ones with hair and eyes totally different from ours, double-lidded and colored.

I keep chewing and watching them before I recognize just which mikarus they are: it's the woman from the airplane from yesterday and her two companions.

One more bite and I finish my meal. Satiated, I gather my bag, rise, ask the girl at the counter where the bathroom is. I've been thinking about this nonstop. If I make a little money as a porter, I could be down the mountain in two weeks, even if I have to do it on foot. Two weeks to the capital. And once there, could I find Nurse Lanja? I could try the hospital where she trained. What was it called...

Still, the first thing to do is earn money.

I stand before the bathroom's dirt-streaked mirror, take out my kikuri. I know what I need to do. I need to become someone else to become myself. I smile, my mother would like that thinking. Thinking in riddles, very Buddhist. Circular logic.

My trembling fingers trace each strand, each lock. My braids are woven so tightly, I've been growing my hair since I was a girl. The corners of my mouth shake as much as my hands, lower lip quivering. I wipe my eyes and raise the blade, hands still shaking. My hair falls in clumps in the sink, tears falling with each clump.

Soon, my hair is the length of a monk's and my braids lay like slain serpents in the sink. Out of the mirror, someone looks back at me. And it's no longer the girl known as Eldest. I'm no longer a girl at all. What kind has hair so short?

On my revealed neck, I can see where my father struck me. I put the knife down and roll up my sleeves: both arms are dark purple. I pick up the knife again, and then the door opens. It's the mikaru woman, frozen in the doorway, startled by the blade in my hand.

Up close, her skin reminds me of fresh snow, eyes green like the mother leopard's.

Another sign?

She looks down at the braids that fill the sink, up at the blade, back to my eyes. Neither of us break the stare—*I must look like a monster*—then she speaks, in Nepali: "What are you doing?"

I'm so surprised, a mikaru woman speaking Nepali, I don't know what to say. When I do find my words, it's as if I'm speaking as someone else. This isn't my voice. "Cutting my hair so I can get a job," I explain.

"What kind of job?"

I've said too much. She puts her hands up slowly, as if to say she means no harm, then takes a step back and out of the bathroom, the thin wood door shutting behind her.

I look at myself in the mirror. I really don't look like a girl any longer. Good. I gather my clumps of hair, throw them into the open latrine and step out.

She's right there, not three meters away. Holding two steaming mugs, she approaches me. Again, in her fluent Nepali, she asks if I would like a tea.

I want to flee, to scream even, but I nod yes and we sit away from her companions, at another table.

This is the first time I've been so close to a foreigner. I study her face. It *is* different from mine. Fuller, and at the same time, slimmer. I want to touch it, to see if it's real. It's all so fine, so perfect. Like a great dream—if I touched it maybe this moment would shatter before me. No one here looks like that. Her nose is more pointy than mine, and her eyes seem alien. Mine are almond shaped, struck in the middle by a dark iris. Sherpa features may be different, but our eye color is always the same. Always solid brown. Shiny bullets. Mikarus, by comparison, show so much white. White eyes. And hers—I can't keep eye contact with her.

"My name is Valerie," she tells me, in Nepali. "Call me Val."
Val.

Sherpa, a dialect of Tibetan, is my mother tongue, but I speak Nepali almost as well. Yet to hear it from this woman's lips...

"Where did you learn to speak Nepali?" I blurt.

Val smiles, her teeth even whiter than her skin—she's pretty, almost pretty enough to be in a Bollywood film, and yet there's a fragility to her. Is that what it is to be a Western woman? And me... in my state, my hair gone, I don't feel feminine at all right now. At the other table, Val's companions don't seem to notice my transformation, both of their heads lowered to their mobiles. The Sherpa girl at the counter, though, the way she stares, she's surely noticed. But if she disapproves of me or my new friend, she doesn't say. Val doesn't seem to care, she just keeps rattling on.

"I've been in Nepal for three years," she says. "I'm an American journalist for the BBC. You know BBC?"

I lie, nodding.

"That's why I came to the Khumbu. Where are you from?"

She asks question after question—nobody has ever taken this much interest in me. I'm more honest with Val than I was with Mashi. I tell her my real name. I tell her that my family came to Nepal after China invaded Tibet. I'm not sure why I say so much. Her manner is otherworldly; I should be frightened, and yet that initial fear passes and I'm suddenly comfortable. Maybe it's just because of that—she has no connection to my world, so there's no threat of her telling anyone.

"Why were you cutting your hair in the bathroom?"

Don't look back.

"I want to work on the mountain, make enough to start a new life. I'm a Sherpa, but I'm a woman, and women aren't usually allowed. Do you understand?"

She nods. "Does your family know you're here?" Pause. I wipe sweat from my face, shake my head. "How old are you?"

"Seventeen." Almost eighteen, really. Old to still be unmarried.

"And that?" She points to the bruises on my neck. "Is that what you're running from?"

I look down. "It's not bad," I mumble. There's a silence I can't fill. Mercifully, Val does.

"When I came to Kathmandu, my boss, my editor, wasn't used to women like me. Women who want and can do everything a man can."

I don't understand. "Why come to Nepal? Why leave your home?"

She smiles. "My boyfriend was in Doctors Without Borders. He came to Nepal, and I followed." Now *she* looks like she's wondering if she said too much. I think back to how casual she seemed when she pressed lips yesterday. What is love to a woman like her? "I had always wanted to be a photojournalist. But we broke up not long after I arrived."

"Why?"

"He...he was seeing someone else. A Belgian doctor. I didn't have anything waiting for me back home. No money, my mom had just passed away, and every time I logged on to Facebook, I would see another one of my friends getting married. So I stayed here and started over. I didn't want to return with nothing, so I built a new life."

Can this really be me, speaking Nepali with a mikaru, chatting about her love life?

There's so much of what she's telling me that doesn't translate, even in Nepali, but I don't stop her. I have the same feeling as I did next to the mother leopard, being so close to something so different.

Val reaches in a pocket, pulls out her mobile. "Hold on, I want to show you something."

Her fingers flit and flick against the screen. I look over at the two other mikarus: they're doing the same. I turn, check behind me, the Sherpa girl at the counter is still staring, leaning against the counter, head propped up by both hands.

"Look," Val says, shoving the mobile in my face. There's a map on the screen, places I don't recognize with names I'm not sure how to say. "This is where I'm from." She places a perfect finger—the nail filed, polished and shiny and painted the color of a mountain sunset—onto the screen. "The other side of the world. That's my home, that's where I'm from, Nima."

I know this much: the world is much bigger than just this mountain. Nurse Lanja showed me in her atlas. "A world beyond our mountains," she would say. Flipping page after tattered page in that old atlas, it was hard to believe as a girl, hard to believe there could be anything on the other side. But sitting here, looking at this woman with her perfect hair and teeth, it's proof. She could never be born in this world. The other side, indeed.

"Very different," Val says, looking straight at me. "Very different for women *here*."

I nod. Is it that obvious to her? Of course. I curse myself for being so slow, so dense. I want to explain myself, what I want, what my plans are, how I would conquer the mountain in order to get down the mountain and start fresh in the capital, but I can't find the words. They're trapped inside me. I don't have a quick wit like she does. I'm graceless, dull.

"How...old are you, Val?" I finally manage before a lump builds in my throat again—in any country it's bad form to ask such a question. I should have asked her about herself, her plans in Nepal, her goals, anything—but my mind doesn't work that way. I have no manners. I don't know how to make friends. Luckily for me, Val laughs. She doesn't seem to mind my question.

"Thirty-one. I'm thirty-one with no husband." My eyes grew wide. "I know, I know, I'm an old maid in this country. Young for the BBC, though."

"What is BBC?" I finally ask. I'm embarrassed, but I have to know.

"British Broadcasting Corporation. It's a news organization— radio, television, online—it's one of the biggest in the world. The BBC. I'm a journalist. You've never heard of it?"

I shake my head. "Journalist?"

"I write about people's lives. I tell stories for a living."

"You write to earn a living?"

I have so many questions. *How much food must her country have, how rich is her homeland, to be able to spend her days studying and writing and not have to grow crops? She must buy all her food in the market. How much paper does she use? How many pens? It's expensive here, paper is hard to get. Sometimes we reuse labels from bottles, or write on the back of cardboard or plastics. But it's hard and the ink always comes off plastics.*

"I've written many stories about Nepal. Stories about the war with the Maoists, the earthquake, the monsoons—about India and China, too."

"And Sherpas?"

She shakes her head. "Not yet."

"But you will now," I smile encouragingly. "On this trip. We have so much to teach you."

She nods seriously. "I want to write about how tourism is affecting the mountain—plants, animals, people. I mean, we're in a restaurant that's a yak version of a McDonald's. There's a fake Starbucks next door. McDonald's, you know—never mind. The point is, there've been major changes here. So much. Yes, some people are getting richer, but I think all this change makes life for most Sherpas harder. Maybe people like you? The ones who own these places are making money, but average Sherpas don't get rich from tourism."

"You must be quite rich?"

I regret the question as soon as the words leave my tongue. Val laughs, those white teeth returning. "Rich? No. Journalists aren't paid well. But a lot of people know about the BBC, even in Nepal. And it feels good to publish, to write about people without a voice and then see your words make change..." She trails off, holds her cup of tea, swirling the remaining liquid as she continues. "Doesn't always work that way, though. A lot of journalism these days is just listicles and puppy pictures."

I nod, not sure what else to say. I'd finished my tea.

"Thank you," I say, rising, ready for what faces me back up the mountain. And just as I'm ready to leave this new world for my old one, Val looks at me in a way that reminds me of my sisters—a way that makes me stop—and then she clasps my hand.

"Where are you going?" she asks.

"To the airport. To look for work as a porter," I blurt out, touching my hair, speaking quicker now. "I told you, I'm no longer a woman—they'll hire me now. I'll wear men's clothes, I—"

I stop, like something's come over me. They have no guide, no sirdar. I feel a cloud lift, the sun filling me. There's a roof overhead, but I still feel its warmth shining right on me.

"I've been up and down these mountains since I could walk," I start, without thinking my words fully through. "You're going to Base Camp, right?"

One of Val's companions yells in English—he must be wondering what we're talking about. Val answers in English, and in Nepali again, to me, "Don't worry, they don't speak Nepali. What are you trying to say, Nima? We're headed to Base Camp, me and these two mikarus." I blush at the mikaru who calls her own people that. "That's right, I know the word for us."

"I will take you," I say. "Let me lead you and the mikarus to Base Camp."

Over her shoulder, the girl at the counter still watches us. She looks away when our eyes meet, goes back to cleaning the counter with a rag. How strange we must look to her: a mikaru and a Sherpa, speaking in Nepali like friends. And a mikaru who is speaking to *me*, no less, a Sherpa who walked in as a girl.

"I already have a sirdar," Val tells me, eyes narrowing, considering me. "Could you work together? I've heard two guides can be beneficial, right, more bodies to carry the bags, one to scout ahead and another to walk with us?" And then, as if she were weighing the pluses and minuses out loud, she speaks to me while looking down. "Locals will trust you more than they will me. You were born here. You'll make a decent wage, maybe enough to start over like you said. But I'm not promising it'll be easy. Maybe it'll be harder, because you're a woman. Will that be okay?"

She looks up, meeting my gaze. Nima would cry, but I'm no longer Nima. I answer yes, to everything.

12

IT TAKES TWELVE DAYS TO GET TO BASE CAMP AND BACK. I'VE NEVER been that high before—I've never been much higher than my old village, but I don't say a word because I know the trail, all Sherpas do: straight up. I'll be making fifty thousand rupees. *Fifty thousand.* That's more than four thousand a day, and Val says I'm getting a quarter to start, the rest when we finish. My wages include food, lodging at tea houses, and a park fee to climb.

Val introduces me to her boyfriend, Ethan—I assume that by boyfriend she means someone she's going to marry. Everything about Ethan is large. His head, hands—it must have cost his parents a fortune to feed him. That giant yeti hand swallows mine, jerking it forcefully up and down. He grins wide, a mikaru with crooked, yellowed teeth. I didn't know they could be like that. Ethan has a full beard of black curly hair, a wide jaw. When he releases my hand, it's throbbing.

"He's an EMT," Val says. "Emergency medical technician."

"EMT," I repeat, understanding individual words in English but not what they mean all put together. The English I've heard, the English I've learned, it's like a completely different language, different sounds.

"It's like a nurse," their companion chimes. He puts down a camera, bows his head, and says, "Namaste." His brown eyes look soft, and he takes my hand much more gently than the other one.

"And this is Daniel. He's the team photographer," Val says.

Val shoots me a look: *See? No one's noticing.*

Ethan talks and Val translates to me. "He says he thought our Sherpa was old. You look like you barely hit puberty."

Ethan speaks again, pointing at my face, how did I get those bruises? He raises his arms, fists clenched, do I like to fight? Then he pokes me with one of those thick fingers.

"You speak English?"

"Little."

"Back off, Ethan. We have a lot of gear to haul." Val points to a stack of packs by the door. "We need two Sherpas, remember?" She holds up two fingers at me, so I catch her meaning. She keeps talking, and once in a while, a word lights up my comprehension like a torch in the darkness. "Sirdar," she keeps saying, an experienced Sherpa guide, someone who knows the mountains and how to navigate them (at least better than me).

Val counts out a stack of rupees, turns back to me and hands me my advance. *Twelve thousand, five hundred rupees.* I've never held this much money, and I stick it into my pocket, fast, as if it might burn my fingers. Now I'll be able to pay back my family for what I took *and* have enough to go down the mountain—maybe even by airplane, like the mikarus.

"You'll be carrying nearly thirty kilos," Val says to me in Nepali.

I nod, trying to keep my face neutral. I've carried thirty kilos before, but only for short distances. I've heard that experienced Base Camp porters carry even more than that. And the ones who haul gear to the summit, they carry twice that. But they get paid more, too. I can only imagine how much, but I know some are quite rich. If I was good, really a good porter, even a woman porter, no hiding, and everyone knew it, would I get the same pay as a man?

I realize Val is staring at my chest.

"Go to the bathroom," she tells me. "I have an idea."

I bow and excuse myself. The Sherpa girl behind the counter looks up from her mobile phone, her eyes narrowing. *Back to the bathroom.* I close the door behind me and look at myself in the mirror and shake at my own reflection. Val comes in a moment later, to the same spot where she discovered me with a knife in hand, barely an hour ago. "They're packing up right now. We have just enough time."

"Time for what?"

She holds a roll of duct tape and smiles. "We're finishing the look. Now take off your sweater."

Val wraps black tape over my undershirt, flattening my chest. I wipe the sweat from my forehead.

"Now take a breath. Deep. All the way in. Hold it."

Around my chest, again and again, Val passes the roll of tape until it gets low.

"How's that? Too tight?"

I stretch my arms, move from side to side, try to breathe normally. It is tight, but I can handle it. And when I put on my sweater, my breasts have vanished.

"Hold on, one more thing."

Val takes out a pencil, uses it to shade in my upper lip. I smile to myself, wondering if this writer has ever penned something like this.

"Keep still," she says. "Just a few strokes, yes, *there*."

I think of Norbu, Father, my sisters, and Mother and what they would say now. Today—*or was it yesterday?*—I was supposed to be a bride. But in the bathroom's tiny mirror, with my hair gone, my now boyish chest and freshly applied mustache, Nima the Eldest, betrothed to Norbu, is gone.

"Good," Val says, looking me up and down. "Very good. And what are we going to call you?"

Without thinking, I blurt out, "Ang."

Val repeats it. "Ang. Very well, Ang."

Forgive me, brother.

13

MY UPPER LIP ITCHES FROM VAL'S PENCIL. IT TINGLES AS SWEAT BUILDS, and I want to scratch it with my nails, but I don't. I'm afraid to touch it. And I want to pull off this stupid knit cap, run my fingers through my short hair. But I don't touch that either.

I must look a fool, but no one says anything. Not the children we pass playing in Lukla's lone street. Not the mikarus I walk side by side with—Nima would never have been able to do that. I finally gather the courage to touch the back of my head, right under my cap, feeling for my long hair and finding none. *That's not Nima*, I whisper in my mind, willing my change while afraid and ashamed to speak my new name, even to myself.

We pass the same group of misfits that unloaded the bags at the airport. They play billiards inside a tiny open-air stall—loudly, pushing and shoving and yelling, just like yesterday, passing a single pole between them. One boy places a coin on the table, hits a white ball with the pole, then curses as another boy scoops the coin up like an eagle snatching prey. Clearly, they are putting their hard-earned money to good use. A boy with a cleft lip laughs as though hearing my thoughts. Another swigs an orange Fanta, finishes it, throws it in a pile of empty bottles. The clank of the glass wakes a sleeping mutt who howls in displeasure, its dream world ended. The dog trots towards me and barks a warning as we pass and the one who threw the bottle scrunches his face at me. He looks a lot like the little boy who pushed me yesterday, the angry one. Another bark, and the boy keeps staring. The mutt takes a step closer, then stops and turns to scratch. The angry boy spits at the dog and returns to the game, laying another coin on the table. We keep walking.

At the edge of town, we meet the sirdar at the domed stupa, just steps from Mashi's home. Lasha looks older than my father, with a craggy, tanned face and graying mustache. His arms and legs are thick and strong, built like a cliff-running goat. He scratches that mustache, and it wiggles, a caterpillar glued to his lip. Val announces me as the second porter and his gnarled old hands press together as he bows slightly, whispering, "Namaste."

If Lasha senses something, thinks that it's odd that I'm a Sherpa without a tokma, with a penciled-on mustache, he doesn't let on. He wiggles that caterpillar, huddles with the mikarus by the side of the road, as they bend, drop, and unfurl their massive duffel bags. The gear is divided—containers of food, water, medical equipment, clothes, shoes, cameras—the mikarus keeping what they need for the day's hike and leaving the rest for us Sherpas to split in two loads.

Lasha must be close to fifty, and though as surely as he had once been a child and would one day be ready for the sky, I can't imagine this hard old goat being any age other than what he is. He looks the age he should always be. Sensing me studying him, he nods at me, then ducks his head back down to readjust the pack. I'm not worth more than a passing glance.

No one has noticed. Val shoots me a look of pride—mikaru magic is strong. I heave my pack on and the straps dig into my shoulders, even through three layers of clothes. As I straighten, trying to pretend like it's all routine, the small of my back tightens. Thirty kilos, but it feels double that, easily, a weight Val can't help with.

Lasha doesn't have to make-believe, he simply pumps those tree trunks of his and heaves the load onto his back in one toss. And then the sirdar's off, leading the way through the stupa, pausing briefly to spin the wooden prayer wheel. He knows it's best to play the game even if he doesn't believe. *Bless us, please.* One after the other, we follow into the narrow space, the mikarus running gloved fingers over the Sanskrit-etched wheel.

"To a good trek," Val says over the chiming bells.

Wheel still spinning, Daniel takes his turn. "A good trek," he echoes, giving it an extra push.

Ethan grips the wheel with those big hands, stops it completely, then flings it so hard the bells clang furiously. He hoots and whistles, an overgrown child.

When it's my turn, I spin it, too. And I don't say a real prayer, I just think of what I'm doing this for and picture the faces of everyone I've left behind. Second, Third, Fourth, Fifth. Mother. Norbu. Father. *I spin the wheel like Father would. I invoke the gods like Norbu.* We pass under the archway of the stone kani. ENJOY YOUR TREK. On the other side, and onto the trail, the sirdar speeds ahead. He's not waiting for the foreigners. He knows to get there as fast as possible, every lingering step an unnecessary delay. In the span of a few breaths, the sirdar is around the bend, disappearing through the trees. I dig my heels, ready to do the same, but then Val touches my arm lightly.

"You don't have to speed off," she tells me in Nepali. "I want you walking with us. I want you to show us parts of the trail that we wouldn't notice. Okay?"

"Okay," I nod. "Okay."

The weight is so heavy on my back—it's nearly impossible to keep my head up to navigate. And *what* am I supposed to show Val that she does not see? I've been along this path only to deliver goods and sell at market, what do I know about the Khumbu? I'm no guide. I feel a pang in my stomach, a slight pain. It's the yak meat—I usually take barley tsampa for breakfast, and my stomach hasn't been right since. Or maybe I just miss home, regret everything. But that's Nima talking, words a scared girl would say. Nima is gone. *Push it away. Bury it.* Do what Val asks: *Look with fresh sight.*

All around, the forest envelops us. Six-foot ferns, giant pines that spring from layers of fallen cones. Branches stacked with watchful birds, bobbing their heads and hooting. Between the trees, the steady rush of the Dudh Kosi below us, an occasional splash as one of the birds dives down to fish a meal. Where the trees thin, I see fields with cabbage and squash ready to harvest, bright yellow wildflowers sprouting in yards. Farmers on plastic chairs rest in front of their homes, sipping black tea. Down here the drought hasn't hit as hard. And next to the flowing river, the Sherpas have all the water they need to feed their crops. Most don't even have to work as porters to make a living.

I watch the mikarus in front of me and decide they are an entirely different breed. The shape of their faces, their noses, lips, eyes, bodies. These men are all jagged lines instead of curves, just like Sherpa men. A woman's body I understand, at least women like me.

Val has a camera around her neck, its black straps hugging her naked nape, bouncing against her chest. Her breasts are clearly outlined through her shirt, visible and unashamed. Her nails, painted a dark red, so unlike my chipped and ugly ones. No woman from the Khumbu would ever dress like that, though in Kathmandu it's different. Maybe Nurse Lanja did when she was there, but here it is strange. And yet on Val, it looks more normal the longer I'm around her. Her way and her world, no matter where she is.

"Hey, you all right?" Val turns to me, slightly out of breath. I nod quickly. The others are already sweating and panting.

"Anybody need to rest?" I ask.

"Let's keep going," she answers for the others.

Val reaches for Ethan's hand, holds it as they walk, displaying affection in full view, with no shame, perhaps even enjoying the stares from the onlookers. *I'm jealous. Yes, I am, I'm envious of her freedom. Free to love whoever she wants, even to do it in public, if she so desires.*

My mother would always say that to make a man happy, a woman must have strong legs, a face flat like a salt lake, and narrow eyes, since evil spirits dive into big ones. *Big eyes show things that are not there.* That was beauty to her. Mikaru skin has no pigment, and it makes their faces plain. Blank. They don't all have the same eye and hair color like we do. They change it.

How different we all must look to each other. If I were to be around them, just mikarus, would I find their form pleasing? Would they find me pleasing?

Despite the heavy pack, I'm walking with a strange sort of lightness. The fear is gone, replaced by a feeling I know monks would call bliss—and I realize that's the power of my newfound freedom. I try to focus on that thought. The trail is a winding path of broken rocks. And with the straps digging into my shoulders, my back, I feel each step.

Not even an hour out of Lukla and everywhere on the trail I am distracted by the signs of others, those who come to the mountain and leave their mark. Even us. The path is littered with things tossed: cigarette butts, candy wrappers, plastic bags, aluminum cans. Sherpas chew tobacco for energy and toss the wrapping. All part of the mikaru world—and if not for the mikarus, then pieces from down below the mountain.

What's *ours* and ours alone is the land and the creatures who dwell here. Pack animals of all sorts: yaks, horses, donkeys, and jobke, a cross between yak and cow, they all traipse in both directions, piled high with supplies, hard at work. Work that makes for quick digestion, everywhere their earthy dung is strewn and steaming in the cold morning air.

The animals are led by boys who can't read books but can command bulls down cliffs. Sherpa boys who walk in sandals and tennis shoes. They don't need boots, they deal with ice, snow, rock, mud, river, feet caked with dirt, toenails like eagle talons, skin and muscle that insulate against the cold and the trail. Sherpa feet walk through it all. I suddenly feel self-conscious of my own feet, privileged in my too big boots. But inside these boots, my feet are the same.

A team of yaks barrels towards us. The boys driving the animals beat them mercilessly with bamboo sticks, pointing them, I realize too late, right at my mikarus. I'm so wrapped in my own thoughts, I didn't sense the danger, didn't understand that the mikarus won't know what to do, how to react.

"Move!" I yell in Nepali, but the yaks drown out my words.

Instinctively, Val hugs the side of the mountain as the bulls charge down—but Ethan and Daniel are right in the middle of their path, frozen.

"Get back!" I scream. They don't understand. I dash forward and in three steps push the men up against the trail's overhanging rock face, just as a big bull swings—he's so close I can see the red of his pupil, the mucus dripping from his nostrils. The bull snorts and trots off as the herders—children half my age—bark and whistle at the old yak, though it seems they're chiding the foreigners.

Daniel rises, panting, his eyes big and darting. "Thank you, Ang," he says, wiping the dust off himself. So strange to hear that name, it takes me a moment to come back to now.

Ethan coughs, his face glistening with sweat. I offer an out-stretched hand, but he bolts up, pushing me back. Val comes over, touches his arm. He resists her, too.

"I'm fine."

"Let's rest for a moment," I say to Val.

"Good idea."

We huddle in a cluster of tall pines and the mikarus all drink, Val from a plastic bottle, Daniel with hands shaking, and Ethan sucking from a long, transparent tube connected to his pack, which he drinks as if his was a dying man's last sip. No one says anything for a long time, more shaken than tired.

"Animals always have the right of way up here," Val says in English, and this time, I understand before she translates.

A woman stops next to us, leaning against a load of oranges and closing her eyes as the sun creeps through the trees. Her face is a row of wrinkles and loose skin. But her hair is jet black. All of us are staring. Daniel raises his camera. *Snap.* When the old woman feels eyes on her, she doesn't turn her head, just murmurs, "Namaste," her lips revealing a toothless hole. "Namaste," I return. She opens her mouth to say something more, but when that hole opens, no words come out, just a string of deep, hacking coughs. Up and down the mountain, all day, every day.

A light breeze sings softly as it pushes the branches. I draw my eyelids closed and see a kaleidoscope of color. I can hear the river, it runs faster and louder below us, the water choked between big boulders. And I hear one more cough, a deep one, from the belly. When I open my eyes, the old woman is gone, as if she was never there.

Trooping down, another platoon of Sherpas haul baskets five feet tall, as tall as they are, loads tipping with firewood, crisps, Everest beer. I lock eyes for a moment with a girl in a faded pink jacket buttoned over an almost breastless torso, hair in braids, feet in pink sandals. She can't be more than fourteen. She reminds me of Fifth.

The girl looks away from me—I'm already acting more like a mikaru than a Sherpa, we don't hold stares, it's bad manners—and she stops to balance her load but doesn't lower the basket, simply busies her hands with retightening the thump line. Biting her chapped lower lip from the effort, she fixes the line, looks up as if to see if I'm still looking, meets my eyes again, and then looks back down. I want to stop her, to find out who she is, where she's going, but she digs her chin into that girlish flat chest and vanishes around the bend.

"How many women work as porters?" Daniel asks, and Val translates. "Are girls ever porters on expeditions? To the summit?"

"Plenty of them are porters," Val answers. "We passed them before, but with their hair short, they look like boys."

"No way," Ethan says, out of breath. "You never see pictures of girls on Everest."

"Is that true?" Val asks me in Nepali. "Are there female Sherpas who've climbed Everest?"

"Lhakpa Sherpa," I reply, remembering her name easily. "She's climbed Jomolangma nine times. She lives in the United States, but she's famous here in Nepal."

Lhakpa Sherpa. Her daughter is named Nima, like me. Other women have climbed, too. I've heard of a group of seven—all Nepali women—who are trying to conquer all seven summits, among them a Gurung, a Danuwar, the rest Sherpas. There is a path to anything. If I climbed the summit, I would be free of all burden, I could truly do anything, and no man would be able to tell me otherwise. I could travel down to the capital and be whoever I wanted. Pick up any book, speak to any boy, eat and dress however I like.

Two girls with baskets filled with tins of coffee and tea trudge past us and my focus follows. One of the girls isn't even wearing shoes. She walks barefoot, her feet and the ground one color. A strange buzzing goes off inside my head just as they pass—I worry it's my intuition, what's called a crying ear. It's loud enough that I expect it to frighten the girls into dropping their baskets. But they keep their gazes forward, keep marching. And then they're gone.

"What does that do to a child's body?" Val asks me in Nepali. "Does it limit their growth, stunt their height, maybe help them build stronger muscles? It can't be good. Look at you, Ang, you barely have any muscle at all."

"I climb better than you," I reply.

Val opens and closes her mouth. It is hard to tell if she is amused or angry. Finally she apologizes: "I didn't mean to be insulting."

Ethan fidgets with the tubing that snakes out of his backpack, notices me inspecting the device.

"It's called a CamelBak," Val tells me. "A backpack fitted with a water container and a plastic tube. So a climber can drink without strain. He sets his watch to ten minute intervals. When the alarm goes off, it's time for a drink."

I nod, not sure of everything she said—some things just don't translate—and I get up so my legs don't get too tight. I pull a purple kerchief out of my bag and wrap it around my face.

"This is what a climber needs up here," I tell Val. We're all moving now, with me leading. I turn to the mikarus and smile, only my eyes showing, and they burst out laughing.

"They say you look like a bandit, Ang."

It's impossible to fight the dust, I reply. You must take precautions. "Wrap something around your face for protection."

"It looks silly," she says in English, struggling to explain the meaning. We don't have that word in my language, but I don't press her.

When mikarus come down the mountain, every one of them is sunburned. Some nod hello, most shun any eye contact. And they can't stop coughing and sneezing. The women look almost disfigured, the men with beards as long as an old guru. Like Val, most don't wear anything around their face—it must be considered *silly*.

When we see a man leading a herd of goats down the mountain, this time the mikarus get out of the way.

"Namaste," he says, pressing his palms.

"Namaste," they each reply.

The goat herder places two fingers in his mouth and exhales a sharp whistle and the goats follow. The bleating faces remind me of the doe back home, the one that would always lick my face or bleat when she was hungry.

Two Western trekkers sidestep the goats, spitting rapid-fire English in between heavy panting. Foreigners smeared in sunblock, steadied by walking sticks, shielded by shiny sunglasses. So strange.

"Namaste."

"Namaste."

Strange to hear this Nepali word coming from white mouths. Most who've been on the mountain at least a day adopt this single Nepali word as their own, the one local word they all know.

"What does it mean, Val?" Daniel asks. "I've heard it before, in yoga mostly, but I never gave it much thought—I didn't know people actually said it and meant it."

"It means 'peace,' 'greetings,' 'thanks,'" she answers. "And 'tashi delek'?" Val asks me, switching to Nepali. "I hear it all the time but I just repeat it. What's it mean?"

"It's from my language, in Sherpa. It means 'good fortune,'" I say, then in English: "Good luck."

"Tashi delek," she repeats, smiling. "My first words in Sherpa."

Freedom is back-breaking work, the dust stinging my nose and throat with every labored breath, even with the rag covering my face. *Maybe this is what drove Father mad, after a lifetime of all this.* My eyes squinting, my mouth and throat hidden beneath my faded purple kerchief, gulping air kicked up by throngs of sandals and boots, hooves and paws, an orgy of dust mixed with drops of perspiration and thick cakes of dung, all kicked up, every step, every breath, tied together from the earth we all walk on. I'm drenched in sweat, feel it dripping down my back, under my arms, pooling at my waist and trickling down my legs.

Traffic is heavy this far down the trail. Girls and boys my age, lugging wood and water atop their heads, sweat pouring from their temples, resigned desperation all over their faces.

What other life is there for us? They heave baskets filled with everything from kerosene drums to furniture, loads stacked above the baskets' rim, each secured right around the forehead, right up against the brain, with a cloth strap that digs deep. But rarely does a brimming load spill onto the trail. Even overloaded, every Sherpa sprints by us, forever hauling their lives up and down the mountain. I have to hold on to my compassion, my joy, I'm the proof that there is another way.

As fast as they go and as strong as they are, man, woman, or mikaru, we all yield to the beasts with massive horns, we all jump to the mountain's edge as they thunder by. And each time, behind them, teens in tattered shirts, miniature masters ruling with sticks and rocks.

Lukla, our start, is two thousand, eight hundred and sixty meters. "More than nine thousand feet up," Val translates. And we've traveled only a few hundred meters in elevation, slow going with unaccustomed foreigners. So unaccustomed, anything could happen to them. They're my charges, my responsibility. My link to freedom. They move out of the way when they see yaks now. They may be older than me, but at times they seem younger, especially the men. Without experience. I have to watch them.

We pass small villages—Chheplung, Ghat—communities that remind me of home. I try to push these thoughts away, but they creep back, like a fox that's been fed. No matter where I go, I'll feel that nagging, until I go back with my head held high.

Then it hits me: all the Sherpas coming back and forth, up and down the mountain—I could be spotted.

That's Nima the Eldest!

She left her groom, stole from her father, what shame. There's a reward for her—100,000 rupees!

Suddenly, my father comes barreling down the mountain on horseback, his kikuri glimmering in the sunlight, eyes black and narrow as he brings that blade down, slicing me in two—

But it's only fear. None of it is real. No Sherpas say anything as they pass. In fact, they don't even raise their heads—Sherpas consider direct eye contact bad manners, a challenge, enough to shift our karmic balance. When the mikarus stare at me, I have to remember that it's not meant as a threat. Try as I do, though, the way the two men look at me now, while we pause again on a rest break, I can see it on their faces. Daniel pulls off a boot and rubs his toes.

Soft white feet. Ethan sucks at the last drops from that tube. Val instructs them about something. I can't understand, she's speaking too quickly and using words I don't know, but it's clear from the way they focus, whatever it is, it's meant to encourage them.

Daniel nods his head up and down, almost as if he's praying. *Daniel the monk*. Ethan coughs and waves a hand, a dismissal that reminds me of Father. With a sigh, Val motions to me to join her, and we walk a few steps ahead while the men keep resting. "How much farther today?" Val asks.

"Two hours, at least," I reply.

Ethan calls out to Val. What are we talking about? Val calls back that she wants to get a feel of the trail. From Ang. *Ang*. Every time I hear the name, it's like my brother's been resurrected.

"They didn't know what they were getting into," Val says to me. "Especially the big one."

"Are they scared?"

Val shakes her head. "No—maybe a little. The yaks. And the dust, and the altitude."

"What about you?"

She shakes her head again, chestnut locks whipping from side to side. "I've been to Namche Bazaar before."

Namche is only a quarter of the way to Base Camp. *What if they decide to quit?* Will I have to return the money, then return home? And then what? If I return with nothing, what will become of me? Will I even be able to make it all the way to Base Camp? What kind of Sherpa will I be if I can't keep up with the mikarus? I feel it again, that familiar ringing in my ear, strong enough that it must be showing on my face from the way Val looks at me.

"What's wrong?"

It's my kan runu, my crying warning. But I don't know where it's coming from. Is it these fragile mikarus? Or is it from something happening higher up the mountain, back home? Another ru'? Or maybe Norbu is searching for me. Or a threat from the spirits of the Khumbu, because I took my brother's name.

"You okay?"

"Sometimes there's red panda in the trees," I say. "I've seen them before here, with my sisters, I was just looking up for them now."

Val looks at me funny, her eyes low like a Sherpa's. She purses her lips. The branches sway with the wind, but I don't see anything in them. I've never seen any forest creatures like that this low on the mountain.

"What about snow leopards?" she asks.

"Higher up, yes."

The crying in my ear stops suddenly. Val stands with arms folded now, looking me up and down. "And tigers?" she goes on. "Have you seen tigers up here, too?"

"No tiger," I answer. "Tigers are scared of the heights." I point to Ethan and Daniel. "Just like those two." Val laughs out loud. So do I.

We keep moving, not talking much. Turning a corner, we find the river far below us, running under a suspension bridge. Multicolored prayer flags flap from the chain-link handrails, and under the bridge, a precipitous drop of several hundred meters.

"The Dudh Kosi," I say to Val. "The milky river."

This far down the mountain, the water is blue like a mikaru's eyes and white from the melt and the rapids. How fast the water hits the rocks, what power to carve and change the mountain.

Daniel comes to an abrupt stop just before the bridge. He lifts his camera to his eye and trains it. Ethan does the same with his mobile.

"I forgot this part," Val mutters.

I place a foot on one of the planks, then the other, the bridge isn't very wide, just wide enough for two, and it rocks slightly. "See? I've walked on this bridge many times and many other bridges like it. It's safe."

Val comes forward and takes a timid step onto the bridge, then another. She turns to Ethan and Daniel and smiles. "Come on. It's fine."

They follow, nipping at her heels like cubs. Next it's my turn. The bridge sways with every advancing step from the mikarus. I try not to look below, in between the metal slats, where my vision drains into the rush. *Keep moving.* The sounds of the river, even from this high up, becomes deafening and I can't even hear what the others are saying a few feet ahead. I run my fingers over the flags, grab one, stop its motion. I let it go and the wind takes it again. I can't help but look. Far below, the angry water churns and crashes. When I bob my head back up, the bridge seems longer, with many steps to go.

Ethan has his mobile trained, snapping photos. "Andanajowns!" he starts yelling. Then the others repeat it—"Andanajowns, Andana-jowns."

"Just like the movie," Val tells me, over her shoulder. "Indee-an-ah Jones. You know, Hollywood?"

I know Bollywood, but what's Hollywood?

A honey bird flies above us, fluttering its wings—a creature so small, yet able to do so much. It flies right up to Ethan, and he holds his mobile up, rolls his shoulder and does a quick turn, the sounds of the river masking his words. The bird buzzes overhead again, pausing in midair, then zipping back and forth, and Ethan shifts his body so quick to keep filming that the force of his weight makes the bridge rock, and I watch as his boot catches in between one of the slats, and he trips forward. The bird shoots away, and Ethan steadies himself. Val and Daniel keep moving forward—no one but me saw—and Ethan smiles in excited embarrassment and keeps moving.

We're in the middle of the bridge, it's that long. Val leading, Ethan right behind her, then Daniel, and me a few steps behind.

The honey bird returns again, its wings are green and blue— how can they be both colors?—and its face a splash of red. Ethan brings the mobile back up, and this time Val trains hers, too. And then it happens so fast—Ethan, looking up at the pretty little bird, taking a step too far back and the railing digging into his back. He puts an arm out to steady himself and grabs Val.

They're about to go over the bridge—they're about to fall over and I'm too far away to stop them.

My ear is ringing. Val's feet slip out from beneath her. Then Ethan's. There is nothing I can do, making it feel too much like what happened to my brother. I can't stop it. The wings of the bird flutter one beat at a time, just a handful of feathers and hollow bone.

Frozen, I watch as Val tumbles back into the railing and begins to topple over the side, just like my black day, all those years ago. And as I hold still, my feet glued together, Daniel lunges and grabs them—at the last moment he collects Val and Ethan with both arms—and pulls them down onto the bridge. They hit with a *thud*, the entire bridge shakes, and the little bird has vanished.

The spell broken, my feet are free, and I rush forward across the swaying bridge.

Val's face is bright red, and she gets up slowly and then vomits over the side of the bridge. Ethan looks worse. He slumps down, stares into the deafening rush of the water below. His mobile's screen is shattered, and when he sees this he starts to laugh.

"You okay, man?" Daniel asks.

Val puts a hand up. "Give him some space."

She crouches down and holds the big man in her arms, and begins stroking his face. The way she touches him, softly, calmly—and when he looks at her it's with absolute trust. She looks back the same way. Is that love?

Finally, Val staggers up with Ethan, each holding on to the railing and the other's hand.

We walk across the rest of the bridge in silence.

14

THE TEA HOUSE IS SMALL. FOUR WALLS FILLED TOP TO BOTTOM WITH flags makes it feel even smaller. I don't know any of the countries besides the stars and stripes of the United States and our own flag with three sides. On the flags, I read signatures from earlier climbing teams. Next to them, expedition photos with mikarus and Sherpas, smiling together, lips chapped, faces baked by the sun. All happy. In some photos, the men's beards have icicles on them. I think of my father, of his own smiling climbing picture. It's hard to imagine him smiling again.

Lunch is black tea and dal bhat: bubbling yellow-brown curry, heavy scoops of lentils and white rice, I spoon it into bowls and bring it to the mikarus. Their voices and accents clash with the sing-song Hindi that flows from the small television in the common room. A Bollywood film plays, and a shiny metal-faced policeman waves a glistening pistol, but the mikarus are busy glancing at the day's pictures on their screens. They barely look up when I serve the food.

"Namaste."

"Namaste, Ang."

"Thank you."

Thank you. That's a phrase I remembered easily. "Thank you," I say again as I wait for them to attack the steaming meal in front of them so I can eat, too.

"Potatoes, carrots, leeks, that's the safe choice," I told Val before they ordered. "All grown locally." I had advised against the meat. Meat served on the Khumbu is butchered in Kathmandu, thrown into sacks and carried up on the backs of porters.

I linger a few feet from the table, waiting, then cross back into their world. Ethan moans. His head is only a few centimeters from resting on the table.

"Hey," Val says. "You have to eat. Today is the easy day."

I chime in, hoping to cheer them up: "Climb high, sleep low," words in English I've heard many times. All three mikarus stare up at me. I keep speaking, piecing together what I once heard from my father, in English before switching to Nepali for the words I don't know. "We climb...a thousand feet a day. Safe. You get head-ache here"—I point to the back of my head—"bad."

Val explains the parts for which I lacked words.

"He's right," Ethan replies. "If you get a migraine at the back of the head, if you're dizzy, weak, nauseous, you have to come down. Right away. The higher you go, the less oxygen. And your heart works harder. It makes your blood thicker, too."

Val smiles, pulls her hair back. "Ang, thank you. Please, go and eat your meal. I'm sure you're hungry."

I had wanted to impress Val and the others, but clearly, I didn't impress them at all. A few yards away, just beyond a screen of beads dividing the rooms, I cross into another world. In the kitchen, I wash my hands in cold water in a blackened sink—no soap— layers of dust peeling off. Splashing my face, I taste the cold water on my chapped lips, feeling how dry the day has been. I close my eyes and feel the sun stroke my face, the pain of the day's steps. Then I finally sit down and warm up with my own bowl of dal bhat. I want to dig in and scoop the rice by hand, but I feel the gaze of Val, Ethan, and Daniel, even from another room.

Next to me, other porters don't share my worries. Their hands knead clumps of rice, scoop up curry with the balls of rice. The woman of the house comes around with a communal water bowl, and we dip our fingers in, turning the water yellow from the curry. The porters burp pleasurably, and when the lady of the house smiles, her eyes disappear within thick folds of skin. She comes up to me, sees I haven't eaten, then reaches into a drawer and hands me a wooden tool surely carved by her own hand. *Thank you.*

I mix the curry and rice with the spoon, mash it all into a paste, and swallow. I've used spoons to cook before, but never to eat. My hand shakes, grains of rice dropping back into my bowl. I eat nervously, even though the mikarus can't see and this woman couldn't care less about me. We're the only people in the tea house, the sirdar Lasha is probably waiting for us in Phakding.

"Base Camp?" the old woman asks. I nod. "One of the new generation—a Sherpa who only eats with spoons, too good for the old ways. Modern."

She takes my bowl, refills it with rice, lentils, curry. I haven't eaten this much in days, besides the yak meat, but this is something I'm more accustomed to.

"Young bodies are never full," she says. "You've been a guide long?"

I shake my head.

"Didn't think so," she laughs. "You look young. Very young."
Preserve the inner secret while only revealing the outer level.

Another few spoonfuls and my bowl is empty again. I thank her for the food, get up before she can ask any more questions and pass through the screen of beads, from one world back to the other.

Val's bowl is wiped clean, not a grain remains. I glance over at the others: Ethan's is untouched, he tosses a metallic wrapper onto the table, leftovers from a foreign treat. Daniel is busy taking a photo of his meal. I don't understand why he'd rather photograph his food than eat it. I come close and he shows me the camera, pointing for me to put my eye into the small window. I see the bowl in sharp detail, half white, the other half golden, with blocks of potato, pebble-sized lentils. I've never looked at food like this before, as a thing of beauty.

"Put your finger here," Daniel says, taking my hand to show me how to hold the machine, his fingers lightly gliding over mine. "Push down here. *Click*."

There it is, captured in the camera's small window. The bowl of dah bhat looks just as good as it does on the table.

"That's your picture," Daniel says, smiling. "You took it."

I feel a flutter in my chest, not quite sure of all the words the mikarus trade, but I feel as if I am finally impressing them.

"Picture," Daniel keeps saying. "Good picture."

Val translates, repeats the word in English. "Picture."

"Pic-ture," I say.

"Picture. Photograph," he says again.

Val leans across the table to look at the image. "Nice. How do you say 'rice'? Not in Nepali, in your language? In Sherpa?"

"Dray," I answer.

Val wrinkles her nose so it looks like the top of a mushroom. "Dray. And potato?"

"Sho-gok."

She tries out the new words on the others. Ethan repeats in a grunt. But Daniel nods his head, listening, then takes out a pen and paper and passes it to me. "Can you write it down? The spelling?"

I haven't touched pen to paper since I last saw Nurse Lanja. It has been three years. I scribble in our script, and Daniel takes the paper and smiles again. "I can't read this, but you said 'sho-gok,' right?"

I nod, look down, then back, and Daniel is still staring right at me.

"Potato," he says. "In English. It's *po-ta-to*. You try."

The sounds drag out of my mouth. Ethan laughs and I feel my blood surge. Just a small ring in my ear this time, an aftershock. But Daniel and Val are smiling encouragingly. It's only Ethan who snickers.

"Time to go," I finally say, in my own Nepali.

"Guys, let's pack up," Val commands.

I collect the plates, deliver them to the kitchen. My neck and back are drenched in sweat. In the kitchen, the woman of the house tallies up the cost. I avoid her eyes as she passes me a slip of paper with the total. I take a breath, cooling off, then part the beads and return to deliver the bill. Each mikaru produces a stuffed wallet, and I avert my eyes, this time out of shame, so much money in those billfolds. *What each of you has there, my entire family could live on for one year.*

A thousand rupee note with a bull elephant on one side and Jomolangma on the other, a five hundred rupee note with two Bengal tigers sipping from a mountain stream, a one hundred rupee note with a one-horned white rhino strutting through the terai grassland, a fifty note with two blood pheasants preparing to mate, twenties and tens with a rutting stag and a family of antelope. My whole world, right here in crumpled notes, passed to me by snow colored hands that even after half a day on the trail look as clean as those of the royal family. And when I look down at mine, hands and fingers speckled in black bruises and red and rough cuticles.

Val told me before that the pay with BBC is low, but I don't believe her. She and the others hold their money fearlessly, trusting they will get more. When I hand the rupees to the woman of the house, she accepts the money with a smile and slight bow, then opens a stuffed box and deposits it. The woman is a Sherpa like me, but a different caste altogether, with her new down jacket —shiny, expensive—she's more like the mikarus than I am. Dozens of travelers pass through her small tea house every day and the tea here isn't even that fresh. No matter, her eyes say. No matter. Mikarus will keep coming, mikarus will keep paying. And where is her husband, maybe dead? Or maybe she's rich enough to not need one. No matter. As long as there's a mountain to climb, they will come. Like a fisherman in the Dudh Kosi, if the waters teem with fish, they will bite regardless of what bait is used.

The mikarus are rising from the table, pressing their hands and saying "namaste." There's no bend to her knees when she bows to her patrons, who smile back.

Smile, smile, smile. The fish don't even know why.

It's late afternoon when we finally stop for the night in Phakding.

With food in my stomach, the trail isn't as difficult as it was in the morning. My blistered feet are getting used to my boots, my shoulders and back to the thirty kilos, my nose to the dust. Val and Daniel are getting more comfortable, too—both have tied kerchiefs over their faces. But stubborn Ethan won't listen. It still must be *silly* to him. I cannot catch any of his English, he speaks so quickly and with so many words I don't understand. But I understand his manner.

Shiny solar panels point skyward along the lodge's long stone walkway. Solar—cheap to use and expensive to install. More well-to-do Sherpas here. No more than a hundred in this village. Inside, the fading sun shines through the lodge's dirt-stained glass windows, but even with the sun, it's empty and cold. I think of my father with his television and solar panels, the prize for my marriage.

Two boys emerge with the jingling of bells on the door, both still chewing lunch. They look barely in their teens, faces small and timid, a touch of down on their upper lips. And beyond them, sitting at a table with cards in his hands, our sirdar, Lasha.

He nods and looks back to his cards, and the boys offer steaming mugs of tea. I'm thirsty, but there's something about the way he looks at me—as if his eyes see through my jacket, my undershirt. I lead the group to a table, then bow, remove my pack, collect the keys for the rooms, steal a sip from a pot of cold water. I gather the empty water bottles, never stopping a minute. I'm exhausted, but I don't want to give the sirdar a good look at me.

"Cards?" one of the boys asks. I glance at the table, a pile of dirty rupees in the middle and a half-empty bottle of home brew next to the sirdar. I shake my head and hear the boys chiding me as I step back into the dining area.

I imagine my father here, whole and with both legs strong and healthy. I can see him with those boys, teasing someone like me. I pass by a map pinned to the wall, Phakding circled in bright red, "2,610 meters." Lower than my home village, much lower. Val says she's been to Namche Bazaar before, but no further. We'll be in Namche tomorrow after a thousand meter ascent, and there's a long way to go after that. A long, long way.

Dinner for my team is fried rice and a pizza made with yak cheese—a Nepali special for Daniel and Val. "Double the C of regular cow milk," she says. For Ethan, *chikken* momos, fried dumplings. Val told him not to eat meat, but he doesn't listen.

"What happens with the empty bottles you took, Ang?" Val questions.

I stare at her a moment, forgetting again that Ang is me. (*Not the other Ang, the Ang wandering in the bardo.*)

"Where do they go? Are they going to be recycled? The bottles?"

"Reused," I say, catching on. "The bottles will hold oil, kerosene. We don't throw anything away on the mountain. And there's nowhere to dump it. We burn. Or we reuse." *Just like I'm reusing your name, brother.*

"What about the trails? They're filthy, worse than last year. Does anyone clean them?"

How can they, dear Val? How can any Sherpa bend to scoop the trash mikarus leave here if they're busy lugging the same supplies that those mikarus bring so as to make more trash? But I don't say that. Nima, Ang, the Sherpa girl, the good porter, whoever I am, I hold back my thoughts.

"More tourists mean more money," I say. And that is true, of course. "Not enough money hurts the people."

Ethan shouts, picking a long bone from a momo.

"What did he say?" I whisper to Val.

"He wants you to learn English."

I nod. "Can you teach me? I know a little."

"Okay." Val rocks her head back and forth. "Okay, starting tomorrow we're going to teach Ang English." Back in Nepali. "Understand? Starting tomorrow."

They've finished eating, and this time, they all ate. Even Ethan.

Without glancing at Lasha, I offer to show them their three rooms—each with two twin beds, pillows, wool blankets. A view of the trail we climbed, abutting the lodge's entrance. No fireplace, but even with these thin wooden walls, it seems fancy compared to my home in Khunde. No, not fancy, but spacious. Private. I hand Daniel a key, "Good night," then one to Val and one to Ethan. Val looks confused. "We don't need two keys, Ang. Just one key, and one room for us."

Another custom that I didn't expect, and I feel a sudden wave of embarrassment. "I'm sorry, Val."

She takes the key, opens the door, "Good night," and she and Ethan leave me in the corridor.

Back in the kitchen, there's an empty bottle on the table, and the boys are still playing cards, but the sirdar is gone.

"Hey, will you sit and play now? We're ready to take your money." Laughs.

"Just two rooms for the mikarus," I say, passing the remaining key to one of the boys. He takes it and throws it into a box piled high with other keys.

"Good," he says. His nose is completely flat, his forehead protrudes farther, his eyes close together. "More mikarus are coming tonight. We need the space. And if you don't want to lose your money, we'll wait for the other Sherpas. We'll take their money—and then the mikarus'."

Then the boy tosses me a key. "Here's yours."

My heart shudders as I trudge upstairs—I should have known I was sharing with him. A pair of cots facing each other. Lasha the sirdar, laid out, strums his wispy chin hairs as I stand in the doorway.

"Either close the door and come in, or close it and leave!" he crows. His breath hangs in the air, and I step in, a frightened girl once again, and the sirdar—he's an all too familiar animal. It's the first time I've heard more than a grunt out of him, his voice like sandpaper rubbed together. He produces a bottle from a bag, takes a sip. It's the first time he's looked at me.

Sweat breaks out under my arms. A shiver crawls along my spine and I struggle to control it—I turn my back and wipe my face with my hand. I busy myself with unloading my gear. I have to pee. I want to cry. I should have kept the key when Val gave it back and used it for myself. When I turn around, he's still watching. His eyes are red, like a lizard's. Two red beads carved into a craggy face.

"Where are you from?" Lasha asks, twirling his chin hairs, studying me.

"Khunde—"

No, why did I say that?

"Khunde? My family is from Khunde. I've never seen you before. I know everyone there."

I turn my back again, parsing through the few belongings I've emptied on my cot. My hands are shaky. I fold my arms, sit on the cot, and meet his eyes. Hungry. And drunk. I bring my feet up onto my cot and hug my knees.

Something flashes in his look, a strange excitement.

Preserve the inner secret...

I doubt, suddenly, if he's really from the same town as me, the town so close to where we'll be passing in only a few days. I've never seen him before, I would remember. He stares without speaking, then he laughs and my throat tightens. That laugh, like a jackal, it burrows deep in me and all I can do is rock side to side on the cot, holding tight to my legs. He cackles until it becomes a hacking, dry cough. Then he drinks from the bottle and coughs again, chang dripping down his chin. He wipes it, licks a few drops from his hand, then sits up at the edge of the cot, inching closer. There's still dew on his whiskers.

"Have you heard of the man who was cuckolded?" A drop trickles off. "What was his name? Nang, Ngung, Nuru...Norbu! Yes, Norbu. Jilted. You heard?"

News travels fast on the mountain, even if it's false.

"Norbu Norgay, the precious jewel, the son of the great Tenzing."

"Godson," I hear myself say. *Idiot.*

"You know him? He's from Khumjung."

"I've heard of him," I say, trying to steady my voice. "His is a famous lineage."

Lasha grunts affirmatively.

"Did the girl not come back?" I ask stupidly.

"Jilted, boy. You know what jilted is? Fool. Even after offering twenty yaks to her father—for only one bride! *Twenty!* What shame. Shame to him and his namesake, all brought from that girl. If that were my son, I would beat him. And if it were my daughter, when I found her—"

"It's not my business," I tell him.

Lasha reflects for a moment, looks at me differently, puts the bottle down. "A girl does not leave the day before her marriage unless she is with another. Or she's impure of heart and body. There's no other reason. No other. When you get to be my age, boy, you know women. You know all about them. All about their tricks, their games. Their masks. All women have a little bit of dark magic. When the sacredness of the ordinary is broken..." He swigs from the bottle. ". . . the answers are simple." He leans back on the cot, takes out a pipe and loads it with black tobacco. "Fool."

He stares up at the wood beams of the ceiling as if contemplating a great thought. But he just lights the pipe and puffs. A cloud swirls around the room's lone flickering lightbulb.

"Norbu Norgay," he says in between puffs. "Hurry up and get undressed, boy, and go make your toilet. I'm turning the light off when I finish this." He holds up his pipe.

I step through the dragon smoke, out the door, down the corridor and into a small bathroom. A mirror, a bucket with water, a hole. From the cracks in the ceiling, the wind howls, and I peel off my shirt, my knit cap. I tear at the tape tying down my breasts, tug against it, stretching my skin and pinching my nipples as it comes free. Such relief, I've wanted to remove that tape all day. There's a mark around my chest, a thick line where the tape was. Something else: a few long wisps of my hair, renegades that didn't make it to the sink when I cut them off yesterday, I flick them to the ground. Here they'll stay.

I rub my breasts, kneading out the pain. In the cracked mirror, I see the pencil marks Val drew on my upper lip are nearly gone, melted by the day's sweat. I squat over the hole— everything back to the mountain. Val's in her room already. With Ethan. I can't knock on her door, I'll have to wait until the morning, maybe get her alone during breakfast? No, I'll have to decide for myself what to do. I have more tape in my bag, I can put that on in the morning. And the mustache? It itches so. Hard to guess if the sirdar would notice if it was suddenly gone. I could have shaved it off, *I did shave it*, that's what happened. That's what I'll say if anyone asks. I wet my finger and rub my upper lip. There. Gone completely. I throw my shirt back on and my jacket over it, look myself over in the mirror. Just an ugly, dirty boy.

Back in the room, the sirdar hasn't moved. He just stares up at the ceiling, pipe in hand. I move my belongings off the cot, wrap myself in the wool blankets without facing him.

I shut the light, and though the room is completely dark, I can still feel him watching me.

15

I'M FLOATING ON A RIVER. TROPICAL. PALM TREES, BLUE SKY, BLUE
waters, like something I've watched on a screen in the cyber cafe.
Smiling monkeys peer down from lush branches. Pink dolphins
sing to me. I'm in the water, but I'm not wet. I'm dry. And warm.
And I feel the touch of the sun shining through the trees. I feel it on
my cheeks, like the caress of my mother's hand. A feeling of child-
hood. I'm happy. Safe. But then the monkeys drop their smiles, the
dolphins change their tune. The palms shake and fall, and the water
freezes. The jungle is gone. And I can't move, I'm frozen in ice.

When I open my eyes, I smell the musk wafting off his breath,
see the devil dancing in his eyes, see every hair of his caterpillar
mustache, that's how close Lasha is. I'm shaking. Like in my
dream, just like those trees before they died. He's right over me
now, one hand tracing my leg, smiling when he grabs me where no
man has ever touched me. And when he smiles, I can see his black
teeth, stained from tea and tobacco, his stink fouling my nose.
Under his weight, I'm pinned—my hands are under the blankets,
and I reach with outstretched fingers—my flailing fingers trace the
wall, flicking the light switch on by chance. Lasha throws a leg
over me, one hand still probing me, the other pulling back the covers. I keep reaching with my free hand, stretching for something
I've kept close—and as the sirdar unbuckles his pants and dips a
hand in his trousers, I grab what I've been looking for and bring
it to his neck.

I can't hear anything over my beating heart. I push into soft flesh and he jumps back, the top of his head hitting the low-hanging bulb with a bolt. The swaying light shines on my kikuri, then swings and catches his shocked face, back on the blade, back and forth, both of us locked on to the other, bathed in light before we're swallowed by the black. Still aiming, I rise, my arm growing tired. But I keep my aim steady. He's off the cot completely now, takes a step back, doesn't say a word, doesn't even put a hand to his neck. When the light passes over him, his lips look stitched together. Red drops hit the ground with a steady *pat, pat.* He takes a step back, away, then another, another, a dance that I lead and he follows. I push closer and we dance until he cowers into a corner of the small room, me pointing the blade like a sorceress wields a staff, Lasha shrinking until he's no longer a lecherous man. Now he's like a child begging for his life. And I...I've grown into something else.

"You're the jilter, aren't you? That's why you knew Norbu Norgay!"

Never breaking my gaze, my weapon still trained, I don't answer. I take my pack and throw my belongings in it, roll up my blankets, and step out of the room.

Only when I'm down the corridor do I lower my kikuri. My heart pumps like boulders crashing, blood so hot I don't feel the icy floor under my blistered feet. I move like a scared animal. Too late for that key and my own room, I settle in the dining hall. But I'm not alone. A few other Sherpas—men from other treks—are sleeping on chairs, under tables. I finger my kikuri, my magic wand, and pick another corner, farther away from the men, keeping my hand on the blade's hilt all the while. Safe. *Safer.* I scan the other Sherpas. Three men. All of them sleeping. *Dreaming of the mountain and the goddess in it.*

The sound of the wind and a faraway wolf's howl blend in the drafty room. Then more howls. Closer. They're singing to one another. A song of night, a song of yearning, of pain, hunger, sadness. I shut my eyes, swallow a deep breath, and listen to the wolves, hoping the mountain song will be my guide to sleep.

I'm up before the roosters crow. Before the sun arrives, I bundle what little I have and creep to the bathroom. Looking at my naked chest in the mirror, marks from the sticky tape still visible, I'm not sure whether to keep up the farce. Then I suck in my breath and tape my breasts down. I no longer have the pencil, no down on my lip. But it doesn't matter. I'm still Ang when I look in the mirror, still Ang when I step out.

When I see Lasha in the dining area, sitting alone, huddled over a cup of tea, he looks at me without blinking, then shifts his eyes and sips from his mug. There's a kerchief covering his neck, right where my blade pricked him. Across from the sirdar sit a pair of trail Sherpas, the men who slept here last night, eating plates of steaming food. None of them speak, not a word, too busy fueling for the day.

I step into the kitchen and help myself to tea and eggs, served out of a huge pan by the blemished teenagers who run the place. They grin at me as I take my food but say nothing. I sit for breakfast at a table opposite Lasha's, scanning the men. Some look my way in between bites or assembling their gear. The sirdar doesn't so much as glance in my direction.

I break the yolk with my knife, mix it with the white of the egg and place it in my mouth, unable to really taste the food. Two Sherpas sit at my table. They nod at me, I nod back. A dozen bites later, I carry my empty plate back to the kitchen. No grins from the youngsters.

When I sit back down, cradling a hot mug, no taste to the tea, the Sherpas get up. Maybe the sirdar just warned them—crazy girl with the blade, stay away. Or maybe they were just ready to return to the trail. The sun peers through the lodge's dirty windows. Soon Val and the others will be up. Across the room, the old man gathers his pack. I try to get a sense of what's to come, but he still won't look at me. Lasha stops at the door, adjusts the kerchief and scratches his neck—and then he's off. Out the lodge and onto the trail, without a word.

An hour later, we're climbing again. No sign of the sirdar— he's surely far up by now— which means I have until tonight to find out if he'll try to tell Val or anyone else. I haven't said a word to Val. Of course not. What would she say if she found out? Will she keep her promise, will she keep my secret? Or will she say I fooled her to save face in front of Ethan and Daniel? The mikarus are quiet as we move. They didn't sleep well on the first night of their trek, I can see it in their faces. Enlarged pupils and red eyes, labored breathing.

Climb high, sleep low.

The air is already so much thinner than they're used to. The mikarus are tiring easily, even so early in the day. An hour more, we stop at a checkpoint, a bamboo hut manned by two soldiers with oily hair and bad skin, sticks for arms and legs. They look my age. Maybe younger. The one with the worse acne holds an old wooden rifle. I wonder if it's ever been fired, or if he knows how to use it. We're the only trekkers on this stretch, and for once, we're alone on the trail.

NOW ENTERING SAGARMĀTHĀ NATIONAL PARK, the sign announces in Nepali, painted in a faded blue, then in English under it. I can see inside the guard hut—no windows, glass is too expensive. There's just a large open space where a window would go, and I see another ancient rifle and, next to it, an open tin of crisps, a small fire warming a water pot, and a sleeping dog who flicks his tail at the buzzing flies. What do soldiers do up here, alone and bored for days on end—shoot pheasants? It's hard to imagine there are Maoists left on the mountain to fight, much less any other reason for the army to remain in the Khumbu. Maoists in the government, I remember Father saying years ago, when they made the peace. *Maoists everywhere.*

"Passports," one of the boys says in Nepali. "Passports," he repeats in English.

My mikarus dig through their pockets, offer them with outstretched arms. The shiny watch on Val's delicate wrist glistens as she holds up the document. The soldier rests his rifle on one shoulder, takes the passports with the other. He scans the passports, flipping the pages with fingernails caked in dirt and grease. "American, yes?"

He looks down at the pictures and back up to the three faces in front of him. Then he closes the passports. "Three thousand rupees," in Nepali first, then in English. The mikarus don't know what to do, then he barks and takes the rifle from his shoulder and points it and they fumble for their money. He turns to me. "Where are your papers, boy?"

"What papers?" I manage before the other soldier grabs my arm.

"Three thousand for you, too."

I try to put my hands up, but he pushes me, then raises the rifle and aims it at me now, then back at the mikarus and back at me. "Please, brother," I say, trying to calm him. "Please."

Behind him, back in the hut, the boiling pot of water starts whistling, and the dog yaps. The other soldier runs to fetch his gun, and the dog squeals. The soldier must have knocked over the pot and hit the mutt.

"I have the money," I hear myself yell. "I have it!" But the rifle is still in my face. I'm so close to the boy holding it that I can count the blemishes on his cheeks, picturing those dirty fingernails scratching at his face. The rifle is just as pockmarked, the wood full of small holes as if termites have infested it.

Click. There's a sound like a twig snapping, and when I turn my head, I see Daniel's finger on the camera, dangling from his neck. *He took a photo.*

One of the soldiers reaches for the dangling camera, pulls at it, and Daniel resists. "Whoa, whoa, here's the money!" He breaks free and offers up the rupees. The soldier grabs the money, flashing a look like he's about to raise the rifle again, then Val steps forward, clasping her hands and speaking so quickly, I can't make out the words. The soldier who pushed me shakes his head and glances at their wallets. "No. Now five thousand." There's a cobweb hanging from the barrel. A small spider crawls towards the hole at the end. Escape.

"Five thousand," he yells again. "Now!"

My mikarus scramble to pull out more rupees. The dog is out of the hut now, barking and slobbering. Ethan flinches and drops some of the rupees. He bends to pick them up. The dog is in his face, canines snapping, he grabs the fallen notes and staggers back up. The boy soldiers collect the extra rupees from him, then Daniel. "Now you," he says to Val, who hands it over. Then back to me. The other soldier points his rifle. "All your money. Hurry up."

All my money? Val gave me twelve thousand, five hundred yesterday morning, a quarter of my wages, but he probably assumes I have a lot less.

"Give now!" he yells again.

I nod. "Okay, brother, okay. I'm getting it. I'm bending to get it in my boot."

I kneel to unlace my boot and the mutt advances on me. I raise a hand—I don't even realize what I'm doing, he's coming and I try to protect myself—and I feel the teeth sink into flesh, right between my thumb and pointing finger. I think of Fifth and how she must have felt all those years ago. The dog tears at the skin like he's tearing paper, and I grab my hand with my other arm and pull back and I feel his jaws tighten their grip—then the baby-faced soldier kicks the beast in the snout and he lets go, whimpering.

There are two small holes in my hand, throbbing and starting to bleed, as I dig the rupees out from one sock, bleeding all over the blood pheasants and rhinos. I had put half of my money in this boot, half in the other. The boy kicks me and snatches the money, wiping the rupees clean on his pants leg. The other soldier lowers his rifle, and suddenly the two squabble over the rupees, just like dogs.

I struggle to my feet, touch the hilt of my kikuri, and a wave flows over me, my whole body a deep drum—and when I stop, I hear Val's voice, still calm. "We want our passports back," she says in Nepali.

I take a cautious step, my hand still fingering the blade. The boy soldiers don't seem to hear Val, and I motion to the mikarus to get moving.

"Passports," Val repeats, facing them again.

"Val, what are you doing?" I ask her.

"We can't leave without those passports."

The one who kicked me still holds the passports in one hand, the rupees in the other. Val takes another step—she's the same size as these boys, and there's a glint in her eye I haven't seen before.

"Val," Ethan hisses in warning, but she puts a hand up, takes another step closer, keeping her eyes on the soldiers. "You have the money, now give us the passports," she commands again in Nepali.

They're listening now, stunned, unable to believe this mikaru woman speaks their language.

Val takes another step, leans in, reaches, and takes the passports from his hand. And the boy soldier lets her, enraptured as if under a lepcha's spell—then it seems to break and he raises the rifle again. The other soldier does the same. I'm sure they're going to shoot, kill her, then us. My hand is right above the kikuri, but what can I do? I'm no killer. And if I pulled out the blade, I'd die.

Guns still pointed, Val takes a step back, then takes the shiny watch from around her wrist and places it on the ground. "A gift," she says, backing up another step. "A gift. A golden watch. For you."

The boys hold their aim, come closer, then drop their rifles and dash for the watch, diving in the dirt. One has the watch, then the other—they're fighting over it. I look at the two rifles on the ground, consider grabbing one, handing the other to Val. No, now Val is motioning to follow, and we all reverse, one step, then another, and dash down the trail—if they pick up the weapons and fire now, they could still hit us. We're circling a switchback, jetting up a small hill, and I hear a loud *crack*—a rock, a boulder dropping, an aimed shot?—which is when we really start running.

I run so hard I forget everything else. When I finally stop and turn around, I've lost them, but I've lost my mikarus, too. I'm scared to turn back down the trail, and I'm ashamed of my fear.

A tall pine juts out by the trail, and I crouch in a patch of ferns, my body and my dark thoughts hidden in the thick undergrowth. There's a deep throbbing in my hand, and it's still bleeding. I tear my sleeve and wrap a piece of cloth tight. The blood soaks through. A few minutes pass, a few more, the cloth has gone from red to black. Then the sound of footsteps. I duck lower and take out the kikuri as the steps come closer. *Loud steps,* I think with relief.

Nepalis don't walk that way, like a plodding yak.

Through the ferns, I spot Val and the others, and I exhale as I sheathe the blade and emerge from the bushes. Val rushes towards me and envelops me in a hug. I don't know what to do—I'm relieved and embarrassed—no woman outside of my family has ever embraced me like this. I laugh nervously, and so does Val.

We are catching our breath, packs off, when Daniel starts yelling. "What happened back there, Ang?"

Val's own voice snaps in translation: "Is that normal, Ang? I thought this was a safe country."

Tired and scared, I snap back: "Something like that has never happened to me. They're bored, they're hungry. I'm so sorry, Val."

Val doesn't say anything, our hug now a distant memory.

"That's not the Nepali way," I plead. "It's not the Sherpa way. Tell them. I want you to explain to them."

Val still doesn't respond.

"It doesn't matter," I mutter. "No one got hurt."

"Ang is right, nothing happened," Val says shakily. "It doesn't matter."

"Doesn't matter?" Daniel blurts. "Where was the other Sherpa?"

"Val just saved us back there, Daniel," Ethan shouts. "We should be thanking her. And moving on."

Val turns to me. "Are you okay?" she asks, switching to Nepali, at which Daniel starts shouting again and I guess what he's saying: There she goes, going native again.

"Daniel," Ethan says, pointing a finger. "Enough."

Daniel sits under a tree, his head in his hands. From yelling to nearly crying—what a reaction for a man. Then Ethan points at me, indicating my wounded hand. "Let me see."

"Let him," Val says.

He unwraps the cloth, now hardened and scabbed, and examines the two holes for a moment. Then he digs through his gear. He douses my hand with a clear liquid and it stings as fresh blood oozes from the holes. "To clean it, to protect from disease." He wipes it dry, then takes a white bandage and wraps it tightly.

Daniel takes the camera from around his neck. I take a step closer and look down at the camera's screen—*he did get a photo*—that soldier with the acne, the rifle pointed right at him. He holds up his camera, looks me in the eye and lets out a whoop of joy.

16

WE DON'T STOP FOR LUNCH. VAL LEADS, NOT SAYING A WORD. THERE'S no talk at all, just the sound of our boots scraping the trail. Marching up the mountain, a Sherpa girl led by three mikarus.

We pass through Jorsale, a cluster of huts wedged along the river. We pass Monju, an even shabbier cluster. My stomach grumbles. Daniel clutches his as he walks. Ethan sucks at that water tube attached to his pack—nothing left. I try a few times to call out to Val, but the words die on my tongue. She won't listen, she won't speak, she just keeps going. So I keep quiet, too, mad at myself for losing so much money.

It's a steep ascent to Namche, straight uphill with no water or tea houses. The sun moves farther over our shoulders, another hour passes, and I muster the strength to call out to Val. No response. I try to touch her arm.

"What?" she almost yells, in English, but I understand her. Her green eyes look almost red. How quickly these mikarus seem to switch from smiles to shouts. Their language, the way it sounds and the way they speak, I can't understand, but I don't need to. There's something about it, even when they're mad, that reminds me of Sherpa, but something softer than Sherpa.

My heart's still beating rapidly and I should still be scared from what happened with the soldiers, but I'm not. I'm distracted by these mikarus, they're all like characters in a film. Being around them feels like I'm in a film. Ethan comes close, Val pushes him off, but he takes her in his arms and she finally buries her face into his chest. Just like Deepika Padukone or Priyanka Karki, one moment strong, one moment feminine, and then a hero's curled up around her finger.

That's power.

Ethan strokes Val's hair, hair the color of wheat ready for harvest. Val starts laughing, looking up at him with a wet smile. Ethan soothes her with words I both don't understand and do. Val wipes her nose, loosens from Ethan's grip and takes off her pack, digs, pulls out a water bottle. She takes a sip, then passes it to Daniel, then Ethan. Half left. Ethan hands me the bottle. "Drink."

Onward. A winding path of broken rocks littered with cigarette butts, plastic, aluminum cans, the mix of mountain and man-made filth. Val keeps pushing us up. Part of me thinks it's foolish to move so quickly, they're all so inexperienced, the surest way to court danger on the mountain is to force the pace. But the frightened girl in me agrees—the soldiers could still catch up with us. I begin thinking crazy thoughts. *That soldier touched my chest—he knows. He's probably thinking about me right now, wishing he was ripping my shirt off, him over me, crouched in that small hut, the dog barking the whole time, the other one holding his gun, waiting for his turn.*

I push the pace.

We pass a pile of construction equipment strewn across the trail. A broken door, pieces of a tin roof, frayed rope—someone's home never made it. The trail is layered with empty packs of tobacco, yellowed tossed wrappers. The pack's logo, a man with a bindi on his forehead, gets torn at every side, corner, or angle, by the impatient fingers of overworked men. My father used to chew this brand. He would always take a new pack when he left for a trek, always bring one back.

The mikarus must be thinking that the hills are never ending. They are. Winding around another ridge, another leg, another switchback. And another. And another. And another. It feels that way to me, too, even though I know what comes next. Two bridges, one after the other, suspension bridges just like the one yesterday. The first sways lightly as we all step on, this time more carefully. The next bridge, we dash across it more swiftly, the wind blowing a sharp whistle like a message from the gods on Mount Kailash. After that, the path becomes more narrow, more crowded. The air is a thick green from the droves of animals that climb over stinking pools of dung. We all cover our faces, even Ethan. The sun pokes in through the clouds and the trees, and we dance in and out, from dry trail to ice, and from ice back to pebbled, frittered trail. Moments ago it was packed, now the traffic has thinned and the rush of the Dudh Kosi echoes louder.

The mikarus are starting to show fatigue from the heights. Val's sinuses drip, even with a rag covering her face. And Ethan has such a fit of sneezing—one, two, three, four, five, six times— we all stop and gawk at him. He sneezes so hard he trips on a rock. "It's okay, I'm okay, it's over." But then he's hit again—one, two, three, four. The rest of us can't help but smile, the spirits of the mountain seem to be playing with him.

"Where's the next tea house?" Ethan asks, trying to hold back a sneeze. I'm sure I grasped the words *tea house*.

Val turns to me, in Nepali: "How much farther?"

I'm not sure exactly. I look up at the sun, it's moved again. Should I tell her? "Two, maybe three hours."

Val says something in English, and I'm sure she gave them a more optimistic time frame because of the relief on their faces. Ethan stops, digs through his pack. He pulls out something in plastic, tosses it to Val, then Daniel. He hands one to me, too. "Eat."

I tear open the plastic, it looks like oats and fruit dried and mixed together.

"Eat it, Ang," Val tells me, softening to me again. "It's good."

I take a bite, I am hungry—and Ethan and Daniel laugh at my reaction. I've never had anything like this. There are grains, oats, but it's too sweet. I eat it anyway.

Ethan and Daniel keep mouthing a word whose meaning I've heard before. Diamox. Diamox.

They're exhausted. I am, too. My back has been wet with sweat since this morning, and I adjust the straps on my heavy load and eat the treat—whatever it is—in a few bites. I've walked these heights my whole life, but never loaded like this, like a pack animal. Maybe it's the mikarus slowing me down? A slower pace means more hours carrying these kilos. That sirdar devil has one thing right—he knows it's not worth climbing at the same pace as the white people. A man on a dark-maned horse rides by, kicking up dust, bells on his saddle chiming. So fast and beautiful—a daikini in the flesh.

"Nepali mountain bike," I say to Val.

She laughs. I've never been on a horse before. I've always wanted to ride. *I will one day,* I promise myself, as I watch man and beast disappear down the mountain. I wonder if Norbu would let me ride, if he took me as his bride. It's the first time I've thought of him today. The clouds build and then break above us, light shining through, and we march, silently, heads down, sliding over the scree.

The lotus only opens when touched by the sun.

After one abrupt incline, we catch up with a group of Sherpas, a group that had passed us long ago. Now they're walking slowly, like us, the hill is so steep. I adjust my kerchief back over my face, but my countrymen are too busy catching their breath to pay attention to me. There is one female porter, with short hair like mine, she must be in her forties. As I pass her, I try to look at her face, but she turns away. I'm gazing at my future, perhaps.

At the top of the hill there's a rest stop where the light washes over trekkers and Sherpas. They both sit huddled together, warming themselves. A young couple—Chinese, maybe—share a boxed lunch, eating rice with chopsticks. Westerners with bright red faces pose for photos at the edge of the hill. No sign of Lasha anywhere. But the peaks are in full view, they circle us on all sides like wolves.

My mikarus are so spent, they barely look at the peaks. This is such a sacred place, our first real view of the glory of Jomolangma. They're too tired to appreciate it.

Ahead, a woman sells bright oranges from a tiny stand. She rests in the sun, leaning back against the load of fruit. Her long fingernails stroke mugju prayer beads. In her other hand, she holds an orange, a bright splash in this gray world.

"Tashi delek," she murmurs from an empty mouth. Her hair is deep black, but her face droops, showing her years. There's a frailness to her, a frailness defying logic, because it seems impossible that she could ever make it up this far. Up and down the mountain—like all Sherpas hauling their lives on their backs, she is no different.

The old woman holds up a perfectly round and ripe fruit to my mikarus. Then she uses a clawlike finger to pierce the skin, effortlessly, and offers it to Ethan and Daniel. She laughs when they peel and eat the fruit, juices dripping down their lips, and when she laughs, a single tooth pokes from her mouth.

"Water?" Ethan asks her, pointing to his mouth. "Water?"

She keeps smiling. Ethan doesn't wait for an answer, walking off, looking for anyone who might sell him water.

"Stay close," Val calls after him. Then she turns to the woman. "Namaste. Can I take your picture?"

The old woman doesn't speak Nepali. I pull down my kerchief and explain Val's request. I no longer have my own grandparents, they had their sky funerals long ago. But they taught me the dialect this woman speaks.

She puts down the beads, motions for me to come closer. "Why would I learn Nepali? I am a Sherpa. Strange that she knows Nepali, though," gesturing at Val.

"Will you let them take your photograph?" I repeat. "Give them your image? It's safe."

She nods. "I used to believe that to give an image would lose one's threnpa inside that picture machine, they'd become a ghost—

trapped forever inside the machine. That was what my mother said to me when I was just a young girl. She heard it from the mediums. In those times, everyone believed their words. Now you can't find a real medium and everyone your age knows you can't lose your soul from taking a photo. Not on this side of the mountain, at least. But I've learned about the world, much more than she ever did. You, too?"

I nod. She rocks her head, that clawlike thumb stroking her beads. "May we...?"

"To all things a purpose, child. When the mikaru takes my image, I only ask that you include my stand, too. This is a business, you know. And this image will go on internet, yes? Perhaps many foreigners will see my stand and they will want to taste the fruit, and then it will help my business, yes?"

Daniel folds four fingers and sticks up his thumb. "Are we good?"

I mimic Daniel's hand sign. Val smiles and does the same.

"Very auspicious meeting, yes? I should say so." The old woman smiles. "Yes, indeed. And how is the fruit? Sweet, yes?"

Now holding a notebook and pen, Val nods to Daniel, who begins taking photographs. Then she asks questions that I translate.

How long have you lived here?

How old are you?

What's it like working on the mountain?

How has it changed? How has tourism changed it?

The woman's name is Dechen. She says her family came over the mountain after Mao's invasion in 1951. Some went to Ladakh, in India. Some came here to Nepal. Just like my family and so many others, thousands fled the plateau and resettled in the south. The most enterprising of our people made the switch to hospitality, setting up tea houses. Today, more of us do that than climb the peaks. Dechen never was able to make the switch to hospitality and the easier life. Life is a maze, some can make it all work, others never do.

"To all things a purpose," Dechen says.

To all things a purpose.

Years ago, Dechen had planned to build a lodge with her husband, but when he died from influenza, there was no money. So she was forced to work. With no land, the only work she could find was as a merchant. But with nothing of her own to sell, her son must trek to the border with India, buying fifty pounds of oranges that she sells up and down the Khumbu.

Dechen picks up one of the perfect oranges, a treasure hauled all the way from the terai. The fruit's color is so deeply orange, its shape so perfectly round with not a single mark visible, it's hard to believe the journey it took to get here. "Would you like to try the sweetness of the Indus?" she asks Val, piercing the skin, just like she did for Ethan and Daniel. "Money flows like a river, you see. If it stays in one place too long, it gets dirty. Just like an orange."

Val peels it and bites into a slice. The juice drips down her chin, and she wipes it with a delicate hand. Dechen laughs, that single tooth jutting out of that dark, empty mouth. "Well?" she asks.

I forget that Val doesn't speak Sherpa, and there's a moment of silence as Val chews and Dechen watches, her mouth open, waiting. Dechen turns to me. "She wants to know if you like it, Val."

"Delicious."

I trust Val. I realize, in this moment, that I trust her in almost everything. When the rifles were pointed at her, she took a heavy risk. How close did she come to losing her life—and ours? A glint in her white eyes, the crack of a twig if she had advanced another step? Anything could have set the soldiers off. And then? None of us would be standing here now. And yet I trust her boldness. *Act, even if afraid. Don't leave fate to chance. To all things a purpose.*

"Everyday life is already so unthinkable," Dechen laughs. "Is not the everyday enough? Is not life, this very thing you hold in your hand, the sand and dirt between your toes, the earth which was here before and will be hereafter, isn't that magic?"

More fruit is peeled and passed around.

"Ask her about the mikarus here," Val cuts in. "Ask how they've changed the mountain."

I translate. Dechen's cheeks sag. "There is always potential for everything, at any moment. Or disaster, at any moment."

"But the mikarus," I repeat. "How have they changed Sherpa life on the mountain?"

"From hardship we grow strong." She pauses, from sadness or fatigue, I don't know. "What is your name?" she asks finally.

"Ang."

"Speak up."

"Ang. My name is Ang."

"Ang. Ang means 'young.' Young life. In my time, every Sherpa had two names, named for the day of the week they were born. I was Dechen Dawa because I was born on dawa, a Monday. How are the mikarus changing the mountain, young Ang?" The old woman turns to Val again, explaining slowly as I translate: "Many Sherpas take mikaru names now, or their parents shorten their names. There are too many of them, too many mikarus. The home of Khumbi Yulha is no longer a hidden valley. And young Sherpas like you no longer have traditional names because the mikarus brought change. Maybe your son won't have a Sherpa name, maybe he won't be a Buddhist." Another pause. Both her hands are busy now, one twirling a prayer wheel, the other tracing the hundred and eight strung beads. "*Om mani peme hung.* Praise to the jewel in the glancing eye. After my husband died, I renamed my son. He was Mingma Babu, but I renamed him Mingma Tsering. Not a mikaru name, but a strong Sherpa name. You know what that means, young Ang?"

"Long life."

"Long life. Tell your mikaru that. Tell her."

So much to explain. Val's writing is a blur as black ink scratches across white pages. "Do you believe the earthquakes and the ru's would have struck anyway, without the mikarus?"

To that, Dechen shakes her head. "No, no. It's the gods' way of showing anger. This is still their home, no matter how many mikarus come."

I keep translating her words to Val, pointing at the peak, the mountain everyone is staring at. Ethan is back with two bottles of water. He passes one to Val, finishes his own, lets it drop to the ground. Val stares at Ethan in disbelief, as if he's just committed some grave mistake.

"What?" he says, scowling. "There's trash everywhere."

Val keeps her stare locked and Ethan mutters something I don't understand, kneels and picks up the bottle, stuffs it into his pack.

Dechen asks me if my mikarus have seen the goddess before. I relay it to Val.

Val stands up, squinting as she tilts her head to the sky. And she sees her. The foremost goddess.

I stand staring, just like my mikarus, and I see her through their eyes. Her body is etched by winds and storms. Clouds swirl around her snow-capped top, before they peel away, revealing harsh streaks of sharp stones, endlessly tall. Peeping through the opening of the clouds, the goddess silently disrobes for us. Jomolangma, she's the reason they all come here. Then, as gracefully as she gave herself, the misty robes wrap back around her. The clouds return, and she's gone.

17

THE NEXT FEW HOURS OF TREKKING ARE A GAME OF HIDE-AND-SEEK: the goddess retreats behind bluffs and crests only to rise again, floating in the clouds, spurring us on. Chasing a view makes it easier for the mikarus to forget their exhaustion, as they crane their necks.

"Everest," they keep chanting. "Everest." I wish I was as easily seduced by that name. The closer we get, the more my mind is back in Khunde, at my home, with my sisters, my mother, even Norbu. *He'll probably just marry Nyi or Soom. Maybe both. He's not a bad man. They should be happy together, they don't need me. But the others will have a hard time now with my father.*

Why isn't what we have ever enough? Dechen's voice echoes in my mind.

Straight uphill, we pass the tree line, into the high country of barren ridges and boulders. The wind is wilder, the air thinner and colder. No snow on the ground here, but all the surrounding peaks are blanketed. Late in the day, we finally trudge into a town that sits in the lap of the range, like a cub in its mother's womb. Namche Bazaar. Three thousand four hundred and forty meters. It's one long road winding up and down the mountain and through the town, and this one is the biggest in the Khumbu.

The aroma of cooked foods leads us from dirt trail to cobblestone street. We pass children in starched white school uniforms running past goats, dogs, roaming chickens. A cyber cafe, a bakery, all closed already, but the scent of sweets still in the air. A police station with a lone officer armed with an ancient-looking rifle—he reminds me of the boy soldiers, but this man doesn't even bother to look at us. We search for a place to sleep as Ethan and Daniel complain about Lasha's elusiveness. Shouldn't he at least wait for us at the end of the day, help arrange things for us? Will he order another room for us both tonight?

The Namche Hotel, booked. Then the Thawa Lodge. The front door is locked, and after I bang on it, a man with a pot belly and a piece of chicken in his hand opens the door. He spits on me when he responds: "No vacancy!"

The sun is down now, and we keep hiking on a dark lane I know well. I've come here for years to sell our produce—back when we had something to sell. When I was small I would come with my father, a farmer between the trekking seasons. Sometimes he let me have a few coins from his sales. How different those times feel now. I exchanged one of those coins for a red kerchief, *for Second*, and with the other I traded for a plastic blue ball, for Ang.

We try three more tea houses—the Trekker's House, Hotel Zamling, and another without a name—no room or no answer at the door, the third shutting its lights as we reach the front step. A curtain parts and a young girl's face looks down with worried eyes. Her mother comes to the window, gives us the same look, shakes her head at the girl, and draws the curtain once more.

There's a hint of panic on the faces of the mikarus. It's common practice to lock up at nightfall to ward off bad spirits. Most Sherpas believe that hungry ghosts knock on doors at night, eager to return to this world. And perhaps they're right: a girl dressed as a man and using the name of her dead brother—I am as good as a ghost to them.

One uphill road, and we're almost at the end of Namche. We pass Siddhartha Bank, shiny and new and with a blinking light. I would sleep anywhere now—my feet feel ready to burst.

And my back, how it burns with these kilos strapped to it. Behind me, the mikarus shuffle, their heads hanging. Something about the bank makes Daniel stop and take a photo. Across from the bank, the Khumbu Lodge and Tea House—the last place to sleep in Namche.

Ethan points to a sign written in red paint in English. ECO LODGE. Val makes a gesture as if she's too tired for his jokes. We don't have a tent or supplies, and it's too cold to bed out in the open. I can see my breath burst out in quick puffs. The three mikarus are all looking at me to solve this final problem. I try the door—fearful to turn the knob—but I grip and turn it, expecting the handle to fight me, but it opens.

Inside, we're finally out of the cold, the warm smells of men hit our noses—but the place is empty. There's a small TV on in the day room: a Bollywood film showing a family dancing at a wedding. The bride in white, her groom in black, Hindi music flowing.

I slam the door to make our presence known. Still no one to greet us. Strange. And there, lined up against the wall, through force of luck or divine intervention, are our team's bags. I rub my eyes: yes, they are our bags. Val, Ethan, and Daniel rush to open them. They dig out water bottles and bags of chocolate and nuts and strip them out of their plastic packaging. They're so hungry. Val hands me a piece of chocolate and I take it and chew without tasting it. Lasha could have foreseen that we would stay here—maybe he, too, couldn't find an open tea house. The magic of the ordinary, according to Dechen.

Other than the low sound of Bollywood chants and my mikarus' loud chewing, it could be a ghost house. Then the sound of glasses being slammed onto a table and a loud laugh. We follow the laugh into a kitchen, its ceiling low, a single bulb hanging from it, just like the room I stayed in last night. And there, playing the card game jhyap and drinking chang, a pile of rupees in the middle of the small wooden table, sit the sirdar and two boys. He doesn't speak any English, an excuse to keep apart from the clients. Just like my father used to do.

"How's your little porter? Is he keeping up?" he asks Val in Nepali. I know Val understands, but she doesn't respond, instead turning from the kitchen to look into the communal dining area.

The old man isn't wearing the kerchief around his neck, and I can see where my blade marked him, a single red dot, scabbed over. He wiggles his mustache from side to side, like a caterpillar above his lips, and looks up at me and slams a card to the table and yells, "Jhyap!" and the boys yell back, "Cheat! Cheat!"

Lasha flushes and his caterpillar twitches. "Cheat? No cheating. These fools distracted you—I jhyapped and reached one hundred points—you saw it! Both of you saw and no one countered. Are you saying I lied?"

"May I?" Ethan interrupts, holding up a few crumpled bills, and Lasha's eyes go from slits to full moons. *Drunk.* He nods, waves the mikaru over. I'm sure Ethan doesn't know the game, but it doesn't matter, he's a man and he sits down next to Lasha, and chang is poured and cards are dealt. Now he's drinking, and one drink is all it'll take at this altitude, all the better to lose his rupees.

"It's nice you speak Nepali," the sirdar says offhandedly to Val. "Maybe we can chat later," he adds.

One of the Sherpa boys gets up. Wobbly from drink, he glances at each of us before tossing his three cards to the floor. "Come, come," he slurs in English to Daniel and Val, leading them through a wooden door and into the dining hall.

The sound of laughter and voices in English, the stink of that all too familiar mountain fuel, they're among a rabble of white faces, men mixed with women, all sitting and drinking tall bottles of Everest beer. Val and Daniel have quickly found seats in the dining area, and I follow. I want to take Val aside to tell her about the sirdar but change my mind. She looks so tired, barely holding her head up at the table.

"Tea?" the youngster shouts at us. I nod and he turns and whistles and an old woman with a dog paw birthmark over an eye emerges—*another conjured spirit?*—holding a tray of steaming cups of tea, and the mikarus take the cups and drink thirstily.

The boy yells again—she could be his grandmother or just as easily hired help.

"Cha," she says, fishing a claw into the deep pockets of her skirt and scooping out three sets of long metal keys. She turns to me. That mark on her face, I can't help but stare at it as she tells me the price of the rooms. Three hundred rupees a night, twin cots, wool blankets, pillows. Standard tea house fare, by now I know.

"Order now, the kitchen will be closed soon," she advises.

Daniel puts down the camera, rubs the back of his head, and I overhear Val speaking to him in English, catching only a few words: "dizziness," "nausea," "vomiting," "altitude."

An empty bottle slammed down at the next table jolts me. Drunks. The same everywhere. One of them has hair so red I can't believe it—it's a girl, probably my age—and she gulps

Everest beer, just like the men.

I pray I can speak with Val tonight, before the sirdar does and poisons her with lies. And if I do, maybe she can start teaching me English, too. If I could speak English with the tourists, I could get work. It wouldn't matter who I was.

"Diamox," I hear Val say before the drunken yells drown her out. My stomach rumbles, I haven't eaten a proper meal since the morning.

"Have you decided what you would like for dinner?" I ask.

Val asks Daniel, who studies the menu as if it were some monk's poetry. Ethan joins the table, empty-handed, having lost his rupees faster than even I thought was possible. He picks up the menu, mumbles a queer poem of his own: "Curey, chikken, feesh." He craves meat. He and Val argue briefly, at the end of which the big mikaru lets out a long sigh and points with his finger: vegetable fried rice. With an egg on it.

The smash of a bottle onto the floor, more laughs from the next table.

"Australians?" Val wonders. Ethan puts his hand on her neck, checking for a tender spot, but she pushes his hand away. She picks up a saltshaker from the table. "What do you call this?"

"Tsha," I answer. "How do you say it in English?"

"Salt."

I smile encouragingly. It's fascinating how things are named— how sounds become words become things. But it doesn't look like I'll get to trade words with Val tonight. I head back to the kitchen, where Lasha is still playing cards, but this time with someone new, a man with his back to me. From his square build and short hair, I think it's one of the boy soldiers, and I freeze in the doorway. Lasha sees me and leers, mumbling something I don't catch, and the unknown man turns to face me. He's the one I've been running from for days, his face tattooed on my mind's eye.

My heart is in my throat, leaping out. Norbu.

18

WAS IT A SCREAM OR JUST THE WIND?

I'm back in front of our old home in Khumjung, watching as my mother and sisters dig through the snow. Dig, dig, dig, they keep digging. However much they shovel, still the same amount of snow remains on the ground.

It's pitch black, and then, behind us, a flare so bright I can't look at it directly—but I know who it is by the way he walks. He takes a step forward, the light gets brighter. I hold up my hands to shield my sight, but I can smell it. The smell of blood, broken bones, and death. He comes closer and closer, and I can't move, and when he's right in front of me, the chang wafting from his breath, the light flashes even brighter. But it's not my father in front of me anymore. In his place, a little boy tosses something in the air—a blue plastic ball. I fumble to catch it, but my feet are stuck in place, I can't move, and the ball rolls away into the darkness.

When the boy comes closer I can see his face. Ang.

I grab him and we fall to the snow. I hold him tightly, refusing to let go. We roll in the snow, me and my little brother, and I shut my eyes hard as the tears build. *I have you, I have you. You're safe. They won't take you away now. I won't let them.*

I'm squeezing as hard as I can, then I feel a hand on my shoulder, shaking me. But Ang is no longer in my arms—all I'm holding is that little ball, cradling it with all of my being. When I look up, the one shaking me is Norbu. I feel the cold suddenly, the wind is roaring now. I'm all alone, darkness on all sides. The only thing I can see is Norbu's hand held out to take me away from all this.

Norbu stands in front of me in the cramped tea house kitchen in Namche Bazaar. The woman with curved fingers looks me up and down and the Sherpa boys swig chang. Lasha utters a high little laugh. It's a warning laugh, reminding me that he knows, that he will speak to Val later. And when Norbu looks at me, I know he knows who I am. He comes closer, reaches out with his hand, just like in my dream.

"Nima."

Terror. All the beatings my father gave me run through my body. I take a step back, then another, and I'm out of the kitchen and back in the dining hall.

Nobody looks up as I stagger in. The door behind me stays closed—the mikarus are here, shoveling food and drink, I'm safe for now. Behind me, the kitchen door opens. Norbu grabs my arm, pulling me close. "What are you doing here? Why did you leave?"

His grip is tight, and I grimace. He lets go and the two of us just stand there, hidden in plain view from the partying mikarus. Norbu places a hand on my right shoulder, aching from carrying the heavy pack. His touch is gentle this time. His hand goes to my exposed neck, touching where the marks from my father still show. He traces up to my chin, a finger on my upper lip—where Val's pencil gave me a mustache only yesterday—all the way to my hair. And then he lifts the knit cap I'm wearing and his almond shaped eyes bulge.

"What happened to your hair?"

"I cut it."

"But why, Nima?"

Don't call me that, I want to tell him, *stop calling me Nima. Just take me back to the village if you must, but don't humiliate me.* I want to say all that and more. But I'm afraid of making him angry. And yet, even after all that I've done to him and his family, there's a look on his face that I've never seen before—he looks hurt.

"Why did you leave? I thought we wanted the same thing. That's why I chose you alone."

I pull back, and that strong hand falls to his side.

"Nima—"

"Don't call me that." I'm more forceful than I intended, but hearing my true name is too painful. "If you're going to take me back, just do it."

Norbu looks perplexed. He spends a long moment studying my face. "What should I call you?"

"Ang."

"Ang," he says, nodding, understanding. "I'm not here to take you back. If you didn't want to be my wife, I would never force you."

He tries to touch my hair again, but I shift and place the cap back on.

"Then why are you here?" I ask, pulling away again.

He straightens, clears his throat. "I'm working as a guide. What about you?"

"The same."

I want to ask him how he manages with the dust, the constant load, the pace and strain, and the clients' demands, but of course I can't. I can't ask him for help. He smiles with those perfect white teeth of his, and I suddenly feel the strain lessen, my mouth isn't as tight. Somehow I'm smiling, too.

"If that's your path to dharma, then so be it. Your father would be proud."

Norbu Norgay, I want to say, *how are you not furious? What kind of man are you?*

Norbu crouches to whisper in my ear, but there's a booming voice to our right—"Oy, boy, more beer! Beer. Now!"—one of Norbu's mikaru clients. Norbu nods, disappears into the kitchen. My feet are stuck in place, my heart beats out of my chest. I pull my knit cap farther down my face and follow Norbu into the kitchen. He's busy loading beers onto a tray.

"The keys," I say to one of the boys who run the lodge.

"Three?" he asks.

I nod. Lasha is still sitting there, cards on the table. His eyes are drunk, and he doesn't say a thing. Norbu disappears with the tray of beers, and the boy hands me the keys—two—"One more room," I tell him. He nods, reaches for a notebook, marks down the room and rate, and then hands me a greenish-gold piece of chipped metal, the number six roughly carved into the key. *My own room.* I step back out into the dining area. The men cheer as Norbu places the bottles in front of them: "Good, good, thanks, mate." And I head to Val and the others, slamming the keys onto the table, harder than I meant, the impact of the jingling metal makes Val spill curry from her spoon.

Would he really have let me go down the mountain to study? Or maybe join him, man and wife, both working together on the trail...

Norbu walks past me silently and out of the room. Gone again.

"Dal baht power, twenty-four hour," Val jokes in Nepali English. She'd said that she wanted to start teaching me *her* language tonight, but I don't remind her. It's the last thing I can think about right now.

"What's wrong?" she asks.

I shake my head. "Nothing."

Val pushes her empty bowl out of the way. "That man you were speaking with—I saw the way he looked at you. How do you know him?"

My mother often said that everyone has white days when their power is high, black days when they're low and vulnerable. If you want to help someone, you must do it when your white days overlap and fall in a row. But to harm someone, you first determine when your white days overlap with your enemy's black days. If you can determine that, you'll perform spells more effectively. Moments like these, or earlier today, with the soldiers, I can see Val tapping into her white days. Able to do things she otherwise couldn't and see things she wouldn't normally see. So what's the use to lie if she can peer through the veil?

"That was Norbu, the one I left. The jilted bridegroom."

I look over at Ethan and Daniel, now done with their meals. The big one massages his temples, the smaller one yawns deeply.

What if they understood, too? These men wouldn't know what to say. They'd probably get rid of me. Taking orders from one woman is enough, right, boys?

"Did he come looking for you?" Val asks. "You're not going back are you?"

"I can't go back, Val. I can't."

"You don't have to, Nima. It's your life, your choice."

But Val looks worried as she picks up the keys from the table. She gives one to Daniel, another to Ethan.

In the darkness, I see Norbu's face. I'm by myself, in a room for a mikaru, my team on either side of these thin walls—Daniel to my left, Ethan and Val to my right. I never ate—too nervous to see Norbu again, or Lasha—and I can feel my hunger curled up with me. Perhaps it's the pain keeping me from deep, dreamless sleep. Then I see my father, then Ang, my mother, each of my sisters, and Val, Ethan, Daniel, and one more I don't recognize. Dirt on the cheeks, bloodshot pupils, short hair, cut unevenly...it's me. When I wake, I'm crying.

19

THE WOMAN WITH CLAWS IS MIXING THE MORNING PORRIDGE, BARLEY
tsampa, and when I step in, she hands me a bowl and a heavy
spoon full of gray sludge. *Thwap.* She tosses a few crumbled cakes
into the stove, that familiar earthy smell wafting into my nostrils. I
can feel her eyes on me, but I scoop the sludge and eat right there,
standing close enough to the flame to feel its touch. My stomach's
settled now, and I eat for the day before and for today, I eat that
gray gruel that has no taste at all. I picture buckwheat, barley,
millet. The woman with the claws is still watching and stirring
that black cauldron, claws wrapped around a long wooden spoon.

"What will you do now?" she asks.

The question startles me, but I close my eyes and keep eating.
A bite of syan dough dipped in ginger, another of turmeric-spiced
potato, a roti smeared with yak butter.

Again, she asks, "What will you do?"

My last bite, transformed into wide thukpa noodles. She takes
the finished bowl from me and, waiting for my answer, taps on its
rim, a sound like a mouse scurrying up a tree trunk.

Once more: "What will you—"

"I'll keep going," I cut her off finally. "I'll keep working."

She sets the bowl onto the counter. "No. I meant what will you
do with your groom?"

"What business is it of yours?"

The words come out harsher than I intended. She's my elder, but I don't bother apologizing. I'm right.

Her fingers tighten around her spoon, while the lines on her face deepen as she smiles. "I am a member of the Norgay household. I was once married to his uncle—*before* he married the others, those sisters."

I shake my head in disbelief—it cannot be mere chance that I meet her now, and under the same roof as Norbu.

"What happened?"

She touches her belly, rubs it with those talons. "I couldn't give my husband a son. I couldn't even make a child. So he took another wife—two wives, to make sure. Two wives and neither could produce for him." A laugh now. Cold. "It seems I wasn't the problem after all. In matters of the heart, expectations, needs, and passions always increase suffering. Always. The only way out of that situation is to dissolve the unrealistic expectations. Spiritual discipline."

Two youngsters walk into the kitchen, the boys from the day before, the ones who played cards with Lasha and Norbu. The old woman fills two bowls. *So she became a mother, and these are her sons?*

She serves that sludge, which the boys happily accept, and I stand there, jaw shut.

One of the boys—at most fourteen—peers back at me and whispers something to his companion, something I can't hear, and they both laugh. I feel the anger and shame bubbling inside, and then something else, a throbbing in my gut. The boys snicker again and before I can put them in their place, the long wooden spoon comes out from the cauldron.

"Quiet," she crows. "If you want to eat from my kitchen, you'll practice respect. Or you won't eat at all."

The boys lower their heads and drop their smiles. She's still pointing that spoon, porridge gathering where the handle meets the tip. The stove crackles and she goes back to stirring the soupy sludge. Her back turned, one of the boys reaches out to touch my hair under my knit cap: "What kind of woman has hair like a man's?"

Whack!

He lets out a yelp. A drop of porridge hits the cold floor as the mother raises the spoon again, then down again. Wet grains of porridge strike my cheek. She pushes the boys with the end of the spoon and they take their bowls and scurry away.

"Ever since their father died, they think they run this place. But not until I'm gone and given to the sky. Do you care for more porridge? The mikarus will want breakfast soon." She slops down another helping. "My name is Dorjee Sherpa. It means 'thunder-bolt.' I was born in a storm," she says proudly. "Or so my parents told me."

"Wonderful name." I don't feel wonderful. My stomach aches.

"Same as the mountaineer, the one who summited nineteen times. His name was Ang Dorjee Sherpa. Like your name, too. Well, like the name you call yourself. Yes, I've heard. You may take that cap off now. And tell me what your parents really named you."

"Nima," I say, keeping my knit cap on.

"Nima. That means Sunday. You were born on a Sunday, yes?" she asks gruffly, as another Sherpa enters, his bowl ready. I'm still standing awkwardly, the pain in my stomach clouding me. The newcomer looks me up and down—*they all must know*—but he doesn't say anything. Dorjee Sherpa's glare is a stern enough warning, he gets his helping and goes.

"Norbu means 'beloved,'" she continues. "And Ang means 'young.' Having a day of the week as a name is not so bad. Be happy you're not Lobsang or Tashi. If your name meant 'disciple' you would be in a shedra by now, studying. And if your name meant 'good luck,' well, that would be no luck at all. Too much responsibility, far too much to live up to. A day of the week is as good as anything to be named after. At least that's something you can count on."

I try to smile, but the fire inside me makes me gasp. Dorjee Sherpa must notice, she picks up a glass, fills it with a steaming brew, opens a jar, mixes its contents into the tea. "Take this," she commands. "For the pain. It won't taste good, but it will ease the trouble."

"Thuuche. Thank you."

"Now go. I have work and mouths to feed."

The tea tastes terribly bitter—Dorjee Sherpa's touch—but I drink it just the same. Then I sit at a table across from three Sherpas. All men, of course. They cast their gaze down, as if looking at me could infect them. Then they begin to multiply, two more Sherpas, and four more, then five more, then six. When the room is full, Lasha marches in. He sits down and eats his porridge without uttering one sound. He watches me, sipping that miserable tea, watching him back.

Then Norbu. He looks tired. He eats his entire meal with his back to me, then he gets up to return his bowl to the kitchen—not looking at me once. Across the room, Lasha rises to take his leave. "Lepcha," he mutters towards me.

A witch, am I? A fleeting moment alone until the mikarus file in now, trampling loudly enough to be heard from the other end of the corridor. Then some of the Sherpas return, too, scampering to take their orders. The white men are those from the night before, the ones who speak the strange English. My own mikarus enter, finally. They move like every muscle aches.

"Did you not sleep well?" I ask Val.

Val, eyes sunken under yesterday's tan: "Not really. Not at all, really."

"Trouble with stomach?"

"We took turns in the bathroom all night. I think I lost five pounds."

"I'll get you tea right away. Very important to drink, three liters every day."

Val burps, nods.

"Eggs or porridge?"

"Porridge."

Daniel's nose is dripping into a stubbly mustache and down into his beard. Ethan coughs deep, an effect of the altitude.

"Eggs," Val adds. "Eggs all around. And coffee if there's any."

She must not be feeling well, she's treating me like most mikarus do Nepalis, as if they're servants first, humans second.

"Porridge, eggs, and coffee, okay," I answer. *I'm starting to talk like the mikarus, too. I'm learning.*

Back in the kitchen, as if Dorjee Sherpa could hear our thoughts through these thin walls, she's already frying eggs and potatoes. There's a line of Sherpas waiting for her to prepare their clients' meals, including Norbu.

"The mikarus are hungry," I announce, looking at Norbu from the corner of my eye. He still won't look at me.

"The mikarus are hungry," Dorjee Sherpa repeats. "Well then, we mustn't keep them waiting. Eggs for three?"

I nod. "And one porridge."

"Eggs for three and one porridge," she repeats back. "And coffee."

"And coffee."

The Sherpas take their clients' meals and shuffle out. Only Norbu remains. Maybe Lasha is speaking to Val while I'm in here. He might tell her I'm a witch, that I'm trouble, say I'm a criminal who broke my family's marriage contract. He might say Norbu is here to take revenge. As the sirdar, there's no reason Val wouldn't take his word over mine.

Dorjee Sherpa flips eggs onto plates, hands them to him. "Here you are, nephew."

He's close enough that I can smell that scent of musk and sweat. Norbu takes a step closer and faces me. "Why did you go?" he asks. "I still don't understand."

The question is so direct I haven't prepared for it. I don't know what to say.

"I wanted you, just you. Why did you leave without telling me?"

I look over at Dorjee Sherpa. She pretends not to be listening, cracking eggs on the wok, the sound of the sizzle filling the air.

"I—I want something more than my mother's life. I don't want to live on my knees and on my back making food and children. I want to see what else is out there. Down in the valley. Or up on the mountains as a climbing Sherpa. A real Sherpa, like you, like my father."

One of the egg yokes pops in the wok. Norbu, holding plates stacked along those tree trunk arms of his, nods with his whole body—the plates look ready to fall.

"I have to decide my own life, Norbu."

"I would have given you that. I would have given you all of that."

"Really, you would have let me travel down to Kathmandu after we'd married?"

He frowned and shrugged.

"My father didn't send you to look for me?"

He shakes his head. "I'm not here to take you back against your will, Nima."

My heart's beating like a drum, my stomach's fluttering, and my mouth is dry. He's doing it again, catching me off guard, speaking in a way I didn't expect. "I thought you wanted tradition—I thought you wanted the old ways."

"Our world is changing. The only way to move is with the stream, not against it." He struggles to balance the plates. "I'm not the same boy you remember from Khunde."

"I don't understand."

"You're going to Base Camp with your mikarus, yes?"

I nod, and he smiles with that too perfect smile.

"Nima, the Sherpa girl. We'll talk again on the trail?"

I nod again. "Yes."

Norbu leaves, and Dorjee Sherpa turns from the wok. I'm staring, losing my sight in the gray sludge, the gurgle of porridge bubbling, the eggs frying. If women and men are *not* so different, then why is the household set up like it is?

"Stomach still troubling you?" Dorjee Sherpa asks.

I've been clutching it without even realizing. The old woman takes out a package, dumps its contents into a pan of boiling water. Long silence.

"Do you think he's telling the truth?" I ask.

She beats the eggs in the wok, the yokes mixing with the whites. "A warrior does not win a battle by virtue of birth. Men always do what they want. So, why won't this one do the same?"

She's probably right, but I can't focus on anything but the food. She dumps the eggs onto three plates. Then she pours the coffee, half moons of dirt under those long fingernails. "Life is impermanence. The only stability we have is the stubbornness of men. You didn't know that, but you should from now on. Men don't give up easily, they don't give up something they want. I was foolish to think I would be kept if I could not bear a son, even if by no fault of my own. And you're naive to think that your fates aren't intertwined. Norbu Norgay won't give you up so easily. Maybe he is telling the truth—I know that's not his uncle's way—perhaps the bloodlines are cleaner on his mother's side. Pray to Mount Kailash that you two wed and you bear a son so he doesn't cast you off, like I was.

Because if he does leave you, what other life is there for a woman on the mountain?"

"You don't believe in another way? You wouldn't have wanted more—more than this?"

She hands me the plates and the coffee on a tray. "What more is there?"

Val doesn't want to waste our rest day, so three hours after breakfast, we're above Namche, passing stupas and grazing yaks. We'll climb higher, then return to Namche to sleep tonight. Still, each time I lift a boot, it's like I'm freeing it from quicksand. When I stop, I can hear the mikarus behind me, gasping for breath. The sun is high but the air is chilly. My old life is still a half day's walk away.

What is my family doing right now?

Is Second cross with me? Is she still crying? Has word gotten back to my father about me?

We climb a rugged ridge. Yaks feed on the short, yellowing grass on the jagged hillsides. Trees don't grow this high up. The pain in my middle has diminished, perhaps from the tea, but my head aches. Perhaps I'm catching mountain sickness from the mikarus.

"I thought this was our rest day. Isn't that what Ang said?"

I learned what "rest" means, and everything else, I can guess. The one who whines it all is Ethan.

"Climb high," Val gasps, "sleep low."

They all laugh, they all look at me—am I one of them now?

The mikarus push on, faces behind polarized sunglasses, sipping water. From time to time Ethan stops, rubs his left knee. Is that an injury I didn't notice, or merely fatigue?

The land flattens and we step over dry scrub invaded by empty plastic bottles. The ground has long, straight markings, tracks from huge wheels. A lone horse grazes among the brush. There's not much to eat here, and he uses a hoof to sift through the dirt, kicks cans and rocks, trying to scrape the hard layer to get to the shoots and seedlings.

"Syangboche airstrip," I announce to Val. "Built by a very rich Japanese to take tourists to his Hotel Everest View."

I step on blackened pieces of rubber, metal shards, broken glass, a bush strung with yellowed papers. Rusty aluminum cans, singed and flaked from sun and snow. EVEREST BEER. Man's plastic touch, everywhere.

"This is the closest airplanes can fly to the summit." My father told me all about it, years ago. Built for the Japanese to snap photos. Just to take photos for the day and leave.

"How high are we?"

No way I can miss the meaning of that. I rummage through my memory, recalling Father's stories. I once memorized all the heights along the trail. What was it here, above Namche? "Three thousand, seven hundred meters," I finally remember.

"That's close to fifteen thousand feet," Val calls to the others. Her hands are shaking as she walks, and not from swaying her arms. All of their hands are shaking, I noticed it when they were drinking water a few moments ago. They took a white pill—probably the Diamox they keep talking about. That's what makes them shake.

Twenty minutes later, we climb a long stone staircase to get to the top of the hill and the door of the Hotel Everest View. Carved stone, carefully cut trees, a flat roof, it all looks entirely foreign. A plaque reads ALTITUDE 3,880 METERS.

We push open a heavy oak door and step inside. More stone, spotless floor-to-ceiling windows, a roaring fireplace.

"Irasshaimase!" a small woman wearing a red sashed dress says as she bows almost to her knees. She doesn't speak Nepali or English, just bits and pieces. She leads us through a long entrance hall and opens a sliding door to an outdoor seating area and a table facing the goddess, clouds swirling her peak like apsara dancers. We sit at a simple wooden table. No one else is here. No sign of Norbu or his mikarus.

"Just front of Everest," the little woman says in her accented English, bowing again as she distributes menus.

"There she is."

"And the peak of Nuptse." I point. "And to the right of the summit is Lhotse."

"Fourth-highest mountain in the world," Ethan adds, as if reading from his guidebook.

A flock of birds flap their wings hard in the direction of the peak, as if they will fly all the way there. Val takes out her mobile and films them as they change their mind, the whole flock all at once, struggling against air and wind.

"Are we done acclimating for today?" Val asks me, pulling her hair back and tying it with a clip. It's after the meal. Ethan and Daniel have moved from the table, playing with cameras and phones.

"I'm up to seeing more. For my story. What else should we see around here?"

She's caught me off guard, and I draw a blank at first. Then I have a vision—of rich gold-and-red mandalas and a giant Buddha shrine. "Tengboche Monastery. I want to take you to Tengboche Monastery. The yeti hand is at Pangboche, but Tengboche is much more beautiful, and Sir Edmund Hillary High School, my old school, I really want you to see it. Don't worry, it's on the way." I smile. "And mostly downhill."

I'd be so proud for Nurse Lanja and Val to meet. Could she really still be working at that school? She'd be so surprised to see me working as a climbing Sherpa. I hope she won't be disappointed in me.

"Wait, did you say a yeti hand?" Val asks, a touch of salt to her words. "I think we can skip that one."

I don't know what to say—I'd already recommended we skip it. So I say nothing. I'm embarrassed. I don't believe in the yeti either, not really, but the way Val spoke—I cannot tell who she is mocking. The mikarus begin talking among themselves and I'm left to stew like a fool. I think of Lasha—maybe he's planted something in her mind.

We stare up at the goddess.

"Do you think you'll ever climb to the top?" Val asks me suddenly. "To the summit?"

"Not all women are meant to be conquered," I say.

My father spent a whole life watching the goddess from afar, never climbing her. Of course, I don't say that, and Val gives me a half smile: "If you had a chance to go up, would you?"

"Wouldn't you?" I ask. She nods. "The risk is an honor for Sherpas. It's in our blood."

"We're all obsessed with getting to the top, but that isn't the story I want to tell. The real story is the people along the way."

I shake my head uncertainly—what kind of story is that?—the story *is* in front of us, I tell her. "The mountain has power, she speaks with the wind, the rain, the snow, the ru'. She always makes her voice heard."

"Good point. So what about your voice? Will you leave the mountain when this is all over?"

Once more, such a direct question. I look over at Daniel and Ethan, busy taking photographs.

"There are other ways for a woman to make money," Val goes on. "Ways besides working on the mountain."

"I know," I answer, though I'm not sure what she's getting at. So I go out on a limb: "One moment I want to stay here, to show everyone that I can do it without a mask. As a free woman."

"And then?" she asks.

"Then I think how much easier life could be in the capital. It is, isn't it?"

"In certain ways, yes."

I tug at my knit cap and adjust my hair beneath it. "The other Sherpas know who I am now."

Val looks at Ethan and Daniel, then back at me. "Still, maybe it's best to keep quiet."

"Why?"

But Val doesn't answer. The way she looked at the others, I'm certain Lasha has said something to them. They must think I'm a joke. Or worse, a liability. The girl who fled down the mountain and left a jilted groom.

"There should be no difference," I begin, "even here in Nepal. Right, Val? Isn't that what equality is all about, to be the same, even if we pretend?"

Val takes in a deep breath. But she doesn't answer.

Ethan turns to her. "Ready to go?" he asks.

Val looks at me, then looks down and takes out her wallet for the bill. She places rupees on the table and starts packing up her gear.

The hills are purple and pink and white, flowering despite the drought. Our boots step over the flowers, from one life to the next. I'm a little girl again, gazing at the peaks we pray to, the same ones that give and then take it all back. Soon we'll be at the monastery and then my old school. I think of Nurse Lanja and my heart quickens. If she's there, I'm going to reveal myself. She'll know who I am anyway, I'm sure of it.

Suddenly, a company of Nepali soldiers in olive green run up the mountain. The sight of them makes us all freeze, reminding us of the two acne-faced boys who almost took our lives. But these ones fly by us, not looking back, none of them the soldiers from the day before. Two runts bring up the rear, struggling to keep up. And then they disappear with the rest of the company.

We go down one hill and back up another, stop at a mani stone wall with flat rocks inscribed in Tibetan, piled eight feet high. Prayer flags stitched with the Tibetan wind horse Lungta flap and flutter in sacred gallop: white for air, red for fire, green for water, yellow for earth, blue for sky.

"Hail to the jewel in the lotus," I whisper to myself, steering the mikarus past a long line of prayer wheels. "Always pass to the left," I caution, spinning the wheels as I go. Val and then Ethan and Daniel add to the spin, wheels chiming loudly from our combined energies. We weave on, wordless and dizzy, and Everest comes into view once more. Not a cloud shields her now. The mikarus take out their cameras yet again. I'd like to be so excited to see the goddess again, to jump from rock to rock and up and down the hills, but I feel something else. A gentle discouragement: *I'm here. I'll be here today, tomorrow, and all the coming days. I'll be here for every day of your life and for all the lives that will spring out of you.*

At a higher bend, an old man is sitting cross-legged on a plastic chair, hood low over his face, bony black hands strumming prayer beads. He wears a multicolored jacket and windbreaker pants, every piece of them torn and restitched. He looks up through wire-rimmed glasses held askew on his nose.

"Namaste," he murmurs. "Tashi delek."

Next to him, on a thin sheet of metal held to the ground with wooden pegs, an inscription in English. Daniel raises his camera to photograph it. The man nods, each eye aiming in a different direction.

"What does it say?" I ask Val.

"Appeal for donation," Val reads. "Dear Visitors, this man Pasang Lama Sherpa has been doing a social work to build mend and maintain the main trail to Everest Base Camp with high spirit, solemn determination. Hearty appeal all the visitors requested to make a small donation to support and encourage this devoted man to continue this sacred work."

There's a box and a ledger to sign. Val writes her full name—Valerie Garcia Jones—puts a hundred rupee note into the box. Then she takes out her notebook and pen and tries to speak to the old man, first in English, then in Nepali. Nothing. He keeps stroking his beads, staring off into the distance. His skin is as dark as the dirt, he's been sitting here for so long. Pasang Lama Sherpa. He's here, but he's not. Namaste for all time.

On a wall, there's a klu-mo, a woman demon with the body of a serpent, a growling face in her chest, a body of coils and scales. We're in the dokhang, a prayer hall filled with red pillows, blankets, and empty rice bowls, everything under the gaze of a life-sized statue of the Buddha. Beside the statue is a raised seat with a gold sash and a small microphone. The head lama's seat. And this monastery's top man, he's smiling, talking to the Westerner with the hair the same color as his robes. His own hair is trimmed to the scalp, splotches of pink and brown all over his head. He wears glasses set on a flat nose, and his lips smile even though they're not curling up.

"The wall paintings," Val remarks. "They're blackened. From fire?"

"Yes, yes, from the fire," the lama answers, insisting on speaking English. "Some paintings were saved. They peeled off from the heat, and we were able to...*reapply* them, yes? Yes. We *reapplied* and then painted over in many places"—he points—"as you can see here and there and here again."

Val scribbles notes. "What happened?"

"Many come here to Tengboche instead of Khumjung, or they come after they see the yeti scalp or the Pangboche hand."

"Is it a real yeti?" Val asks sincerely.

The lama smiles without moving his lips. That all-knowing smile of the divine. "Who am I to say? Many things special here. Tengboche Monastery was built in 1916, by Lama Gulu. Construction begun by Ngawang Tenzin Norbu, the reincarnation of the great Lama Sangwa Dorje, the fifth in a line of reincarnation going back to the ninth century, before Sherpas left Kham." He raises a finger for emphasis. "In 1934, everything destroyed by earthquake. Lama Gulu died, too. Then we rebuild. A second monastery was constructed on top of the ruins, and in 1989, all destroyed again—this time by fire—electrical short-circuit burned everything to the ground. So, once more, we rebuild, stone brick by stone brick, with the generous help from Sir Edmund Hillary and the Himalayan Trust. Much history tied to this place. Sacred history. This is why we stay. When Sherpas first settled in the Khumbu in the 1400s, there was a powerful lama named Pachen. He lived in a cave on the eastern slopes of Kongde. One night, a group of ghosts came and lit a large fire at the entrance to the cave. But he was in a deep meditation, so deep he was able to escape right through the mountain rock. Pachen flew across the Dudh Kosi, leaving his footprint in solid stone where he landed on the other shore. That place, which still bears his mark, is called Phurte, from the word for flight, 'phur.' You can still see it, when you pass."

Val smiles, repeats: "*Flew* across the Dudh Kosi."

"Lamas today don't travel by flight." He curls his lips. "At least, we don't talk about it, if we did."

"Wouldn't that make people believe?" Val wonders aloud.

"Belief doesn't come from seeing. Belief comes from inside. From knowing. You don't need to see to know."

"So why study—why spend your whole life here?"

"The true fulfillment of knowledge is overcoming mental obstacle, gaining insight into one's own truth and self. Ours is but one world of many, one plane of existence. The great field of knowledge is as tiny as the universe is a speck. This is Buddhism. This is why we believe."

20

SO MANY GREAT MEN IN OUR HISTORY: MILAREPA, LAMA SANGWA
Dorje, the Dalai Lama, Tenzing Norgay. But where are the women?
If our path to enlightenment is the same as men, if we are truly
equal, then why must we always be seen and never heard? We are
like a vast unknown. Watching Val, I know that's not the case in
her country. The way she moves, she talks, it can't be.

> *I am a woman — I have little power to resist danger.*
> *Because of my inferior birth, everyone attacks me.*
> *If I go as a beggar, dogs attack me.*
> *If I have wealth and food, bandits attack me.*
> *If I do a great deal, the neighbors attack me.*
> *If I do nothing, gossip attacks me.*
> *If anything goes wrong, they all attack me.*
> *Whatever I do, I have no chance for happiness.*
> *Because I am a woman, it is hard to follow the Dharma.*
> *It is hard to even stay alive.*

These are the words of a great woman, told to me by a sacred
woman who didn't let on how deeply she thought and felt—my
mother. Could it be that these words were taught to me for a reason,
lessons to feed my mind and soul, and perhaps find a riddle in
them, a guide to this mandala maze we call life? Walking down the
hill towards my old school, I am filled with sudden regret. How

silly, how small it must all look to *her*. This is what I was so proud to show Val?

I want to hate her, living so removed from my troubles, but I can't. I want to trust, I want us to be friends, and those desires consume me, no matter what nonsense Lasha or whoever else has said to her. *We'll talk when we're alone. I'll set her right and she'll understand.* It's that simple. Right now, her face looks twisted, as if in great pain, and I can't help but be concerned.

"How's your stomach?" I ask.

"It's my head. Migraines. I used to get them sometimes from reading on my iPhone. I can't focus, and I can't write when that thing keeps buzzing. By the end of the day, my head is pounding. That's how I feel now."

I reach in my bag, pull out a plastic pack, rip it open. "Take this, put it on your tongue. Herbal root."

I dump some of the bag in Val's hand. The root looks wormlike, brown and dry, tiny chips like pencil shavings. "Take it with water. It's all natural, and good for head and stomach pains." I put some in my mouth to show her. "Don't think like a mikaru, think like a Sherpa. It's good for your story."

Ten minutes later, we arrive at my school. It doesn't look any different from how I remember it, just a few dusty old buildings made of splintered wood and flimsy plastic. Except, instead of children, there is a group of weathered men sitting in front of my school like a bad joke, their faces so tanned they look mummified.

I don't know how it's survived the wind and the snow. We march past the old men, who pay no attention to us, through a yak gate and into a courtyard, towards a smiling man made of bronze surrounded by solar panels and a plastic trash can. The bronze man wears a fedora and a sporting sweater. SIR EDMUND HILLARY, 1919 TO 2008, FOUNDER AND PATRON OF KHUMJUNG SCHOOL. The solar panels I haven't seen before. I'm surprised no one has stolen them. Probably too heavy. The only thing impressive here, I realize, is that statue. But Val walks right by it. The school is empty, no students here, no children. Is it a holiday—is it already Mani Rimdu? No, it cannot be, the monastery would have been celebrating.

"Where are the children?" I ask one of the living dead slumped at the entrance.

"Work," says one with dark sunglasses and an ugly black mole on his left cheek, a long strand of milk-white hair growing from it. "Most children are working this season. Thank the drought. And the price of yartsa gunbu!"

I know his face—another bad man from my past. One who touched me when I was a child. He was such a monster then, a monster that sent chills through me. And now, he's nothing. He only wears the skin of a man, a wrinkled, dirty husk that's left to rot under the cold sun. I walk past him without looking back, searching for traces of the school girl me amid the cheap wood and plastic buildings. How fast the years have flowed since the last time I visited Nurse Lanja. No telling where she is now. She gave me the confidence to come back here, to lead three mikarus into this ramshackle place.

Nima, you've learned so much. And on your own.

I'm standing in front of a building, a shed really, it's inscribed CHILDREN'S ART GALLERY.

Despite the sign, I recognize the place. It's the old infirmary. But remodeled. The one structure here that seems different. Khumbu's lone female nurse, erased. Was it the doing of the monster with the mole, that lazy tshera lang dozing at the entrance?

Where there were once medical books and supplies there are now dozens of crude drawings stuck to the walls, pasted to old wooden desks, strewn on the floor. Nurse Lanja is gone. In her place, mountains, yaks, snow leopards, gray with white specks, orange tigers, huge elephants, pictures made by children, free to dream. I never made pictures like that—certainly nothing displayed on the walls. Things have changed, and maybe not all of them bad. In the corner, two old worn chairs—where Norbu held my hand for the first time; where I sat and watched my father die and be reborn into something less than a man; where I promised myself to leave this place. I catch a glimpse of myself in a mirror hanging tilted on the wall. My face is so thin—the cost of freedom. *Nurse Lanja could be speaking to me through Val, even if she isn't here.*

Next to the mirror, right where Nurse Lanja kept the syringe with the medicine, there is a drawing of a muscular ape with long teeth and a yellow stare. He stands over a pool of blood, a half-eaten yak at his feet. A Sherpa woman is running away from the slaughter, off the page.

"Yeti?" Val asks, behind me.

The picture is simple, but it tells the story well, a story I've heard more than once. I don't care if Val believes, it's a story many do, and even though I'm not sure, I feel a certain pride to recite it. "A woman close to here was attacked several years ago," I begin. "She was walking with her yaks in a field and then fell asleep while they grazed. When she woke, two yaks had been killed, heads and bodies ripped apart."

Val laughs, a single *ha!*

I feel the blood cooking in my veins but say nothing. Realizing her mistake, Val adds quickly, "But surely it could have been—"

"The scalp is in a monastery not far from here, you heard the lama talk about it. We have no time to go now, it's in the opposite direction, but it's there, I've seen it."

I'm lying, I've never seen it, and I'm defending what must be nonsense, but I want Val to stop being such an all-knowing mikaru.

She doesn't say anything. She nods, looks away. Val pulls out her notebook and scratches a few things down, but it looks like she's pretending. She's not really writing anything down. I can tell she's just moving her pen so she can turn away from me.

Next to the yeti picture, there's another in pinks and oranges and reds. I instantly recognize it's made by a girl's hand even before I realize what it is: a girl surrounded by jewels and smiling people, stick figures and shiny stars all around, but it's obvious. It's a dream wedding.

"This was my school," I tell her finally. "This was where I learned so much. I wanted to show it to you, it's important to me. I wanted you to meet the woman who reminded me of you."

Val doesn't have a smart response, I think I've finally gotten through to her and she nods, hanging her head.

For some reason, I know the girls being taught here will have a better chance than me. Just seeing those pictures, they've been taught something important. Whether it was conscious or not, they've been allowed to dream, even if that dream is something that now seems so old-fashioned: choice. Something that took me so long to learn.

I lead us all back out, and it's likely none of us will ever return here. Just beyond the gates, just thirty minutes from our return to Namche, we pass by a pair of girls, girls my sisters' age, their heads weighed down by heavy baskets and supported by thump lines and tokmas to help them up the trail. Ethan says something I can't understand and Daniel laughs. The two girls trudge up the trail, heads hanging not from the weight, but the shame of the foreigners' jibes. I open my mouth, but no words come out. And then I cry. I cry with all my heart for everything. And I do it right in front of my mikarus, who stop, stone still, not knowing what to do.

"Why's he mad?" one of the mikaru men asks.

Val keeps her mouth shut. I can feel her eyes on me even with my own overflowing. The men are puzzled, they begin to roll their eyes and laugh nervously, making me more upset. I was wrong to listen to Val, wrong to hide my true nature. Val never had to hide who she was.

She's not afraid to be a woman, she's proud. I should be, too. I am young, but I'm not inexperienced, suffering was revealed to me at a young age. My pain is age old karmic residue which must be erased. I was never Ang. I was always Nima. I shouldn't have pretended otherwise, I know that now.

I pull off my knit cap and strip off my pack at the edge of the school where the Khumbu's first female nurse taught me so much about myself. This is the place where I first became proud of the sex I was born, the first time I felt unashamed of what I was.

I take off my jacket to reveal that I have breasts, to reveal who I really am. "Woman," I say in English, staring straight ahead, a word I've been repeating in my mind. Then I turn to the mikarus, feeling my voice grow louder: "I am a woman."

21

THE RETURN TO NAMCHE IS A BLUR. I DON'T REMEMBER ANY OF IT, except for the mikarus talking among themselves. *Arguing*. And Val was defending me, that I know. And now, they're nowhere to be seen. Still arguing, they disappeared to their rooms, and I no longer am sure I have a job.

When I open my eyes, I'm in the dining hall and all the climbing Sherpas are standing in a line, Lasha at the front. Their arms are folded, jaws clenched. Val stood up for me, I remember that—but what Ethan and Daniel thought, I couldn't say. I was so full of pain in that moment that I blacked out. I led us here without really knowing where I was going, walking without thinking. And when we got here, Lasha was outside to greet us, whispering to Val as she went by him.

And now this roomful of Sherpa men arguing:

"It's bad luck to have a woman porter, bad luck for all of us," Lasha bellows. "She has magic, she used it on me in Phakding to cut my throat."

He pulls down his collar to show where my blade poked through soft flesh.

"There was no magic," I yell, "just my kikuri to his neck after he tried to have his way with me! If I was your sister or your wife, would they do any different?"

"She's a lepcha!" he yells back.

"What should we do?" one of Dorjee Sherpa's sons asks.

"I don't want to sleep under the same roof as a witch," his brother responds. "We should throw her out."

Lasha shakes his head, takes out his kikuri and holds it at his side. A hush falls over the room. "We know who you are. We know who your family is. The ru' that struck four years ago and destroyed Khumjung, was that your making, too?"

He takes a step closer. I'm frozen, watching a glint of light shine on the steel.

"Is that why your brother died, so you could steal his soul and live as a man?"

Lasha grabs my arm. And then all of them reach out, too. Hands on my arms, grasping everywhere, they pull and push me towards the door. I drag my feet, thrashing and screaming, the rubber soles of my boots shrieking. The wind hits as I'm heaved outside and away from the lodge. I fight with every fiber of my being, and then I feel my body go limp. Looking up, through an army of dirty hands and contorted faces, it's there, the same view I was faced with when the ru' struck four years ago, when it took my father and my brother. I was frozen then, I'm frozen now. The color of the leaves on the trees—turned from green to a petrified gray. The air feels heavy and the wind blows. Then I hear pounding footfalls and heavy breathing and something else I haven't heard in I don't know how long: rain. Real rain. It comes down like bullets, a hard, wet gift to the farmers.

I focus on the feel of the shower instead of the hands on me, watch each drop drip down and hit my naked skin. I open my mouth, let a drop find my tongue. I go deep inside, far, far away like I have so many times before. And under that steady fall of rain, there's a scuffle, a fight: it's me, swinging and kicking wildly at Lasha and his Sherpas. Their hands won't let go, they're too strong. Raindrops hit me right on my brow, where my third eye hides. Arms like tree trunks are tearing me to pieces. And then the dirty hands release me. Everyone steps back. Only Lasha remains, still holding up his blade.

"Stand aside," he growls at the figure making them all cower. "She's a lepcha!"

Norbu hits Lasha with such force, it sounds like Sangwa Dorje has landed back on earth. Lasha crumples to the ground and stays there. The others scatter.

Norbu Norgay lifts me into his arms.

I'm nervous, so is he, I can tell by how quiet he is. We're lying side by side on the cot, both of us careful not to touch the other. I'm afraid to turn and look, to see if his eyes are open. He's a man, I know what men want—even good men like him.

"What do you think will happen?" I ask finally.

"What do you mean?" he answers, both of us staring at the wooden ceiling.

"Lasha. And the others—"

"They won't bother you again. They don't matter, they're the past. Scared of women, scared of change."

I hope he's right.

"Nima, the real question is what do you want?"

"What do you mean?"

"What do you want from life?"

No man has ever asked me this before.

"I want to finish this trek. Whether or not the mikarus decide to keep me around. I want to do it for me."

"And then? After you finish? What then?"

"I want to start my life over."

Why didn't we discuss this before I left home?

Next to me on the pillow, he nods. "How?"

"I don't know yet. I don't know. I know I want more than what my mother had. I want to lead treks up the mountain or go down to the capital and study a trade. But I want to finish this trek first. Then I'll decide."

"You wouldn't be scared to go to the capital? You'd be all alone."

"Before I left home, yes. Now, I don't know. A part of me wants to be scared, wants to feel something new, something different."

"You're not one of the mikarus yet. And you're not even really Nepali. You're a Sherpa."

"Why should that matter?"

Long pause. "Do you want a Sherpa husband?"

"I want to be the one who makes the choice of who my partner is. Marriage is forever, they say."

He nods again. "Yes, yes. At least it should be."

There's a long silence between us. Then Norbu shifts on the cot—he's moving towards me. "Norbu, no. I can't."

He sits up. "I only wanted to take another blanket. It's cold in here."

It is cold. *All men can't be scoundrels and monsters, can they?* Norbu stretches to take a yak wool blanket from the foot of the cot. He drapes it over me. Itchy and warm.

"Thank you."

"Better, no?"

"Much."

It is nice under the blanket. Warm. And nicer still to have warmth from a body right next to me. A strong body—a man I can trust. The blanket is wide enough for two, and I drape it over his strong frame. There's room for both of us. When I close my eyes, I feel safe for the first time in as long as I can remember.

It's early morning when I wake, and the cot is cold. I rise with a bolt—he's at the foot of the cot, lacing his boots.

"I have to be ready for the mikarus," he says. "We head off today."

"Us, too."

"You'll continue with them, even if Lasha has been planting bad seeds with your mikarus? I heard it last night."

"I told you I'm going to continue, whether with them or on my own. We'll see if they still want me."

Norbu nods, pulls on his blue coat. Still under the blankets, I'm suddenly shy to be so close to a grown man. But I'm fully dressed. We're looking at each other, him and I. I feel a flutter in my stomach and run my hand through my short hair.

"Do you think I'm ugly, like this?"

"No. I liked your hair long. But I like it like this, too. It's different. It suits you. Maybe that's what they wear in the capital."

"It's not by choice. I did it for the mikarus—so they would hire me."

"There's that word again." He smiles. "Choice." Norbu rises and strides to the door. "On the trail then, I'll see you on the trail. And when we both return from Base Camp... ?"

"When we both return from Base Camp." I smile—I can't help myself.

"You'll make some choices?" He's smiling wider now.

Before the door shuts behind him, I feel the cold air rush into the room and a shiver down my spine. Soon, I'm dressed, packed, and out of the room, but before I'm two steps down the corridor, Ethan blocks my path, holding something in his hand. I'm not sure what he's doing. He comes close, and as he opens his mouth all the yelling between the mikarus—Val defending me, Ethan arguing angrily—it all floods back in sharp detail. But his face, it doesn't look angry—it's between emotions, like he's unsure of what he's doing.

Get out of my way, I want to shriek, but I don't have the words in English.

"I'm sorry," Ethan says, lifting the pack off my shoulder, so carefully I'm not sure what's going on. "Please."

He goes through the bag, takes out the team's gear: plastic wrapped food and folded clothes, bundled wires and batteries. An extra notebook for Val's story. My heart is beating wildly as he collects it all. I mouth the English words: "Where is Val?"

He straightens and stuffs a wad of money into my hand. "Take it." He can't even look me in the eye when he speaks. "Paid. For-a-week. Understand? Paid. Please, just go home. We don't want trouble. Just go home."

Ethan leaves me in the drafty corridor, holding my fistful of money. After the span of seven breaths, I pace to the door, push it open, and peer out into the dining hall. Val, Ethan, and Daniel all have their loads already strapped to their backs. And Lasha is with them. He has a welt on his face from where Norbu hit him. None of them notices me. Val's in the middle of saying something to Ethan—she looks upset—but I don't understand what she is saying.

I open my mouth to yell out, to tell Val to stop—she knows why I did what I did, she helped me, Lasha's lies are polluting everyone—then someone pushes me hard from behind and I stumble forward, falling to the floor. It's one of Dorjee Sherpa's sons, the youngster who hit me yesterday.

"Lepcha," he sneers. *"Dirnmu."*

The door to the lodge slams shut. Val and the team are gone.

I get up, dust myself off, watching from the doorway as something in my heart holds me back from running after them. The other mikarus—the ones who speak English different from Val— they're preparing to leave, too. But I don't see Norbu with them. He must already be on the trail, but his words ring in my ears: *You're not one of the mikarus yet.*

There's a plump mikaru girl with hair the color of fire lying back on a bench, mouth agape, holding a mobile to the sky. Another girl stands next to her, blond and waifish, doing the same with her mobile. A mikaru man with a thick gray beard and a hanging belly hands Dorjee Sherpa a stack of rupees. She bows to him slightly, and he turns and shakes the girl's foot. "Come on."

The girl pulls her foot free. She won't get up. She's arguing— it's something about her mobile. The other girl joins her in complaining. The red-haired one wheezes as she runs her finger across her mobile's screen. Then she takes her finger off the screen and sticks it in her mouth. It's truly miraculous they've gotten this far up the mountain. If that pot bellied man were my father, he would have snatched that toy and hurled it into the stove without a second thought.

I count the members of their group: more than ten, all with faces as red as that girl's hair. All large, loud, clumsy. The pot bellied man yells something that might mean "we're leaving," and the girls finally gather their things, join the rest of the troop. Dorjee Sherpa bows her head at the departing guests. I feel her eyes on me. *Go, girl.*

Back on the trail. The forever frittered trail.

Dorjee Sherpa, the remover of obstacles, didn't have any wise words to offer me before I left. She only looked at me with a mix of purpose and pity. *Find what you're looking for.* I hurry to catch up with Norbu. He must be ahead. I'm doing this for myself now, but if I can walk with him, my journey isn't for nothing. At least I'll show him, too. I've earned more in the last few days than Father has earned in years.

Soon, I'm striding past the red-faced mikarus. They're stirring so much dust and dirt that even with my kerchief as a shield, I'm choking. I hustle to get by. I give a side glance to that girl with bleeding crimson hair. She's even younger than she looked at the lodge, her and the other one. No Sherpas with them now, and I can see why. I hurry on.

Out of Namche and over the mountain, beyond the airstrip and the huge mani stones looking down over Khumjung, past the mutely watching Pasang Lama Sherpa, with his legs crossed, still stroking his prayer beads. I climb past it all, through the tiny villages of Kenjuma and Sanasa, no sign of Norbu or Val. *Too wrapped in thought, I've either somehow passed them or they're far faster than I would have thought possible.*

The trail descends once more to the Dudh Kosi, and I cross bridges and hike into a cluster of huts. Phunki Thanga, I recognize it from the water-driven prayer wheels that give its lodges electric power. I poke my head into a tea house perched on the river's edge—a very skinny cripple sits inside with his equally skinny wife, feeding an even skinnier goat. The goat crunches a ginger tuber, bleats when I slam the door shut.

I try the next tea house, right next door, this one's completely empty.

I walk to the river and sit by the water's edge, flipping stones into the fast-moving current. It's less cold down here, the water free to move, free from freezing. Yellowing grass grows by the riverbanks. The aphids climbing the stalks remind me of the hill overlooking Lukla's airport. *When was that? And what happened to that girl?*

My mother's words, words of the great Milarepa, flood my mind.

All beings tremble at punishment,
To all life is dear.
Comparing others to oneself,
One should neither kill nor cause to harm.

Just a few days away from my mother's home, yet I am so different. And another woman's words have begun to dominate my mind:

Val, what does the ocean look like?

It's been so long since I've seen it.

But you must remember. Tell me.

Look at my eyes, Nima. In places the ocean is as light as my irises. In other places, deep, deep in the middle, it's as dark as the center of my pupil.

Staring into the river, it's all just one color. *Change is an illusion,* I told her.

The deeper the water, the darker it becomes. The water just looks transparent, but anything below two hundred meters is pitch black, no matter where it is.

Does it really change, though? Isn't water the same in all places?

Well, it changes for you and me, Nima. It's the look of it that changes, but the water doesn't really change. Like a person's perspective. The deeper the water, the deeper the person, the more different they become. Or at least appear to be.

Change in water, change in people, we see what we want to see. What a fool I am to think Val and I were two of a kind. Foolish to think like one of them.

I pass by Khunde, just over the hill. I could have stopped. I could have run home, flashing my earnings. But what life would I have returned to? I would have liked to see my sisters, to explain to them what happened and what I've decided to do. My father surely would have punished me, but he wouldn't have sent me to the sky. No. He would have beaten me harshly, to remember, despite the pride that would have come from me, the runaway, and my money. And then...no. I stop thinking about it. Even if my plan is foolish, I keep on. I need to finish what I've started.

In Tengboche, I stop for the night. Half a dozen scattered lodges shaded by pines, all dwarfed by a hilltop monastery—all this I know from memory, I can barely see in front of my face. The fog is thick, just like yesterday, and the only thing I can see in the distance is the gompa, the top of the monastery, shining from the dying rays of the sun. The all-seeing eyes of Buddha painted at the top of the white-and-gold kani tower. My cold and calloused toes keep marching, grass crunching under my boots, the squeak of rubber on slick earth. I reach into the fog, tripping on an empty gas drum, and open a door. Yet another tea house, full. "Get out, girl!" I try another. I search for any familiar face. "No room."

The last one in the village, I knock on the door. It creaks open, revealing an innkeeper with a wide face and a wider middle. "Many, many mikarus tonight," he tells me, spitting as he speaks. "No room."

"I don't require much space. Just a blanket, if you can spare it."

He looks me over before speaking again. "Food?"

I nod.

"Three hundred rupees."

I dig out the money, hand it to him. "Come."

Dark inside with a low ceiling. Smoky and cold. Full of people, their faces shrouded, their breath visible in puffs. The cold feels the same in here as outside. Music plays softly out of a small radio. Radio Kantipur. The song ends and the box squawks the day's headlines, something about congress and Prachanda.

What place does the government have here on the mountain? With its squawking box that not even all Sherpas understand. So many native tongues and ethnic groups crammed together: Sherpas and Tamangs and Brahmins and Chhetris and even a few Tharus and Newars, all sitting together at a dozen wooden tables, at random, no attention to status or rank or caste. They're all bundled in their climbing gear, the terai and the hill people look so cold, so out of their element. But there they are, my countrymen, and not a woman among them (except me, of course), all of them sipping steaming tea, holding their hands out as if in prayer to a divine dented stove in the center of the room. A young Sherpa boy, less than a meter tall, feeds the flames with flattened dung cakes.

"Namaste."

"Tashi delek."

Searching, I spot Norbu's mikarus, then some of the Sherpas who attacked me the day before. I'm careful to keep my head low and not make eye contact. They're here, but no Norbu. No Val. It's so dark I don't think they've noticed me. And I'm close to the fire, and I feel sweat beading on my temple, so I gamble and take off my knit cap, my gloves.

The spitting Sherpa who let me in takes me to the last seat available at a table crammed with empty bottles. He has that drunk glint in his eyes, like he's looking at something far off. "How pretty you are under that cap. Thirsty, girl? Hungry?"

The fat man smothers my hand with his, and I pull it away. He whistles at the boy feeding the flames: "Cha tang! Dray!" The boy drops the cakes, wipes his hands on his shirt, and nods.

The innkeeper turns back to me. "Why all alone, girl?"

The boy places a pot of tea and a bowl of rice in front of me. The innkeeper takes the pot, pours two cups, pushes one towards me. "Drink, drink," he says, white spittle sticking to the corner of his mouth.

I feel a hand on my leg, under the table. I spill the tea trying to pull away. He looks at me with such lustful eyes and as he squeezes my upper thigh I pull my kikuri from its sheath and stick it into his happy hand—he pulls it away and lets out a yelp just as the door to the lodge swings open and two cloaked figures step in. The strangers are holding something between them—it's hard to make out what it is. The innkeeper rises from the table, looks at me with scorn, and puts his paw to his mouth and sucks the blood. The strangers come closer, each holding a length of old rope tied around a box. They heave and drop their load onto the table right in front of the innkeeper—and a high-pitched squeal comes from inside the box. Like an infant's cry.

"Sit, sit," the innkeeper commands the strangers. They keep standing. The stove crackles, that earthy smell wafting into the air. The innkeeper wipes the sides of his mouth, scraping crust and flicking it to the floor. I sip tea and scoop clumps of rice with my fingers, grateful to finally be eating, but still holding the naked blade under the table with my other hand. One of the men takes off his cloak, a shiny watch on his wrist reflecting the light, a rifle slung across his chest.

That watch...My eyes widen. The other has blemishes on both cheeks and a rifle slung around his chest as well. The stove crackles again, and another squeal leaks out of the box.

"What do you have?" the innkeeper snarls.

The two men are dressed in faded green fatigues. Army green. The one with the blemishes looks in my direction and I look away, stroking my hand where his mutt bit me, still sore under my bandage. I pull my knit cap low over my eyebrows. Glancing down, so as not to meet their eyes, I notice that each wears shoes without laces.

"Something special in here," one of them says. "Very special. The mikarus will pay to see this."

"Show me."

"Patience, sahep, patience. We must set a price first. Then you will see."

"Let me see now or I'll throw you out."

The one with the blemishes scans the room like a hawk. He lifts the black cloth covering the box, and the innkeeper bends his head to look. I glimpse a wire cage and inside it, two little, shiny orbs. The creature utters a squeaky chirp and the soldier drops the cloth back over the box.

The boy soldier leans over the box. "Well?"

The glint in the innkeeper's eyes brightens and the soldiers smile at each other. "Where did you get it?"

"Poachers. They found their lair—then *we* found theirs. It's too bad we couldn't bring you the other one, but it was too hard to transport. Too large."

"What happened to the skin?" The innkeeper keeps looking at the box as he negotiates.

"Gone. Sold."

"And the bones?"

"Over the mountain," he answers. "The Han are willing to pay."

"If you do business here, Deenabandhu," the innkeeper rasps, "I get half."

One of the soldiers jumps from the table. "Half? Come on, we'll take this to the monastery. The lamas would pay good money to raise one of the gods' pets."

"Yes, good idea, Alok."

"Wait—let me touch it, let me see it closer—"

"This is a serken, dear sahep, not some common jackal or wolf. *Serken.* And if you don't want to be fair in business, we could take it to the monastery or down the mountain, to Lukla.

Much more money in it for us."

In Nepali, Alok means "brightness," Deenabandhu means "friend to the poor." So now Brightness and Friend to the Poor pretend to lift the box and head out with it. The innkeeper jumps to stop them.

"Thirty percent," he says. The soldiers keep quiet. "Maybe you would get more elsewhere," the innkeeper continues, "but it's not easy carrying this thing all the way down to Lukla. I see how heavy it is. And the cub may not survive the trip—it needs milk. I have milk from my goats. Do you? Without me, what will you do, milk each other to feed it? Thirty percent!"

The boys lean in and whisper. Then the one called Alok, the one wearing Val's gold watch, he faces the innkeeper and nods.

"Good. Do it now," the innkeeper commands. "They've eaten and their purses are loose."

The boys throw the cloth off, and now I see him, behind the bars of a wire cage, a trembling snow leopard cub.

Alok grabs the cub by his scruff, hoists him out of the cage, and the cub erupts into a birdlike shriek, paws flailing, claws out. "It's a male," Alok says, flicking the tiny penis. "A male snow leopard. Truly one of the gods' pets."

Alok ties a collar made from dirty shoelaces around the cub's neck and plops him down onto the table for everyone to see. Mikarus and Nepalis crowd around the cub. The little snow leopard shakes like a leaf. "Come, it's safe. Come." Alok tugs at the shoelaces, but the cub won't move. Tiny claws dig into the wood table. His ears turn and his tail curls between his legs. The cub hisses and snarls—the other boy, Deenabandhu, plucks one of his whiskers and the snarl becomes a sharp cry.

"Grind and mix the whisker with tea. Good for curing rheumatism."

The innkeeper considers the whisker, his stubby fingers measuring its length. Alok and Deenabandhu go from table to table, displaying the little serken. Rupees start dripping into their hands. A mikaru with a bushy mustache scratches the cub's muzzle with a curled finger, another poses for a photo with the little thing, holding its mouth open to display the tiny jaws. *Snap. Snap.* And another and another and another. So many hands, petting and grabbing and touching. Yesterday's attackers flash before my eyes. But where is this one's savior?

One of the outstretched fingers comes too close, and the little cub bites down with those needlelike teeth that remind me of Nurse Lanja's tools. The mikaru screams, jerking his hand away. The innkeeper laughs as the foreigner scrambles to stop the bleeding. Alok picks up the cub by its scruff. "This is a wild creature. A very valuable and rare wild creature." He holds the cub above his head, and the little leopard pees all over him. More laughs.

Alok throws the cub back into the cage, his small body crashing into the wire. "No milk for you tonight, baby serken. We'll teach you respect." Alok, whose shirt is now soaked a darker shade of green, begins wiping himself off.

My eyes meet with Alok's and hatred builds in my beating heart. I touch the hilt of my kikuri—and just as quickly let my hand drop. He doesn't recognize me. And that poor cub, I can't save him. Even if I somehow did, I wouldn't be able to feed him or me.

We'd both die.

I bolt from my seat so fast that the chair falls behind me. No one notices, all still enraptured by the cub. I slink to the door, twist the knob, then slip out of the lodge, back into the cold void. *I'm sorry, little serken.*

It's dark and the fog is thick. I can't even see my fingers in front of my face. I'm walking blindly. Then I hear a *ding* in the distance, and I instantly recognize it. The call to eat, from the top of the hill. I walk faster, by memory, up and through the fog, heading for the only light source I can see, just a flicker on the ridge: Tengboche Monastery.

22

'BUT YOU'RE A WOMAN,' THE LAMA REPEATS. 'A WOMAN!'

The wind is so strong on my back and exposed neck, it shoves me against the oak door.

"You must go to Deboche, to the nuns, it is not allowed for you to be here!" He tries to push me back into that merciless wind. But I push back.

"Please, the nunnery is too far and I am too tired. I would never make it in the fog. Let me in. Just to sleep. Please. Let me in!"

"What is going on out here?" A rumbling from behind. "Brother Dolma, explain yourself."

Dolma bows to the older monk—I recognize the lama I met with Val and Daniel and Ethan only yesterday.

"Tashi delek," I say, pressing my hands together.

"Tashi delek."

"Sir, *sahep*, I was here a day ago. We spoke, don't you remember?"

"I do."

"You spoke of the dharma, how the bodies of men and women are equally suited for enlightenment. I lost my way from my group. I implore you for a place to stay for the night. Only for the night, I will leave by morning. Would gracious monks turn away a fellow Buddhist, a low-born woman in need?"

The old lama looks at the younger one, furrows his brow, deciding what to do.

"I apologize," Dolma says, half prostrating in the doorway. The wind bites at my neck. "I told her no, Lama Tsering, I told her she must go to Deboche, and now she will not leave—"

"Please," I beg.

The old crow adjusts his glasses, purses his lips, and I feel his gaze on me, tracing my shape. "She is a woman, most definitely. And she is right. It is too far, and too late in the night, for such travels. Let her in, brother."

"But, Lama Tsering, what will the others say?"

"What will the others say?" With an open palm he whacks the younger man on the crown of his head, firmly but not without tenderness, something a father—*not my father*—might do if their child spoke out of turn.

"Gong dhaa."

"Don't say it to me, say it to the girl."

The younger lama bows to me, knees bending.

"Refusing a wayward soul in the dead of night, is that what the dharma teaches? You're not in China any longer, Brother Dolma. This is the land that birthed the Buddha, helping a traveler in need is always the way. What will the others say? The others will look beyond the dogma. Secular ethics, as his holiness preaches, secular ethics. Come, girl."

Full of monks in saffron gold and crimson robes, the monastery is transformed. Shangri- La, maybe not, but something so welcome in my current state. Lamas, old and young: some my father's age, some twice that, some as young as my brother would have been. All very thin. Thin arms and thin legs, thin bodies with large, hairless heads. They sit on burgundy pillows, blankets pulled over their feet, hunched forward as they empty shiny silver rice bowls into their open mouths. A roomful of heads as shiny as the bowls they eat from. The herd turns as I walk in—a woman in their midst.

"The temptation of food, the temptation of physical consort," the head lama whispers, noticing the monks' surprise. "Perhaps it is better if men have had intercourse before taking a vow of celibacy. Just as someone who has eaten or drunk too much will retch at the sight of food or drink, so too will people who have had much sex find it easier to renounce it."

He leads me to an open seat, motions to an underling, who hands me a bowl and a cup of tea. I bow my head in thanks, and the old man takes his seat beside the statue. It is the raised seat of the head lama. He adjusts his glasses, leans into the small microphone attached to the seat. "We have a visitor this evening." There's a murmur all around me. Lama Tsering holds his hands up, quiets the dissenters. "Please, brothers, please. We've all seen women before. We all came into the world by a woman's strength, raised by a woman's grace. Treat this one with the same respect you would treat all the mothers or sisters on the earth."

Another grumble. The lamas' shadows are dancing over the monastery's wall paintings. I feel eyes on me and turn to the brother to my right. He quickly looks down and rice falls from his mouth. He can't make eye contact with a woman. The flickering of the candles makes Buddha with his green halo, the deities with human faces and animal bodies, twist and writhe. And above the paintings, the window to the goddess, ever staring down, illuminated by the moonlight.

The monks return to their places in the center of the dokhang after the meal, bending and crouching, resuming their work. Even at this hour, they work. Red and blue and black and yellow, they carefully move and place grain after grain of sand, using long metal rods called chak-purs. Others crush stones with mortar and pestle, collecting the stone particles in golden bowls. They use the chak-purs to arrange the sand, their hands moving so feverishly that their vibrating tools make the grains appear to be flowing like liquid. Even at this hour, they work.

"Have you ever seen a mandala before, girl? Have you ever seen one being made?"

I shake my head. Old Lama Tsering smiles like a young boy. "Come." He gets up, leads me to the edge of the diagram. "What do you see?"

Lines and boxes, boxes within boxes.

"This is the entire universe," he explains. "Balance, life, death. Everything, contained here. Everything. We offer the universe to the Buddha, as an aid for meditation."

I watch how carefully the monks work, how finely they build, slowly lifting and placing each grain of sand.

"It will take one hundred thousand of these offerings before a lama can begin the tantric practice. And then, once the ritual is complete..." Lama Tsering stamps a sandaled foot on the ground, a centimeter from the mandalas. As if snuffing the life from some unseen demon. "Impermanence in all things. Even things of beauty."

"Why destroy something that took so long to create?"

"Everything is eventually destroyed, even pure creations like this. The protection that we need from destruction and decay is in *here*." He taps his forehead. "In the mind. Separation, protection, that is what you see before you. The four outer circles, all protection from samsara: the purifying fire of wisdom, the vajra circle, the lotus circle, the circle with eight tombs. We build it all, sometimes for weeks or months. And then the sand is brushed together and spilled into the Dudh Kosi to spread the blessing."

The mandala looks like a giant map of the Tibetan plateau—in the east is a mountain like a heap of flowers. In the south, a pile of jewels. In the west, a stack of stupas. In the north, shells.

Next to the giant Buddha shrine is the history of the Khumbu painted on the walls. Every centimeter is covered in rich gold, dark red, emerald green. Hundreds of mandalas, buffered by miniature sculptures of smiling deities with human faces and animal bodies. Buddha in various stages of his ascendance to Nirvana, freedom from malice and lust, a green halo around his head.

On a wall, I find myself staring at the klu-mo: the demon with the body of a serpent and a face in her chest. The lama notices me staring at it.

"She gives rise to the world," the old man says, watching my eyes trace the painting. "Her head becomes the sky, her right eye the moon, her left eye the sun, her teeth the planets, her voice thunder, her breath clouds, her veins rivers."

"A woman gave birth to all that?"

He nods. "A violent conception."

"Do women have the same potential as men—for enlightenment?" I ask.

"The human body is the basis of the accomplishment of wisdom. And the gross bodies of men and women are equally suited. But if a woman has strong aspirations, she has the higher potential. The words of Padmasambhava the guru. True words."

Lama Tsering gives me a yak wool blanket and a place by the mandala. There's no stove for warmth, so it's the closeness and body heat that keep the place from freezing overnight.

Even with the blanket over my head, my knit cap on, and the brothers at an arm's length, I'm still shivering. Perhaps the absence of a burning stove brings one closer to enlightenment.

Tengboche is the ancient and revered home of Sangwa Dorje, a powerful lama said to be the reincarnation of the Dalai Lama. My mother would tell me these stories as a child, every night before bed. A child never forgets adventures when she doesn't want to go to bed. All Sherpas know this story. Sangwa Dorje was so divinely gifted, he could read hundreds of pages merely by glancing at them. He had other powers, too. Spreading a shawl like wings, he could soar through the air, what the ancients called wind meditation. Once, when the great lama took off at the confluence of two rivers, the Langmoche and the Nampa, he left imprints of his hands and feet that can still be seen. He flew toward the Dudh Kosi, where he left his mark again, then he flew to a hill where he left the marks of his feet and rice bowl. He named that place Tengboche and vowed to build a great monastery there. In Sherpa, Tengbo means the "imprint of heels," and che is "village."

When I shut my eyes, I see Norbu flash by, then Val, my father, my sisters, my mother, my brother. Then that poor snow leopard cub. To save a life intended for slaughter, there is no higher act of charity. But I failed. My mind flashes to Norbu, to Val. *Why didn't they come to look for me?*

If Val doesn't want me anymore, I could stay with Norbu's mikarus. I should have joined them on the trail this morning, they would have surely led me to Norbu.

Stop and start and stop again, always at the same branch of the tree.

The morning comes, the light streaming into the dokhang, a greeting from the gods.

Through a window, the goddess stares down at us. Wind comes into the cavernous room, chanting to us: *I'm here. I'm everywhere.*

Most of the monks are already gone. Lama Tsering still sleeps—loudly—and so do a few other abbots, but all the other beds are empty. I get up and stretch, fold my blanket, walk over to the mandala. So much work, just to cast it to the heavens. I look down at my hands, flex my fingers and touch my bandaged palm. Their hands must ache at the end of every day from such hard labor. I wonder if monks feel pain the same as the rest of us. Maybe not, sleeping in a meditation box for a year, this room must be a luxury.

Perhaps some of them *are* enlightened—although I can't imagine that one who's enlightened could snore like a moon bear—but how naive they seem, too. It's a better lot in life to be among people, to be an actor in the world, than apart. If I were a wife in a kitchen, cooking and lying on my back every night, making meals every day and babies once a year, that wouldn't be much different from living in a shedra. What would Buddha say? Was there even such a person? *Suffer for me like I have suffered, face heaven and hell if there is such a thing.* If not, that's the cruelest cosmic joke of all.

The head lama stirs as a coughing fit comes on. Still in the lotus, the way all monks sleep, he slowly uncrosses one leg, then the other. After the coughing passes, he puts his glasses on, a worldly possession in itself, and scans the room.

"Shokba delek," he says, clearing his throat.

"Shokba delek," I respond.

I'm not wearing my knit cap, my short-haired womanhood on display. But if he's bothered, he doesn't say. He gets up, regards the three sleeping abbots to his right—old men with round bellies that move up and down like waves—pauses by the microphone, seeming to contemplate whether to wake them by speaking into it, then he shakes his head. "I'll let them sleep until the morning meal. They'll wake for that."

Lama Tsering walks towards me. It's the first time I've noticed: one of his legs is a few centimeters shorter than the other. Then we stand over the mandala, just like the night before.

"You don't think we should scatter it, do you?"

"Why keep something so beautiful hidden away?"

"We won't. Ten days after Mani Rimdu, when the sand takes to the sky it will be a blessing to the people, a blessing that will bring rain and end the drought, if we are fortunate. Perhaps the gods are listening. It rained two days ago, did it not?"

The door to the monastery creaks opens and I turn, hoping to see Norbu—instead it's Brother Dolma. He walks up to the old lama, never once making eye contact with me.

"Should I make a bowl for our guest?" he asks, keeping his gaze low.

"Of course, Brother Dolma, of course. The girl must eat if she is to continue up the mountain. That is what you plan to do, yes?" He turns to me. "And where will you travel to?"

"Base Camp. Everest."

He nods, his whole body rocking. "Very auspicious day for travel. Today will be the new moon. You can see from the direction of the sun, see there?" He points to the window, the light shines directly to where I slept last night. "Very auspicious."

Soon I'm back on the trail, alone.

The dog bite still hasn't healed. When I make a fist, my hand cries. When the wind blows, my face and neck sting, but at least the load on my back is gone. Dewa and dungal, happiness and suffering. And all my suffering is the result of something I've done in a previous life. But this time, come what may, I'm suffering as a woman, no hiding now.

I pass the shedra that Brother Dolma wanted to send me to last night. Life as a nun. Life in a box.

I go for refuge to the Buddha.
I go for refuge to the Dharma.
I go for refuge to the Sangha.
I go for refuge to the Triple Gem.
So that I and all sentient beings, my mothers,
May be led to complete and Perfect Enlightenment.

I don't prostrate myself enough before the gods, but I have enough compassion, I'm sure of it. When the lama said those words just as I was leaving, was it a mantra to bless me, or just his regular morning incantation?

The trail changes as I start back uphill, colorless hillsides, a sweeping blanket of dry gray shrubs. I hope the gods do listen when the monks scatter the sands. The land needs it. At the top of a crest, just outside Pangboche, I come across Norbu's mikarus once more, this time with two Sherpas. I recognize them from Namche, but no Norbu. I decide to follow anyway, and these Sherpas don't say anything to me when they see me. Maybe they're too tired, maybe they finally respect me, maybe I'm too far behind. It doesn't matter.

There's an upsurge of voices—someone stumbled, that red-haired girl. She tosses her walking sticks and the bearded older man picks them up. She's barely moving, on her knees now, and the whole group is backed up. Her father offers her an energy bar, but she shakes her head.

He shoves it in his mouth and tosses the plastic wrapper on the trail. He's decked out in goggles with polarized lenses, an ample parka, leather gloves. He, too, has walking sticks, shiny, metal plated, with black rubber grips, wrist straps looped around his paws.

"Freddie," he calls to the girl. "Freddie!"

Two guides hurry over to her, each grabbing an arm to prop her up. With help from the Sherpas, the girl takes a step forward. Slowly. Her companion, the blond waif, wipes a tear that leaves a streak from the dust. It's hard to watch. The whole group is stopped now. I decide to keep moving. A few minutes later, from a jagged perch above, they all look like dots. And they're still trying to help that girl.

Out of water, I stop at a roadside stand, halfway between Pangboche and Pheriche. I buy a bottle of water and a tin of crisps, still plenty of rupees left. There are even a few trekking poles and tokmas for sale.

"How much for a tokma?"

Later, while I rest on an old stone wall next to a row of fallen mani, two little boys make faces at me as I eat crisps. One puffs his cheeks, the other sticks his tongue out. They must be the stand owner's sons. I hop off the wall, raise my arms and contort my face like the lepcha I've been called so many times now, and the two little ones run and hide. I chase after them, cornering one. He picks up a bamboo stick and points it threateningly. I lift my new tokma and we sword fight, swinging and striking, he laughing in delight as I fall back and he slays me. Dead, I give the tiny warriors the last of my crisps, which they grab.

"Another demon slayed!" one yells before fleeing.

I feel a slight tug from my crying ear as I keep walking.

Up ahead, a trio of figures rest on their walking sticks. Men from Namche. Men who deserve just retribution in this life and the next. I expect a confrontation, waiting for them to rise, approach, attack even. The sirdar Lasha and the others don't even sling an insult. I'm without a mask, but they don't even look at me, only *past* me, sitting and chewing their tobacco, like spiders, waiting. It feels like a trap—and then he comes out from behind a bush, zipping up his trousers and jacket. Norbu. Now I understand. It's because of him that they don't say anything.

Just like dogs, these men, and what do dogs do when confronted by a bigger breed? They surrender.

Lasha spits brown juice and rises from his tokma, his face still bruised from where Norbu struck him. Without words, the trio hoist their packs and continue on the trail, leaving me alone with Norbu. He doesn't seem to notice their departure. We stand in front of each other, close enough to touch.

"You're Nima again," he says, reaching out his hand to touch my face. But I pull back.

"Why did you leave me yesterday? Where did you go?"

"Nima, I didn't leave—"

"Where did you go?"

For all his strength, Norbu's suddenly a little boy, looking down now that he's chastised.

"One of the mikarus got sick," he answers, still looking down. "I had to take him to

Syangboche. I carried him part of the way. It was nightfall, and I was too tired to return. I looked for you in Tengboche. Are you all right? Why are you alone? Where's your group?"

"The sirdar didn't tell you? They let me go."

Norbu shakes his head. "None of them will talk to me. Not since Namche."

"Did you really look for me?"

He nods, opens his mouth to say something—then doesn't.

A horseman gallops past us. Then a troop of people emerges from the dust stirred by the rider. All the women wear fur hats, their noses glistening with gold rings. The men march behind them, in plain robes, all except one who wears a fedora and tennis shoes. And behind him, a young girl, so effortlessly radiant, so ready for what will come into her life.

They beam with happiness. Norbu turns to me and a bolt of shame flows through my body. It's a wedding party.

23

of us speaks much. A light flurry of snow begins to fall. A pair of birds call overhead, hidden in the trees. Yaks graze everywhere, their thick hot tongues digging through the frozen dirt to scoop roots. Not much else on four legs can survive up here, except the Himalayan tahr. Those creatures have huge curved horns and ebony spheres for eyes. They've become rare, their meat and horns prized by hunters and serken alike. A small herd grazes in a corral of boulders, their lower jaws moving side to side as they chew. Sacred animas. Where there are tahr, there are snow leopards. I think about that poor cub, never to grow up free, never to be wild. *How many serken are left in the Khumbu?*

The tahr hop over the corrals effortlessly, not in the least bit worried by our presence. Too many mikarus here, too many Sherpas, no predators left to be worried about. They pick through the frost in search of hidden shoots of grass. But there is not much in Pheriche. No trees, no river, just boulders and yaks and shallow, icy riverbeds. Each village is smaller than the last, smaller the higher we get, this one just a handful of piled stones and tin roofs. A wind funnel between the peaks, there's not much life, but there's a stillness, a cold power to the mountains that gives it a stunning beauty.

Norbu and I climb over stone walls, about a meter high, not to keep animals out, but to keep them in. Work animals, farm animals. Hogs, fowl, skinny horses. Enough to sustain perhaps a dozen people year-round. And the people rely on every one of those creatures to keep them going. Farming is slow here, trade equally slow. Over the pass to Kham or down into the lower valley, both take time. The constant battering from the wind and long winters govern the farming schedule, same as in my home village. You can barely grow potatoes and roots, and never out in the open, always in a shed or storehouse, the only place to dig where it's not iced over. Some build special huts with roofs they can remove on the days the sun cuts through the clouds.

There's only one lodge here, just across another wall, its stones caked with black ice and snow. I lift a foot and come down slipping on the ice, but Norbu steadies me before I lose my balance. We don't waste words, both of us focusing on our steps and the uphill journey, but I feel calmer just walking next to him. We each swing our legs over the wall, carefully, hands entwined, all the way to the lodge's door.

We sit together by the stove. No longer holding hands, but our feet touching just slightly, toes aimed towards the flame. There's a bucket stacked with pressed and hardened cakes that Norbu feeds to the flame every few minutes.

One by one, Sherpas who called me names bring their plastic chairs closer until we form a circle around the stove. The bad luck woman isn't so bad, not when it comes to getting warm. And up here everyone just wants to stay warm, even Lasha, he isn't part of the circle, not quite, but he isn't apart from it either. He doesn't have the nerve to open his mouth or look at Norbu. He's sitting in a plastic chair, just a pace beyond the circle. Up here, it doesn't matter. The bad feelings I had, they don't quite disappear, but I know they can't harm me any longer.

It's hours before the first of the mikarus trudge in. I'd dozed off briefly, awakened by the rattling of the lodge doors. First, Norbu's group comes in. Norbu lets go of my hand and rises as they enter— was he holding my hand while I slept?—tending to the needs of food and drink. As the mikarus strip off their packs and gear, the circle breaks until all the seats are filled with Westerners and all the Sherpas are busy scrambling to serve. All but me. I have no clients to serve, not anymore, and I keep as close to the flame as I can. My chair next to the mikarus, right next to the stove, on the same plane as them.

The door swings open again and in come Val, Ethan, and Daniel, their faces red and chapped, lips smeared with dried blood—and when they step in they're reeking of dung and dirt. Lasha bolts up to take their order: hot tea.

I'm not sure if Ethan and Daniel see me, but if they do, they don't let on, slinking down at a table, dragging their legs. I thought I would be furious to see them. Instead, I don't feel anything. Val doesn't break stride, peeling off her gloves and heading straight to the fire where she holds her arms out, hands shaking.

"Lasha said you left," Val tells me, not wasting any time. "He told us you left to get married."

"Lasha is a liar," I say quietly, watching the sirdar tending to the men. Maybe it's the altitude, but I don't want to pretend.

"Lasha told us that Norbu tried to take you by force back to your village. He was trying to protect you and Norbu beat him. Then you agreed to go. We saw his face, we saw how upset you were after Namche—"

"All lies," I say, cutting her off.

Val rubs her hands together close to the fire, studying my face. She's seen so much in her life, but there's something about the way she looks at me. She's never dealt with something like this.

"Lasha attacked me. Twice." I take a breath, then continue. "Norbu saved me the second time." She's still quiet, her face a mask. "Ethan gave me the rest of my wages and told me to go. Did you tell him to do that?"

"Nima—" Val's voice cracks.

"I want to finish the trek, Val."

"Nima, I'm so sorry."

"I plan to finish, with or without you."

Val looks over at Ethan, considering what I've told her.

I dig into my bag and pull out the money. "Here. All of it, Val, except for what I spent on the tin of crisps." Val puts her hands over mine, pushes the money back. I shake my head: "I want you to tell Ethan that I forgive him, too. I understand that he was scared."

"No, no," she says in English. "This isn't what I wanted, Nima," switching back to Nepali. "I should have talked to you myself, I was wrong. I was scared about getting too involved, Nima. Ethan and I talked and he said he would fix the problem, and I let him—I'm so sorry, you deserved better from me."

The sirdar appears holding a tray with cups of tea. Lasha the sirdar. This time, in the safety of this place, he somehow has the nerve to look at me. *Coward.* He hands Ethan a cup of tea, then Daniel. Then he comes closer to Val and I, and hands her a cup. In between sips, Ethan rattles off something to Daniel, and he lets out what sounds like a pained, nervous laugh. I can see the blood rushing to Val's face, the veins in her neck coursing under her skin. Lasha isn't important anymore. All of my anger washes away, shame receding with it, replaced by a deep need to be understood. To be equal.

"I don't work with women," Lasha sneers.

Val pivots like a mantis. "You'll work for a woman, but not work *with one*?"

Ethan looks up from the stove's flames. I can feel his eyes searching for mine.

"Miss, these are just stories from a dishonest girl who abandoned her family," Lasha says, trying to tame the mantis. "A woman porter is bad luck. It makes the mountain angry. It's not done."

"Enough." Val digs into her pocket, takes out a billfold, and counts off rupees. "Leave our bags at the door."

"But, miss, she's just telling stories—"

Val holds out the rupees. He looks less like a man than a hollowed, leafless tree. Lasha the sirdar isn't one any longer, not on this trek.

"Tashi delek," Lasha says, smiling. He takes the money and slinks away.

Norbu is at my side now. He puts his hand on my shoulder. *Steady.*

I thought I would have something to say to Lasha, some gloat, but I don't even want to look at him. I don't even want to be in the same room as him.

"I have to go back to my clients," Norbu whispers.

I nod. "Go."

Val puts her hand on my shoulder now—then pulls me towards her, holding me close, like a sister, an equal.

"I'm sorry," she says. "I'm sorry. I'm so sorry."

My face is buried in her shoulder, and when the tears fall, no one can see them.

24

THE PILL IS CHALKY WHITE, MARKED WITH THE CODE NUMBER 250.
It reminds me of the pills we swallow for Mani Rimdu. Pills for
life, pills for health, pills for spirit. How can something that small
truly calm one's mind or feed one's soul? The mikarus are haggard
and weary, they've waited too long to take them.

Ethan gives me a crooked smile and swallows the Diamox
with a guzzle of Snowy Geyser bottled water. A moment ago, he
held his hand out to me and I shook it, accepting his apology when
he finally mustered the courage to face me. "We were wrong," he
told me. "I was wrong."

I knew Val hadn't coaxed him into saying this—I saw the same
look in his eyes when he gave me the money in that drafty hall-
way. A mix of shame and remorse. Daniel wasn't as expressive,
he mumbled sorry a few times, but he also held out two hands to
me and shook them in a way that felt like I had earned his respect.
And I understand. It makes sense: Why would these travelers
want to get in the middle of a local drama? Of course they would
try to move on from me. They would respect the old, more experienced sirdar. Val, even Ethan and Daniel, none of them cared I was
a woman—they cared that I was being chased by my family, by
Norbu, that I could be a danger to them.

Val is now with her notebook in hand, scribbling things
down—maybe this very scene. Ethan is working with Daniel,
cleaning camera equipment, all of them already moving on to the

next problem. So unlike the Sherpa, but I am beginning to understand. Better to move on from things, in their way—very similar to us. Don't dwell, move forward. Life is too impermanent to waste time. Ang is now Nima, a man is now a woman, but it really doesn't matter.

I want to laugh, but I hold it in. Val must have a similar feeling, since she decides to put down her pen and pick up the teapot on the table. And then—*how often does a mikaru do this?*—she serves me tea. I wait until she sits and puts the mug to her lips before I dare take a sip. A guest, even if she serves me, must always remain a guest. Still, here I am: a girl porter sitting at a table with mikarus, despite all that's happened. Meeting Val in Lukla less than a week ago, but nearly a lifetime now—if they came to the restaurant only a few minutes later, we never would have met.

The lodge door opens and four figures shuffle in, wind screaming behind them: the two girls with the wild hair and their pot bellied father, along with an exhausted Sherpa. The one with the fiery red hair stumbles, collapsing on the floor.

"Freddie! Freddie!"

They pick her up and place her on a bench by the door. "Tea! Bring tea!"

Norbu emerges from the kitchen, cradling a steaming pot and a cup. He hands over the tea, and the girl's father and her guide hold her head up and drip hot liquid in her mouth. The other girl begins crying.

"Not good to lie down," the guide advises the bearded mikaru. "Not good for head. Lift."

They make the girl sit up and keep dripping tea in her mouth.

"Is there a doctor? Anyone here a doctor?"

The father looks around wildly as we huddle around the girl—me, Val, Ethan, her father, the exhausted trail Sherpa, and the girl with the blond hair.

Nurse Lanja taught me what happens when the brain swells. You stop walking and talking normally, you become confused and aggressive, like a drunk. For a foreigner, someone unaccustomed to the high altitude, it's common. Even Sherpas can get it. Eventually, the lungs fill with liquid, you get so weak that you can't move at all. All the great mountain mikarus suffered from these conditions. That's why so many are still on the mountain, forever entombed in ice.

Looking over at this red-haired young thing, with her head slumped, slits for eyes, it's clear she needs to descend. Now. The Sherpas are trying to tell her father, but he's not listening. Hundreds of muscles and bones in a human's body, hundreds of hurts. When altitude sickness comes, you feel them all. Thumping pain. Tormenting pain. Pressure in the skull, the mind, everywhere. Kneeling, I stroke the girl's head.

"Ddaaa, whyss ma headdd hurtt sssoooo?"

"I had to carry her for five kilometers," the exhausted Sherpa says to Norbu and me. "The father is so stubborn, he doesn't want to turn back—he kept accusing me of making her condition seem worse in order to collect some kind of travel insurance money. He's a fool. She needs to descend. Maybe he'll listen to someone with the same skin color."

The girl lets out a catlike moan, startling enough to cause the hair on my arms to stick up.

Ethan breathes deeply, closes his eyes—is he praying? Then he searches frantically for something in his day pack, pulling out a small blue bag with a white cross on it. "Let me," he says to her father. "I'm an EMT." He places the same tool I remember Nurse Lanja used on my father on the girl's chest, then places those metal tongs in his ears, listening. He looks at me, no malice in his eyes now, then flings me an order: "Raise her head."

And Norbu and I jump. Ethan puts his palm on the girl's forehead, touches under her ears, her throat, the inside of her wrist.

"No fever," he says, taking those tongs out of his ears. The heart rate must be fine, but Ethan still looks concerned. Might be a chest infection. Either way, she has to go down as soon as possible.

The girl groans, like a sick dog. *Snap*. Daniel shoots a photo.

"Get her into bed, keep her hydrated, and keep her head elevated," Ethan instructs. "You have to leave in the morning, understand? Take it slow, but get down. The lower she goes, the better she'll feel."

The girl's father rakes his fingers over his face. Sweat drips off his cheeks. Ethan puts a hand on his shoulder. I hear the word "helicopter."

"Won't fly up here," the guide who carried her says in slow, deliberate English. "Air too thin, too dangerous. If she can stand and walk, she can walk down."

"This is the last place for something to go wrong, get it? Tell your mikaru that," Norbu says to me. "A chopper can't rescue her any farther up."

Ethan searches through his medical bag again, finds what he's looking for. "What's her name?"

"Freddie. It's—it was her mother's name."

Ethan holds the white Diamox in one hand, shakes the girl's shoulder with the other. "Freddie, Freddie?"

"Nnnnnnwwwwhaaaaa?" the girl mumbles.

"Can you tell me your name?" Ethan asks. "What's your name?"

"Fff-ff-reddeeee."

"Okay, Freddie, I'm going to give you something, I want you to swallow it, okay?"

She nods. "Oookkkaayyy."

Ethan motions to Norbu and me, we prop her head as he puts the pill in her mouth. "Tea." The guide pours tea. "Swallow it, Freddie."

"Taayss lyyykke cha-awwk."

Snap. Daniel crouches low and close, camera in hand.

"Piss off!" the old mikaru yells, waving a hand at Daniel. Then he gently brushes his daughter's cheeks, a bit of color slowly returning to them. "Thank you, son," he says to Ethan.

"Get her to bed. And take this." Ethan hands him a sheet of pills in plastic.

All of us help the girl up, slowly, supporting her weight. Her legs are so wobbly, she can barely lift them. Her father and the guide help her make it to the doorway and then down the corridor and they disappear.

Ethan walks over to Val, takes her hand. They don't say anything, just embrace.

When Norbu looks at me, I see both worry and relief in his eyes, and then something else. He motions to me, shifting his head to one side. *Follow me.* I take his hand.

25

Everything is burning.
What is burning?
The eyes are burning.
Everything seen by the eyes are burning.
The hope is burning.
The mind is burning.
We're on fire. We may not know it, but we're on fire, and we have to put that fire out.
We're burning with desire.
We're burning with craving. Everything about us is out of control.

WITH NO EYES TO WATCH US—NO MONKS TO PREACH, NO CLIENTS to disapprove, no parents to disappoint—my heart beats like a prayer drum. His beats just as strong.

This isn't how I thought it would happen. I thought it wrong to lie together before becoming man and wife. And I am scared. I never got the chance to ask Val how it's done, I've never placed my lips onto another's, and when I try, Norbu pulls back in surprise. How many times in the last few days have I watched Val stroke Ethan's face, press her lips to his. How easily this touch came to her. It made me wonder what it was like, to touch, to be touched, and when I try it now, I feel a suppressed joy spring from my body. A flutter in my heart, my lips. And something from him...something I only now understand.

Norbu doesn't pull back the second time. I lace my fingers with his and rest them on my chest, place them over my breasts, feeling the up and down of my breathing, the beat of my heart under our intertwined hands. And then I take his hand and place it lower, feeling his touch inside me and my flower spread. His finger dancing nervously, then slower, more deliberate. My heart flutters now more than ever, spinning like a prayer wheel. I'm no longer the girl from the mountain. Eldest was left behind in Khunde, and scattered in Khumjung even before that. Maybe she died when my brother died.

The choice is mine. I get on top of him, this mountain of a man who I never fully understood and never gave a chance to. My skinny legs wrap around his torso. As we writhe together on the narrow cot, bodies sticky and hot despite the cold, I'm not sure of anything but this moment. And it doesn't feel wrong. His touch, his smell and taste, it mixes with my own. There's pain at first, sharp and pulsating, but it goes, filled with something else, something beyond our two bodies.

Animals have no guilt—why should we? We lie on top of each other in that narrow cot, just like I imagine two mikarus might. Like Val and Ethan are right now, I can hear their moans beyond the thin wall—*or maybe it's just the wind*. Regardless, we are suddenly as carefree as any pair.

So what if we are discovered. My reputation cannot become any worse and I don't care. I've already become everything they fear, and I've come out better for it. An affirmation, a new mantra, a rebirth. I wanted this to happen, thought of it every night even if I was ashamed to admit it to myself. What men tried to take by force, I'm giving to Norbu—and what would have happened on our wedding night, as strangers, is happening now, as something more, because it's something we both choose, not an act forced upon us by circumstance. This is purer, this is more virtuous, because I made the choice, tradition be damned. His and mine, mine and his, mixed together in all the ways that matter. I didn't ever think it would be like this, but it is. And I don't feel an ounce of guilt that I enjoy it.

When it's over, I keep my eyes open. And watch him. Counting the hairs on his chest, noticing a small scar under his nipple, another above his left eye. Like the moon when it's skinny. He is doing the same with me. Norbu runs his fingertips across my cheek, tracing the line of my jaw, past my ear, touching my short hair. I shut my eyes and rub my cheek on that rough palm of his. Pressed against his body, I don't even feel the cold. And in the morning, I'll make sure I wake before him. I won't be left alone this time.

"Two days to Base Camp," he says as I'm lacing my boots. "Tomorrow, take them to Kalapathar if the weather's no good for BC. Excellent views. Then do Base Camp after. If not, do it the other way around."

"Kalapathar," I echo.

"The monks say it's the passageway used by the gods to climb Jomolangma. It's the best views of the peak, exactly at sunset. And be careful in the ice fall. And in the glacier. Watch your steps, it's full of crevasses."

I nod. I know.

"Are you feeling the altitude?" he asks.

"I don't think so. I have a small headache. I think it's my nerves."

"You didn't seem nervous last night."

"I was."

He nods, finishes lacing his boots. "I was, too." He puts on his shirt. I'm already fully dressed. "When we're done up here, I'll visit your father, we'll smooth things over. All will be as before."

It'll never be as before, Norbu, you must see that.

His eyebrows scrunch together, pulling up that crescent-shaped scar. "I told you I would let you go to the city. And if you stayed here, you wouldn't have to work. You won't even have to cook or clean, I'll hire a servant. Everything will be taken care of. You'll be happy—I'll make you happy."

"And what happens to you if I go to the city? You said you hated it there. And if I stay here? Become a mother when I've barely become a woman, become old before my hair goes gray?"

He wrings his hands together, bites his lower lip with those white, white teeth.

"Norbu, I can't go back to what I was. I'm someone else now."

He doesn't say anything, looks down, then back up at me.

"If I go home after all that's happened and get married now, I can't set my own path. I need to do that or I'll never be happy, no matter what happens between us. Do you understand?"

"What if we work together?" he asks. "As man and wife, leading climbing teams? Would you consider that? Would that be enough?"

I shake my head. I don't know if I'll take my wages home or straight to Lukla and board one of those metal birds and leave, never to return. Maybe I would be happy to work with a man I trust, a man I love. But right now, I only know my path is to finish this trek and keep moving forward, not back.

"Nima?" he whispers, leaning towards me.

Norbu, I'm ashamed and afraid to tell you all this. Instead, I nod my head and do what's easiest. For the first time, I lie to his face. "Yes, it would be enough."

I curse myself for how easily I'm able to do it. And when I swallow I feel hollow inside.

Three hours later, we stop at Thukla Dhuka's Yak Lodge. Norbu and I are separated again. Dal bhat power. I can't even taste the lentils, my mind won't stop replaying the morning's episode with Norbu. Our groups aren't traveling together. Different paces, different sizes, different clients. Perhaps fate will pair us together, in Lobuche and Gorak Shep, or a few days later back in Lukla.

Could we work together, leading treks up the mountain, as man and wife?

"Nima. Nima!" Tugged from dream by Val's voice. "We're ready."

There's a change now. An unspoken difference I notice as I continue on with the mikarus. As if a higher social status was granted me when I transformed back into a woman. Now all of them—Ethan and Daniel included—look at my face when they speak to me, treat me the same way they might a mikaru woman.

Are they any different than us? It's not a simple yes or no. It's both, really. So deeply beyond any words, theirs is a reflection of my own future, different, and yet still the same.

We reach the Dughla Pass. It's like the gods had flattened this place with hammers and lightning bolts. Massive ancient boulders scrawled in Nepali and English. Stone manis. And everywhere funeral plots and sacred flags—blue, yellow, green, red, white—sky, earth, water, fire, air.

"What is this place?" Daniel whispers, raising his camera.

"These are tombstones, Nima, aren't they?" Val asks.

"Yes, but I can't tell you much. I've never been here before."

"I thought you'd been all the way to Base Camp."

I shake my head and smile. "I thought you'd made it to Namche."

"We're both heading into unknown territory," she says, smiling.

Val touches a massive stone, reads the name on it, touches the faded white kata scarves and prayer flags draped over the stone, scrapes ice and dirt off the bronze plate at its center. "Who was Babu Chhiri?"

My father, when he was still my father, often spoke of Babu Chhiri. A great man, he said, even though he had six daughters—cursed to be without an heir, just like him.

I say what first comes to mind. "Babu Chhiri once spent twenty one hours on the summit. Without oxygen!"

Val scrapes ice from the plaque. "June 22, 1965 to April 29, 2001. Says he summited ten times, even spent a night sleeping on the summit—how is that even possible?"

"My father told me that Babu Chhiri had the courage to try because no one thought it could be done." I once thought of my father the same way. He was Babu Chhiri to me as a girl. *Once.* "If you try when everyone thinks you will fail, then you cannot fail, that's what my father used to say."

"What happened?"

To my father or Babu Chhiri?

"They say he was taking photos and didn't watch his steps. Strange way for a climbing Sherpa to die."

"Do you think something in his life, his karma," Val responds, "do you think it had something to do with it?"

Ten meters away, Daniel, camera pressed to his face, trips and stumbles on a block of ice. He doesn't fall, doesn't even look down. He steadies himself, adjusts his machine, keeps shooting.

"Babu Chhiri fell into a crevasse," I continue. "One of the greatest to ever set foot on Jomolangma. Killed by carelessness or karma, does it matter? He left behind six daughters." "Six daughters," she repeats. "Any of them become climbers, like him?"

I shrug. I don't know. The wind becomes a harsh whistle, like a warning from the great Sherpa's spirit. Then Ethan yells and gestures for us to continue—he's already several meters ahead of us. It's not safe for any of them to be on their own, so I run ahead.

"Let me lead," I tell him.

He nods and I step forward. I've never been up here before, but I follow the cairns, the three-foot piles of rock that mark the way. When I don't see the markers, I use my instincts and follow the tracks from boots and cloven hooves etched in the snow and ice.

"Dying on the mountain is an honor for a Sherpa, isn't it?" Val says to me, catching up. "Regardless of how."

"Yes, but who wants to die frozen, or suffering great pain for hours, at the bottom of a crevasse?"

Val's eyes shine with curiosity. "And yet, if you die in great pain, your soul is trapped, wandering for all time, right?"

I nod in agreement.

"Do you believe in the afterlife, Nima?"

"I'd like to."

A single flake of snow drops between Val's eyes. A white bindi. *What use is there to ponder the afterlife if I haven't yet lived fully in this one?*

Every breath containing less and less oxygen, I feel as if my head is somehow less connected to my body—and like someone is watching over me. My brother, Babu Chhiri, some other spirit from the past?

Apart from the snow falling and Val's boots and mine stomping, there are no sounds. No life this high. No yaks, no tahr, no serken, no plants. No grass beneath our feet, just rock and ice. That's all there is: massive boulders and stacks of ice, each the size of a house. Nor is there a path. We're single file, me in the front, Daniel at the end, trudging through a wide, high valley of black ice, white snow, gray stone. The snow stops falling and the sky becomes misty, like it's crying.

I know that Lobuche, where we'll spend the night, lies just west of the Khumbu Glacier, the world's highest chhaaram. At the glacier's upper end, the Khumbu Ice Fall. There's enough hanging ice here to crush an entire village. Our route to Base Camp will take us across the glacier and under the ice fall. I keep following north, always towards the goddess and the next cairn. The next twelve kilometers will be like this. The mikarus don't know this, and I don't tell them. They're walking even more slowly, Ethan limping slightly, Daniel still with the camera pressed to his face, and Val, who keeps staring at the frozen sky.

In between the towering ice slabs, we stop at the edge of a dark crevasse. Out of breath and thirsty, we're surrounded by so much ice, all of it frozen and locked away. I look into the crevasse, kick an ice chip, sending it into the black abyss. I can't hear it hit the bottom.

Daniel points with shaky hands. "You'd never get out of there."

This I understand instantly. Daniel's hands shake so much he has trouble screwing the cap onto his bottle, and Ethan helps him. How can he take pictures with hands like that? I wonder.

"It's okay," Ethan says. "Diamox side effect."

Daniel nods, puts his hands in his pockets.

The snow stops falling, but the wind blows harder, piercing my coat, pinpricking my arms and legs. I adjust my kerchief over my face, pull my knit cap snugger, all to no effect. My ears feel like they're encased in ice.

My father used to tell me that the glaciers move. Hard to believe, looking at them. It's a sluggish creep down, to be sure, a creep that uproots dirt and boulders. Like a very slow ru'. That frozen dirt is what we walk on now, the moraine. "In summer, when the sun makes the glacier retreat, what's below is exposed like a rotted tooth," he told me when I was just a girl bouncing on his knee, eyes wide with wonder. "In winter, the cold makes it expand again."

We crunch along on that path, children in a temple of chhaaram, weaving past hanging ice towers. I've never seen all this, and I'm as awestruck as the mikarus.

Suddenly Val falls on the ice. "It's okay," she insists. "I'm okay."

Ethan kneels, touching her leg, taking her foot in his hand.

"I said I was okay," she says.

Val starts to pull her foot away. He pleads with her.

"Let go!" She kicks at him like a dog, and Ethan loses his balance, falls back and hits the ground. I don't think she meant to hurt him, and Ethan grits his feet and rises.

No words now. Just the sound of four bodies panting on the frozen pathway.

Keep moving.

Below us, like giant open pores, lie the deep crevasses that can shift without warning. All around us is the blue, black, and white ice in different stages of melt and freeze, the stones bleached by wind and water. Everything is alive in its own way. And above us, the bright cold sun creeps through the clouds, as snow falls again. Sun and snow, a sign from the heavens.

Everything is dangerously beautiful up here. I understand why so many foreigners want to see this and why it's such a holy place for us Sherpas. I can't see the goddess, hidden in mist, but I'm beginning to feel her attraction. I can picture Norbu and I traversing the South Col, tied together on one rope, reaching for the summit.

The far off crack of ice smashing against ice sends a billowing white cloud of snow and ice. The sight takes me back to my village. I'm a girl once more, watching the ru' wipe away my world.

All summiting teams have to conquer this passage. When ropes snap, when ladders break, even a Tenzing Norgay or a Babu Chhiri can die. And many have. The route to Base Camp takes us right along the edge of the ice fall, two days of hauling your weights beneath an awning of ice.

We follow the cairns, dung mixed with snow and ice, once part of an animal's warm body—a sign of life, a sign that we're closer to Lobuche. I lead the mikarus over the ridge and we claw our way out of the glacier. At last, with that monster of ice behind us, we look over a cluster of wood and brick. Lobuche. Another village without villagers.

Everything is white from snow. Too cold to grow, too cold for animals either—a sheer miracle of will that these people hauled rocks and logs to build a life so close to this vast glacier, to choose to make something *here*.

We try the doors to one tea house, the Himalayan Eco Lodge: locked. Bright Lady Hotel: locked. Norbu's group must be in one of these places, since they started earlier this morning. But if they are full, the lodge keepers won't open. The last, Mother Earth House, is two stories high, a doubly difficult construction project. The sign in front reads: 4,940 METERS. The doors are unlocked. *There are no thieves to come because there is not a thing to steal.* We walk in...

We eat tasteless food in a barren room. Empty plastic chairs, empty plastic tables. No other trekkers, just us. This tea house is a massive cave, cavernous enough that it feels colder in here than outside. The tiny stove in the center of the room isn't even lit, so I set about my first task: convincing the lodge's keeper to light it.

Val wants to work, she tells me. Can we talk to him? Ask a bit about what it's like to live here? I've finally understood what she does—she learns people's stories and then shares them with others, who hopefully share them with others. So much Sherpa history is passed from generation to generation, and so much of it has been lost because it's not written—that's what makes Val's work important. She uses ink while we tell our stories to whoever will listen. She can reach so many more, she can preserve my culture in a way that we cannot. An honorable endeavor. But what will she do with my story? What will outsiders think about a Sherpa woman who isn't defined solely by climbing the peaks?

"The owner is back in Kathmandu," the headman complains as I translate to Val. "Wanted me to close for the season, but I told him more trekkers were coming. 'Americans don't follow rules, they'll be here,' I said. He's going to be mad, mad there aren't more of you. Double price. Must be double price, for each. You, too."

If he notices I'm a woman, he doesn't say anything. Up here, any guest and any amount of money is appreciated. The meal is more water than curry, the rice stale. But we eat it anyway.

Every scrap. There's a worn, old map on the wall next to the kitchen. The village's location is circled in red, and above it, I read Gorak Shep. To the left, Kalapathar. On the map, the trip looks easy.

The mikarus have heavy circles around their eyes, dirt lodged in the creases on their faces. Val coughs, deep. Ethan props his right leg on a plastic chair, carefully, rubbing his knee. Daniel's hands shake as he puts down his camera. He takes out a vial of those white pills and swallows one. He passes the pills to the others. All three are shaking now.

"Depending on the weather, tomorrow we do either Base Camp or Kalapathar," I tell Val.

"What do you mean, either? And what's Kalapathar?" She looks like she'd have trouble crawling into bed.

"If the weather stays like today, climbing Kalapathar gives us the best views of Everest, exactly at sunset." I'm repeating Norbu's words. My father told me about it, too. His clients would be so impressed it would result in a bonus when the trip was over. But I don't care about the money anymore. I just want them to be impressed.

"And if it's not clear?" Val asks through another throaty cough.

"Then we head for Base Camp."

Val translates to the team. They all start speaking at once, talking over one another. Val gets up, then Daniel and Ethan follow, heading to their rooms to sleep, I hope. I hope they sleep. I hope I sleep. The mikarus move as if their feet are encased in boulders. I had hoped tonight Val and I could trade words, and I could learn more English. But Val doesn't even bother to say good night, just trudges along down the corridor to her room.

26

are starting to blend together.

The cold wind blows right through the lodge's thin walls. I'm bundled up in the cot, wishing Norbu was beside me. I pull my knees to my chest and stare up at the ceiling, remembering his warm body. Mismatched paint flaking off in the corner. I could never be a typical Sherpa wife, waiting for Norbu, knowing what he faces on the trail. But I'm something else now. When Val writes about me, Sherpas will see—all Nepalis will see—there are choices for young women like me. We aren't defined just by the past. And what about Soom, Shi, Nga, little Doog, when Father sells my sisters off as brides? Will any of them protest that they want a different kind of life? They'll read about me and become inspired. And reading those words will take the place of all the guidance I *didn't* give them.

I flex half-frozen fingers—there's still a mark from where that stupid dog bit me—then I put my hands in my armpits, where they're not quite as cold, but I'm still shivering. Last night, I put on every layer I had, I slept with the blanket over my face, and when I awoke, the top of the blanket had iced over from my breath.

A multitude of words express cold in my language. Sīl, "to be cold." Khyēwa lang, sīlwu, threngge, khyak—all mean "to feel the cold." Dang mo for "cold weather." Kyag-pa for "ice," gang for "snow." And so many of our mountains are named for snow and ice. We call snowy mountains "gang-ri." Then there's the Gangdise Range. Mount Kailash is known as Gang Rinpoche or Gang Ti-se.

The night comes and goes, and a rooster announces the morning's trek—a creature somehow able to survive the dang mo with just a few feathers to keep warm.

I lace up my boots and head out. As I follow the corridor, I rap on the mikarus' doors. "Breakfast," I call in English, a word I've been eager to test.

The lodge keeper's eyes linger on me as we leave an hour later. Woman porters are bad luck, they tell me. Very inauspicious. Eat. Pay. Go. Still stuck in the past, he'll learn. *I'll make him.*

I catch another glimpse of that map when I dole out the rupees, then it's back to the glacier. I don't need a map to know where we're going, it's in my bones. It's north, after all, uphill, easy enough for a child to understand.

We wind left and right, up and around hanging ice and boulders. There are no more cairns up here, just a narrow between the slabs. I'm relieved when we have dirt under our boots instead of ice. I use the sun and the mountain to navigate: keeping the goddess straight ahead, that's my guide. Truthfully, I'm as untested as my mikarus, but I follow the sun and the mountain's direction. How much more confidently I'd lead if I'd done this just once before, following someone who knew the trek.

Our march is as quiet as the morning meal. No birds calling, no chiming bells from yaks. After the rooster this morning, nothing suggests life. An hour of walking like this. Then another hour. I can only imagine what's going on for my mikarus. It's a short way from Lobuche to Gorak Shep—at least that's what the map suggested—but we're all weak and the going is very slow. Another hour later, we see tin roofs glistening in the sun. We must be just outside Gorak Shep. We break. I think of my father:

How does a Sherpa's body do this every day for an entire climbing season? Of course the men turn to chang, there's nothing else for it.

Behind us, more mikarus. They file past, some nodding their heads, some puffing out a mumbled "namaste." A few faces I recognize—white men with beards, Norbu's group—but I don't see those two girls with wild-colored hair. And then I see him, shoulders rippling under his blue jacket, with his confident stride. I see him in the distance, leading from behind. As he comes closer, our eyes catch.

I expect him to stop, to touch my hand, to smile, to say something, but he doesn't. He walks right by, his eyes locked on mine, the only dialogue he's willing to share. I can feel Val watching so I look away. *Don't say a word. Don't.* We're not mikaru. We're Sherpa. We don't show the world what goes on in our heart.

At Gorak Shep, we stop at the Buddha Lodge. ALTITUDE 5,164 METERS, written in blue ink on a sign. The last outpost on the trail, in a windy bowl right at the glacier's edge, this village is the saddest and smallest of them all.

It's been about an hour since Norbu passed me on the trail, I can tell from the sun's place in the sky. Hands buried in my pockets, I sit on a yellowed plastic chair outside a square cube of wood and tin, a shack exposed to wind from all sides. We're waiting to see if the weather holds. Kalapathar's peak is three hundred meters higher than where we are, and we would have to scale it before sunset. That means a return in the dark. The only light will be from the mikarus' headlamps.

"How do you feel about that?" I ask Val.

"If Ethan and Daniel think it's all right, I support it."

One hour until decision time. I rub my legs with icy fingers. If the clouds roll in, we change course and head for Base Camp.

Norbu's group isn't staying in our lodge. I thought if I sat out here, I would spot him. I hoped we could talk and agree that our groups could finish the journey together.

At one in the afternoon, we hit the trail. Clouds gather, scatter, gather again. "We go to Base Camp," I announce.

Ten paces in, the sun winks his return. "Sorry, we do Kalapathar."

Val kicks at an ice chip with her boot. We trudge over a dried-out lakebed, silt and stone crunching under us.

We're halfway up Kalapathar when the wind pins us against the mountain. The clouds roll in so thick I can't see more than a meter in front of me. No trail to follow, we move from boulder to boulder, me leading, slinking and shifting, using my whole body to lift myself. The wind doesn't stop, blowing loose rock, dust, ice, my right hand clutching the kerchief over my face, the other attempting to shield my eyes. Then my cap is blown right off my head.

My nose burns, dripping into the rag, and the wind howls maddeningly, sending loose shards into my eyes. The wind pushes us all like we're made of paper. When I turn around, the mikarus are battered, but battling.

"Just a bit more," I coax them on.

Three quarters to the top of Kalapathar, the summit comes into view, just the very top, the clouds and the wind blocking the rest. I check back on the mikarus, to show them, and find that they're barely moving. They can't take out their cameras, that's how hard the wind is blowing.

They shuffle together at the edge of the rock face.

I squint through cracked eyes, looking back at my charges. Ethan takes a step forward, and his knee buckles and he rolls back off his feet. He's too far away, he's going to fly right off the mountain—he's hurtling toward the void, then he reaches a hand and stops himself on a rock face. Val screams his name and dives into the wind, grabbing his arm. The gods of the mountain shriek in answer, drowning my voice completely. I have to shut my eyes against all the debris the wind is slinging at me. I can't see anything in front of me now. Then the outline of a body appears—it's Daniel. I push him behind an icy boulder.

"Ethan and Val?" he asks.

"Follow me!" I yell in English.

One hand in front of my face, the other held out to feel my way down, I lead. Daniel's behind me. And behind him, Val and Ethan reappear. Ethan limps, but he's on his feet.

We start heading down. Val, her chin tucked in to battle the wind, steps on a loose rock and chirps in pain, rolling an ankle— Ethan grabs her. Somehow they both stay on their feet. We keep lurching downwind, and I hit a patch of hidden ice and someone stops me from falling. I think it's Daniel, but I can't be sure, the churning elements are too overwhelming. I stagger on, and then, steps lower, the wind lessens. I can open my eyes fully, to check— we're all together. Climbing back down, Ethan's again favoring his right leg, but still he's walking, and Val seems to be moving without trouble.

We shuffle back toward Gorak Shep, close enough to grip each other, the blind leading the blind. When we finally hobble into the lodge, everyone gathers around the stove. The Sherpa owners, a family of four, jump up to offer their chairs. "Where'd you go in this wind?" the patriarch asks. He has a stringy black beard and wire-rimmed glasses, and he takes them off and cleans them on his shirt repeatedly as if the action helps him hear better.

"Kalapathar."

"Is it even possible, in this weather?" he asks, rubbing those frames. "You're lucky you weren't hurt."

"At least nothing life threatening," I murmur, watching Ethan massage his leg gingerly.

"How is it?" Val asks.

Ethan shakes his head, takes out a pill, a different color from the Diamox.

Daniel is holding his boots close enough to the stove that I smell rubber burning. I hurry to fetch tea. "Help her," the owner tells his wife. I must have a wild look, my short hair exposed without my knit cap, and she tells me to go warm up by the stove. She'll prepare the tea. The wife is no more than a girl, barely older than me, but her face is so much more dried and withered from living in this place.

Soon, I'm handed a mug of tea and I put it to my lips. Val takes my arm and pulls me down onto a plastic chair, next to her and the others.

"I'm sorry," I say. "I lead the group, I put us in danger. It's my fault, I should've known."

"You couldn't have."

Norbu would have known.

We sit for a moment, staring into the stove's open flames. I throw a cake in, watch the flames take it.

Ethan looks like he's in pain. Val leans over and brings her lips to his. Those are the moments I want.

"When you placed your lips on his—what's that called?"

"Kissing," she tells me, staring at me strangely. "It's called a kiss. You don't have that word in your language?"

I shake my head.

"You should try it with Norbu," Val says, smiling.

"I have," I say, feeling my cheeks redden. "I've decided, Val," I go on, feeling my voice get stronger. "I want us to work together, if he'll have me. And I'll use the money to help my family, pay for my sisters' dowry. I'll save the rest."

"Good." She nods again, not prodding, giving me the chance to share. "And what about leaving the mountain?"

"In the off-season, I'll go down to the capital. Maybe I'll study, maybe I'll roam like a tourist. Like a mikaru. I'm not sure yet."

"Good. Good plan. Lots to see in Kathmandu."

"And you?"

"Ethan and I are going to do the same as you, we'll keep trying. When you have someone you care about, you have to keep trying. I don't want to ask what if."

"I don't either," I answer.

"So tomorrow's Base Camp?" Val says in Nepali, so weakly it's almost a joke.

"Tomorrow's Base Camp," I answer. Too tired to say anything else, I stare into the flames, rehearsing all the things I want to say to Norbu, all the things I've held back.

27

THE WIND BLEW ALL NIGHT, GUSTING AT THE TIN ROOF, MAKING RICKETY music. Another sleepless night. In the morning, the four of us gather in the common room for porridge and black tea. The wind is still furious.

"Felt like I was upside down last night," Val tells me. "Couldn't sleep at all."

I couldn't sleep either. "Oxygen's fifty percent now," I say to Val. She's even paler today. Ethan and Val adjust their packs and cameras in slow motion.

"Ready?" I ask her.

"Will the weather let us?" she wonders.

"Isn't that why you came here, for your story?"

She nods. "I'm not sure what I've got, to be honest. The story is different now. This trip has turned into something else. Not what I expected."

"But still good?"

"Still good. Just different. Deeper. More personal."

"And how do you feel? Headaches, stomach?"

"I took a lot of ibuprofen last night. So did Ethan, for the swelling. He's fine, just got scared. We're both a little groggy. Nothing a strong cup of coffee can't solve."

Brave woman, but she speaks with bravado.

When we step out of the lodge, it's so cold I feel the porridge icing up in my stomach. The skies cry like some poor creature caught

in a hunter's trap. "The wind is strongest here in between mountains," I say, raising my voice to be heard. "I don't think it will be
as bad further up."

Daniel and Ethan curl their fingers into fists and throw up
their thumbs. Val takes my hand and shows me how to do it. An
hour later, on the glacier again. White, blue, black ice covers rocks
waiting to crack and fall into frozen caves no human will ever ex-
plore, and if they do, they're caves they'll never escape from.

An hour later we are still battling a strong wind like we've
offended Khumbi Yulha and Jomo Miyo Lang Sangma. We walk
on a moon of ice, and in between the blocks of ice, crevasses as
deep as the mountain is high. If I fell and survived, what would
I fill my mind with until death came for me? How long would it
take to end it all—and how would I do it?

Two hours pass. Three. Nearly four. I'm using the terrain as
wind cover. *I'm pushing them hard. I'm pushing myself hard.* My
knees burn, my face burns, my stomach is churning. The others
plod along, slowly, puffing and wheezing. Daniel doesn't bother
with his camera today, no jokes or chatter from Ethan or Val. They
walk with their shoulders slumped, barely picking up their feet,
Ethan especially. Val said he was okay, but he's so slow and stiff.

"Conserving energy," she answers when I ask how they're
doing.

The sun starts vanishing behind the ridges. After what happened yesterday, we have to be careful—I don't want the group
trekking in the dark. Nothing can go wrong today. Between two
huge frozen slabs we stop, and Ethan sucks from that tube, and
Daniel finishes his water. They're dripping sweat, and I watch it
harden instantly on their faces, crystals of ice streaking down their
temples. Val uses a handkerchief to pat their faces dry. Onward, in
that same slumped formation. I keep watching the sun. It's gone
now, descended beyond the ridge. An hour, maybe two, until it's
fully dark. And then? We'll have to head back downhill, but still
partly in the dark. I'll give it fifteen more minutes before we turn,

that's it. Then I see something ahead, a few kilometers in the distance...they look like yaks or ibex. Little brown dots, moving on a slab of frozen rocks. "What is that?"

We get closer, but they don't move like yaks. Whatever it is, they stand on two feet, and there are many of them. A dozen or more. Maybe two dozen.

"Are those people?"

They are: ants floating on a vast boulder pile with tiny prayer flags and multicolored tents. We made it: *Base Camp. The doorstep of the Earth Mother.*

I pick up my feet and break into a trot. The mikarus follow without instruction, and we're all running now, hopping over stones older than the dharma. We catch up with two Sherpas and two red-faced Westerners, a couple in their thirties, I recognize them from Norbu's group. Each Sherpa holds an arm around one of the mikarus—they look sick, their eyes sunken, cheeks sagging, victims of altitude—nothing we can do for them, and we're too excited. We dash past them without even pausing to speak.

Val starts filming on her mobile with giddy drunkenness, all of us forgetting our pain. We hoot and whistle, closer and closer. *We made it.* Before us the great mountain pierces through the clouds and into the sky.

"So tell me again, for you this is no big deal?" Val rasps in between steps.

"All this, for a pile of rocks," Daniel spouts, a huge smile blooming on his face.

"But what a pile of rocks," Ethan grunts.

Staring straight up at the pure white pillars, I know this is a mountain monastery, a holy place. And far beneath it, Base Camp, a smattering of little brown dots, sits as if in worship—it's too cold and too late in the season for the masses to be climbing.

Val takes off her pack, guzzles water, craning her neck. We all stop, perhaps a thousand meters from Base Camp, with the sun creeping lower. But we're so close, the little dots aren't so little now—and beyond them, the endless ice fall. Pure white. We can't even see the mountain from here, Everest is hidden behind the ice fall, that's how imposing it is. Val opens her bag, hands out tiny flags with stars and red and white lines. "For when we get there," she says, and laughs. "A little piece of home."

Flags are typically placed at the summit, but teams to Base Camp often place them here, too. I hope we can all write our names on the flags when we get there.

"Good trek," I say to Ethan, another phrase I've just learned. I hold out my hand like I've seen other mikarus do. He looks at it, then takes it firmly and pulls me in and hugs me. Then he lets go and Val hugs me. Then I hug Daniel. The mikarus laugh between sips of water. I ask Val what she will eat first when she returns to mikaruland.

"Chicken."

"Just chicken?"

"Kentucky Fried Chicken. A whole bucket. No more curry. I want KFC all day."

"KFC?"

"KFC, baby."

"Me, too," Daniel clammers hoarsely.

They're excited. They should be. We did it. And I got them here, safely—by myself. No one can take that away from me. And in the moment I realize this, I begin looking for Norbu—I want to share this with him.

Val still holds her mobile in one hand, the little flags in the other. *Snap. Snap.*

"Nima, lean in with me, I want to take a selfie with you."

She pulls me close, and we grin widely as she holds the phone out in front of us. *Snap.* She places the mobile in my hand. "Here, you try." With the camera before me I can see my face peeking from behind wisps of my hair, tired, haggard, and happy. So happy to be here.

"Try to get Base Camp in the background. Yeah, like that."

Snap.

Around us, Daniel and Ethan howl like mad dogs, their echoes bouncing off the peaks. "I can't believe we made it, I can't believe we did this."

Val hands me one of the flags, holds up hers and waves it as she trains her mobile. *Snap.* Moment after moment gets trapped in that little device. We're walking again now, over jagged boulders, deep snow, and navigating through pieces of ice shards, every step getting closer to the tents, orange and red and black, colors that pop against the white background—all of it populated with men and women preparing to scale the peak. Mikarus and Nepali of all kinds, Sherpas and Dolpas, Brahmin, and Chhetris—many more than I expected at this time of year, all in the shadow of ice and rock, and framed by those sacred flags. We're on a ridge now, just above the camp, the final descent, the final steps.

Snap.

"You think Norbu's down there?" Val asks.

So many mikarus. That big group milling about and taking photos, that must be Norbu's. I scan the rocks. If I squint, I think I can—yes, I make out Norbu, even from here, I recognize his broad shoulders, the way he stands, that blue jacket. The prayer flags flap right over his head. His group must have noticed us, because they're shouting at us now. Strange. His group and ours haven't had any meaningful interactions—why would they be greeting us?

Norbu's blue jacket sticks out among the white snow and ice. He's looking at something in the distance. Then he turns and begins to run towards me, perhaps a thousand paces away. All the mikarus around him are running now.

I glance up, above the camp, and it looks as if the mountain is moving, as if the glacier's coming closer. Next to me, Val drops the little flags she's holding. Then there's a sound I had hoped I would never hear again, a deep, thunderous *tuuuuungg* that drowns out my crying ear.

I reach my hand up my sleeve, tugging my arm hairs to make sure I'm not in dream. I keep tugging despite the pain. And I can't stop watching. Norbu is still running towards me—and I start running towards him.

That blanket of white rises high above the ants, right over Base Camp and Norbu's team. It goes so high that the sun is gone. I reach out to Norbu as everything turns white, and the white comes crashing down just before I can touch his outstretched hand.

28

WE'RE RUNNING THROUGH A WHITE MIST, RUNNING WITHOUT WATCHING where we land, trying to avoid falling rock and snow and ice, trying to outpace the storm. I was just out of reach of Norbu's grasp before it hit—I stretched and touched him—when the ru' came down, its impact sending me flying back, and now I'm still running, Val, Ethan, and Daniel and I, each of us hustling to keep the ru' from dragging us under and burying us.

I am the bad luck woman that they say I am.

The haze begins to lift, the ice flow has stopped, and we stop moving. I try to keep my focus where that white blanket first landed. Or where I think it did. And then I rush back into it. The sound is worse than the sight. It's the sound of screams.

Base Camp is gone, and in its place, slabs of white.

One hundred yards away. Fifty yards.

Twenty. Ten.

The air clears, and I follow the moans, the screams, men and women, arms and legs poking out of the snow, some buried to their necks, some hidden but screaming all the same. There's a hand sticking out of the snow. Thick fingers, strong. I reach for it and pull.

Norbu's hand.

I pull with all my might, but it won't budge. I scoop snow, clawing at the ice with my fingers, stripping my gloves to get a better grip. Val helps me, both of us burrowing.

"He's not moving," I cry. "He's not moving, Val!"

"Keep digging! Just keep digging!"

We manage to dig out the whole arm, but the jacket the arm's attached to is black. I keep digging anyway, find the man's broken face—a frozen caterpillar, those craggy cheeks—Lasha. I let go of him and he falls limp onto the snow.

I'm a girl being carried back to Khumjung. I am cursed.

"Nima! Val! Over here," Daniel is calling.

I feel myself falling, scattered in the wind, lost on the mountain.

"Nima."

Val pulls me back to my feet.

Ethan and Daniel have uncovered a few mikarus—alive. One has a bloody face, an arm dangling from his side. Another, a man with a beard and broken glasses, a cut running along the bridge of his nose, is on all fours next to Daniel, digging. Ethan has his medical kit out, helping whoever he can. There are three bodies, all Sherpa, all facedown in the snow. Two of them are fully dug out, one of them is still partly buried. So much snow and ice has fallen that I can't even see the tops of the Base Camp tents.

I lift their faces. One of the boys who beat me outside of Pheriche. The other, same age, maybe a little older. His brother. Two fallen brothers, Dorjee Sherpa's sons, they didn't deserve this. The third Sherpa—he wears blue and my heart seems to stop—but when I turn the body over, it's not him.

I'm on my knees, watching it all as if through someone else's eyes. I'm losing my grip on this plane of existence. My soul is escaping. Then I hear a child's voice: *Eldest. Get up. Get up, Eldest. Get up and dig.*

I can see Val beside me, watch her talking to me. But it's not her voice I hear.

Eldest.

I still feel as if I'm floating, but there's a tug now, something weighing me down.

ELDEST.

My brother's voice brings me back. I wipe my face, get up, and turn to Val. "Show me your mobile."

"What?"

"Your mobile, give it to me! Show me the last photo you took—of Base Camp."

"I don't—"

"Just give it to me!"

Val pulls out the phone, hands it to me. I open it, too many buttons—Val takes it and pulls up the last photo. I grab it from her and look at the small screen, searching for Norbu. *He was standing next to two other mikarus. By a cluster of rocks.* I look up from the mobile and try to judge his location—I count his paces in my mind as I run ahead. Then I drop to my knees and begin scooping piles of snow, first with my kikuri, then, afraid to strike flesh, using my hands, pile after pile, my arms burning. *Keep going,* the ghost commands. That little shoe we found back in Khumjung, that was all we could save.

Keep digging.

Norbu wrapping me in his jacket, taking my hands in between his, rubbing them to keep me warm. Carrying my father on his back to Nurse Lanja. Gently holding my hand while we waited to see if my father would live or die. Believing in me. Seeing me.

There are as many types of ru' as there are people, my father would say. We and filled with sluffs and slabs, ru's that glide when the entire snowpack moves as one, or slush, like a flash flood of permafrost. And this one? A hard slab ru', the most deadly. When Father was coming down the trail, waving, calling our names, did he realize he was in its path, *or was he realizing who else was in its path, further down*?

So many things can cause a ru'. Layers of fresh snow weighing down on the ice crust, or a bed of large-grained, wind-hardened snow made loose by the sun's rays, or ice calving in the heat of the day, or rain, which can cause a melt-freeze. Wind, trekkers, climbers, so many things can be the cause. Some even say it's just the mountain's way, a reminder of its power.

Eldest.

A red streak appears with each pile of snow I scoop—a dark red, almost black. My fingers, numb, torn to pieces, keep digging.

Keep digging, my ghost commands.

Don't stop. I hear my mother calling now, too.

Keep digging, my sisters chant.

Eldest. My father's cold bark sends a shiver through me.

"Nima," Val says over my shoulder.

I can hear Ethan, too, like he's far off somewhere. "Val, look at her hands."

"Nima. *Your hands.* Nima, that's enough, please. Please, Nima stop."

I can't. I can't stop. I can't leave him; I never told him my choice. *The one man who believed I had a choice.*

"She's gonna catch hypothermia, Val."

He deserved that much. Norbu deserved to know my choice.

There's a wail, a strange shrieking howl. It sounds like the screaming deities and daikinis you tell children about to scare them into going to bed. There's something familiar to the cry.

And then I realize that it's coming from my open mouth.

Don't look back.

I keep scratching at the void. My fingers hit something that's neither snow nor ice. They tug at wisps of thick hair. I keep digging, harder than ever now, freeing him from Khumbi Yulha and Jomo Miyo Lang Sangma—I was a fool to doubt their power, a fool to lie. I hit something.

There's a pocket of air—that's the kind of ru' it was, blessed with enough space to breathe, the gods are looking down on me, they can't take another from me—I scoop free a massive chunk of ice with both hands. I see him, just a fingertip away. So still. Ethan and Daniel and Val, Sherpas and mikarus whom I've never seen before, they all help and we pull him free from the mountain. But he doesn't jump up, doesn't wraps his tree trunk arms around me. He can't even stand. Norbu Norgay lies slumped over, his eyes shut, his chest flat, and I reach out and hold him in my arms and don't let go.

I cry. And as I do, I tell him: my plan, my choice. I tell him our life as I know it will be. Suddenly, his chest moves—Norbu coughs and his whole body shakes. His eyes are open.

"Ethan," Val says over my shoulder. "Quick."

The mikarus rush to help, but I won't let go.

"Norbu," I say, focusing on his dark eyes, not the darkness pooling in the hole where we scooped him free.

"Gimme your belt," Ethan yells. "We need to wrap it around the arm, above the wound."

I stroke Norbu's face with my torn fingers and he smiles at me the way he should have when we took my father to see Nurse Lanja so long ago.

"Keep the pressure on it."

He touches my lips and whispers in my ear, and we both laugh.

"My choice," I whisper back to him.

Then he lets out a cough again, wincing and smiling at once. I lean in, wrap my arms around him, and don't let go.

ACKNOWLEDGMENTS

There were many people who breathed life into this book and helped bring it to fruition. I want to thank my family—father, mother and sister—for always giving me the most honest feedback, even if it wasn't what I wanted to hear. There's nothing more important to a writer than honesty.

To my Gina for giving me the confidence to keep working even when it felt like the summit was so far away, and it was. We made it, G.

To my friends in Nepal who through their love of this complicated country planted the seed for what would become *Nima*: Suman Thapa, my brave guide in the Solukhumbu; Cody and Cheryl, the marines who trekked with me into the sky; and the journalist Deepak Adhikari who stoked the fire. Thanks as well to early readers Ammu Kannampilly, who generously alerted me to errors; Parag Khanna, whose own work on Asia was a guiding light; Lisa Choegyal, an expert in all things Nepali; and Dr. Lhakpa Sherpa who has done so much to promote and improve the conditions of Nepalis. To all of you I owe a deep debt.

As a journalist, I am acutely aware of errors and inaccuracies in my work—it's what we all fear most. That being said, any inconsistencies in this work are my fault and mine alone. This is a work of fiction, and I did take liberties. But in doing so I hoped to tell an honest story about these mountains, and the inspiring people who call the Nepal Himalaya their home.

Reading past and present greats filled my sails: Lil Bahadur Chettri, Manjushree Thapa, Jamling Tenzing Norgay, James F. Fisher, Sherry B. Ortner, Rita M. Gross, Janet Gyatso, Karma Lekshe Tsomo, Lhakpa Norbu Sherpa, George Schaller, John Whelpton, Bruce Temper, Janice D. Willis, Peter Hopkirk, Peter Frankopan, Dr. Hemanta R. Mishra, Jim Ottaway Jr., Sam Cowan, Fitzroy Maclean, Arnold Henry Savage Landor, James Hilton, Sir Rudyard Kipling, Lobsang P. Lhalungpa, His Holiness The Dalai Lama, you were the guides. I would travel with you anywhere.

A very special thank you to my agent, Pilar Queen of United Talent Agency, who had the vision and the guts to take a chance on this story. To Chris and Olivia at The Unnamed Press, who nurtured and believed in *Nima* from the beginning. Your enthusiasm and feedback are unrivaled.

To Nima, whatever path you chose, thank you. This book is for everyone who stares up at the sky and wonders *what if* and then pushes towards that unknown. Push.